PROPHASE

PROPHASE

DNA STRAND 1

JORDANA WELLS

Prophase
DNA Strand 1
Jordana Wells

Edited by Karen Robinson
Proofread by Jennifer Oberth
Formatted and Typeset by Jo Michaels
- all of INDIE Books Gone Wild
Cover Design by Robin Ludwig Design Inc.

CONTENTS

CONTENTS

PROLOGUE

Tuesday, November 4, 2014, 11:38 PM
Belleville, Illinois, USA

Dog food. Shampoo. Vitamin C.

Oh, and peroxide for the blood.

I pulled into the Wal-Mart lot and parked my car under a light. I was glad Paul wasn't around to give me crap about stopping on my way home from school for the second night in a row, but I had forgotten dog food and Jackson's bowl was empty.

I had to stop taking night classes. They wore me out, grinding me down until little details slipped through the cracks.

Did I have enough cash to get more than the small bag of dog food?

My stomach clenched. Paul's paycheck wasn't stretching as far as it used to, and I hadn't figured out how we were going to make it to the end of the month.

I *would* take more night courses. I had to. If I hadn't taken the complex variables class at night this term, it would've thrown off next semester's schedule. I wouldn't graduate on time, which would make me wait even longer to get a good job in a bad economy.

I could go without vitamins. I could use bar soap on my hair for a few weeks, too. I'd only get dog food. But what was that last item on my list?

Shuffling toward the entrance, I automatically gave a wide berth to a pair of men arguing by a worn-out van.

Peroxide. I needed peroxide for the blood.

My cell phone signaled an incoming call with the generic ringtone. Who'd be calling at this hour? "Hello?"

"Hey, it's me."

"Don't tell me they're still preempting our lab time for that high school tour."

"Let me repeat that: Hey, it's me."

With a tired chuckle, I said, "Sorry. Why didn't you call me on your cell? I thought you were Ruis."

"I did use my cell," Paul countered, yawning. "And after all this time you still can't tell my refined Pittsburgh accent from that hick one of his? Maybe I should take the dog and move in with someone who knows me from Adam."

"So, Adam, when are—"

One of the van guys took the phone from my hand, saying, "You won't need this anymore."

The calm, dispassionate way he looked at me chilled me to the bone.

Paul's panicked voice sounded tinny and far away, and the man lifted my phone to his ear, pale eyes never leaving mine.

"Boyfriend?" the man asked me.

Wide-eyed, I corrected him. "H-husband."

He gave me another questioning look. "Mira?"

"It's short for Miranda."

With a pleasant smile, he told Paul, "Miranda has pretty eyes. I wonder if they'll still be pretty when she's dead."

He closed the phone on Paul's roar and tossed it aside, the plastic clatter loud in the momentary stillness of the parking lot.

Do something. Don't stand there like a cow about to be slaughtered. Run, scream, plant a foot in his balls, anything. At least go down with a fight.

He aimed the gun barrel at my forehead. "Let me tell you a secret. If you hold very still, you won't die. Do you understand me?"

"W-why?"

"Shh," he admonished gently. "Calm down. You're shaking so hard I might shoot you in one of those beautiful eyes. It's not like I do this every day."

You don't have to do it today. Not to me.

He lowered the pistol, his brows knit together. "I'm trying to put you out of your misery, but I can't pull the trigger. How perverse is that?"

With unwilling hope and crazy, irrational disappointment, I watched him stride away.

He whirled, raised the gun, and said, "It's only those who're strong enough to survive the darkest storms who can change the world. And, Miranda, tonight we're going to make history."

"Oh, crap," I whispered, fingers tightening on my purse strap.

He pulled the trigger.

CHAPTER 1

RESCUED

The deep, hollow sound of my breathing filled my head like I was submerged in water except for my mouth, but no sign of liquid warmth surrounded me. Filling my lungs deeply and slowly, I felt the rawness of my throat and a bone-deep ache in my chest.

I was so tired.

The wind swirled around me, and I caught the comforting musty smell of a forest before a cloud tasting of burning plastic choked me.

I tried to open my eyes, but they didn't respond. A claustrophobic kind of alarm hit me when I repeated the attempt.

I tried to bring a hand up to my face, but I couldn't do that either. Struggling against the restraints that pinned me from end to end, I felt the frantic fear increase until my breath came in short, biting gasps.

"Stop," a deep male voice demanded breathlessly as a callused hand took mine. "You'll hurt yourself. What's your name?"

My head rolled disjointedly as I tried to look toward the source of the voice. Why couldn't I see?

"Miranda." It hurt to force the word out, and my voice sounded hoarse and strange from disuse. "Where—"

"Miranda, you need to be very quiet and do everything I say, okay?"

I nodded sloppily, my head weighing more than my neck was used to supporting.

He loosened my restraints, and I breathed more easily.

With a weak, shaky hand, I touched bandages over my eyes and then followed a ragged line of scar tissue from my temple into my hair. Instead of falling halfway down my back, my hair stuck out less than two inches. I felt naked without all that hair, and I could feel color rushing up to flood my cheeks.

An explosion close enough to make my ears ring spurred the man to throw his body across mine, protecting me from most of the flying chips of wood and rock. Dirt rained down. A burst of gunfire drove him to haul me over his shoulder and scramble through the underbrush.

Disoriented and sick to my stomach at the rough ride, I welcomed the blackness that took me under.

The faint didn't last nearly long enough. I came to as we were jerked from the ground with a force that tore a gasp from my throat. My rescuer held me tightly, pressing my face against his chest as we ascended. I felt the calluses on his hand scratchy on the back of my neck.

Another pair of hands guided us into a helicopter. The vibration increased, the engines howled at a higher pitch, and we shot forward. I tried to catch myself, but muscular arms guided me to a prone position in a snug cradle.

The whirlwind inside the cabin died down with ear-popping haste. I was glad. I needed everything to settle down for a minute so I could think.

"There's no medical transport on the manifest," another man said. "How're we supposed to do our job when we aren't given an accurate count? What if both members of the crew had survived, too?"

"We would've managed. We always do," my rescuer said. "How're you doing, Miranda?"

"Okay," I said hoarsely, wondering what to use as a frame of reference. Honestly, I'd never felt worse, but I suspected I could've been a lot worse off.

He tucked a wispy sheet of fabric around me, and I caught myself before I asked for a more substantial blanket. I was cold, that wet, bone-deep cold that takes forever to get rid of.

He asked, "What kind of eye surgery did you have?"

I bit my lip. My mind couldn't produce an explanation.

"Were you in an accident?" He touched a sore spot on my temple. "Do you know how you got this? It looks freshly healed."

I had pulled into the parking lot at Wal-Mart, but what followed was a mystery. "I don't know anything about that, either."

The other voice spoke up, sounding puzzled. "Click off a minute."

"Make it quick."

"Miranda? That's Marco. I'm his partner, Red. I need to know where you're from so I can notify your clan as soon as possible."

Clan? "My husband's stationed at Scott, but he's—"

"Where?"

"Scott Air Force Base in Illinois. He's in the field a lot, so I'll give you the phone number for his unit."

I had to repeat it several times before they read it back to me right. Did I slur or transpose the digits? Even though my blindness spared me the sight of their irritated expressions, I still wished I could see their faces. The weird weakness in my body made me feel crippled enough as it was.

Red spoke to his partner in a low tone. "Let's ignore the obvious problem and talk about her bloodwork. Blue's finally identified some of those unknowns as antibiotics and a tranq cocktail."

"I can't say it's a surprise."

"Well, what's bothering me are the drugs that can't be identified."

Marco said, "You've got to stop thinking everything Little Blue can't identify is a biologic weapon. Look at her. She shouldn't have been transported in the first place, so I'm sure a Big Blue scan will show the drugs to be more support therapy."

"Her condition brings me to the next point. It was too risky to jack her with a fast burn stim given the obvious dehydration and malnutrition. You know that."

"It was safer than extracting her gurney." Marco's voice dropped so low I had to strain to make out words. "This wasn't the crash we were sent out to handle. The scan of the pilot shows a different blood type than on his ID. The copilot's ID was a straight-up fake. On top of that, the position of his body shows he used his last breath getting her a safe distance from that transport. You heard what she said, and you saw the way they attempted to protect her. Coupled with the bogus IDs and the fact that someone was shooting at us, we have to treat this as the real deal. The question is, what are we going to do about it?"

"It's not our problem. If we see a crash and bodies, we go help. It wasn't our fault her flight was illegal. If your gut's saying she's not a biologic weapon, then all we have to do is keep her stable until we touch down. We play dumb and wipe her medstats from our Blues. Then we walk away and never look back. This doesn't concern us."

"They'll be busy. We could sneak her out of there."

"Marco, do you know what they'll do to us when we get caught?"

I'd never been in the hands of emergency services before, but I was certain that being confused and afraid was supposed to occur before they showed up, not afterward. And I was feeling worse by the moment. Weren't they supposed to be comforting me?

Marco said, "I'm doing it. If you won't help, at least look away. How wrong could it go?"

Red burst out laughing, the sound bitter and pained.

The sensation of a thick, dark liquid pulsing inside my skull with each heartbeat grew until the pain was more than I wanted to take. It spread through me, making me heavy, making it hard to breathe.

"Hang on, Miranda. Stay with us."

It was too hard. I let go, and the blackness obliterated me.

CHAPTER 2

WAKE UP CALL

Despite the expectation that I'd wake surrounded by the sounds and scents of a hospital, I found myself in a warm, quiet room that smelled of sage.

Soft tapping on the door announced I had company.

"Hi, I'm Dr. Antonius Rainer, but you can call me Tony. My nephew Marco brought you to my house three days— No, don't do that. You'll dislodge your IV line."

"Sorry," I croaked, putting my right hand back down on the sheet. I felt the IV line move as he checked it. "Is my husband here yet?"

"I'd like to discuss that with you after I ask you a couple of questions."

I didn't care for the evasion but recognized Paul wasn't the easiest person to contact when he was out in the field. I answered the doctor's questions about my date and place of birth, my medical history, and how I felt with the excruciating detail he requested.

"The last area that concerns me is your temple," he said.

I touched the tender, nascent skin of a fresh scar and was revolted by the feel of it.

"Marco said you don't know what has occurred. Is that true?"

I couldn't remember past my arrival in the parking lot, but Tony didn't seem concerned.

"Sometimes with a head wound, people lose the memories that haven't made it into long-term storage yet," he explained. "Marco found residue under the skin that suggests you were shot, so—"

Brow furrowed, I motioned for silence.

The memories slipped and slithered, and I grasped fractions of the whole. Plastic hitting the ground. The sour taste of fear in my mouth. The musk of a man's cologne assaulting my nostrils.

"Miranda?"

No, that wasn't right, either. I had explained that Mira was short for Miranda. That man who took my phone had said that I— Desert Eagle. He had a Desert Eagle with the triangular muzzle that Paul said was cool, which was the sole reason I knew the name of the gun at all. The van guy had scared the bejesus out of me because he carried an old Desert Eagle.

"Miranda, I need you to calm down. You're safe."

I gripped the sheets. "He had a gun. The guy who took my cell phone in the parking lot had a gun, and he told me..."

Oh, crap, my eyes. My poor, bandaged eyes. For a moment, I was afraid to open my mouth. I could feel a scream rising, fighting to escape.

"What did he say?" Tony coaxed.

Swallowing hard, I concentrated on forcing the breaths to come slowly and more evenly. With my voice sounding unnaturally calm, I said, "He told my husband I had pretty eyes and that he wondered if they'd be that pretty after he killed me."

Tony made a shocked noise.

"We'd better see what the damage is before my husband gets here," I told him. "I need to have my game face back on by then."

His ragged exhale was the only indication he was still in the same room with me. Maybe his medical practice revolved around kids with fevers, sniffles, and the occasional broken arm from falling out of a tree house, not victims of a sadistic eyeball collector.

Neither of us seemed to breathe as he removed layer after layer of swathing, so his voice startled me when he said, "Whoever did this was a pro. That's a good sign."

But he didn't sound so confident of that, and as he progressed, his hands slowed.

When he stopped altogether, he explained, "There's a circular patch over each eye with a curved, hard shell underneath. I changed the outer bandage when you came in, but from what I read I could damage what's below if I remove the shells wrong, so I wanted to wait until you were conscious before I did anything more. I was really hoping you would be able to tell me what kind of surgery had been done."

"Curved shells mean curved eyeballs underneath?"

"Not necessarily," he said, snuffing my spark of hope. "I'm sorry I can't give you a better response, but Blue can't see beneath them. That's been the difficulty all along."

"Blue?"

"The bioscanner."

After the removal of the outer patch from my left eye, I felt unpleasantly cold moisture on my eyeball as

11

the inner layer of the eye shield became saturated with saline. When the saline ran down my cheek like tears, he lifted off the first eye shield.

He said, "There's going to be discomfort, but I want you to keep your eye as still as you can. Just close your lid."

A light moved from one area of my uncovered eye to another, and I fought the urge to look away. "That's bright."

He took the light away, and it returned much softer as my other eye was freed from its restraint. He toweled away the moisture on my skin and asked, "You want the good news or the bad news first?"

"If the good news is that I've got eyes, and I can see light, I'm way ahead of you," I said, almost laughing. "I thought for a while there that he'd cut out my eyes."

Silence, but that was okay.

My eyes felt achy and gritty like I'd worn my contacts too long. The brightness of the room made my eyes water, but the moisture eased the discomfort as I continued to open and close my eyes at a measured pace. A hazy face came into focus. "You don't look much like a doctor."

He was a tall man approximately thirty-five years old, with short, black hair and somber, form-fitting clothes. Even in the dimly lit room, his amiable dark eyes and generous smile couldn't counter the harsh lines of his features.

"Slow down," he said. "Don't try to focus. I probably shouldn't have even gone this far, but since I have, I want you to give those eyes a chance to get used to their new surroundings."

His words struck me as odd, but not for long.

"You've had eye transplants," he said. "The eye cups were used to hold your eyeball stationary while your eyes were healing."

First his discomfort dealing with the unpleasant possibilities of what lay beneath my bandages and now this?

"Don't believe me?" he asked. "Close your eyes so I can turn on a light."

"Why?"

"So I can find a mirror."

I barely recognized the woman in the reflection. My face was gaunt, my skin ashy in a few places and downright scaly in others, and the blue veins and red, wrinkled depressions from the bandages stood out garishly against my paper-white skin.

"What the hell?" I said, following the shooting scar from my temple into my hair. Even in the low light, my hair didn't look right. It was my natural light brown instead of the strawberry blonde I'd been dyeing it since I was thirteen.

With my heart beating hard, I reluctantly looked into the windows of my soul.

These were definitely not the blue eyes I'd used for the first twenty-four years of my life.

"They're a light golden brown," Tony said.

I looked at him so abruptly my eyes blazed with pain, and I fought to keep my voice calm. "I've got pieces of another person, presumably a dead person, in my head because I was violated in a fairly horrific way. Do you think I care what color they are?"

A knock on the door made us both jump.

"You in here?" a semi-familiar voice murmured as he pushed through the bedroom door. "I talked to— Oh, she's awake. How are you feeling, Miranda?"

I smiled tightly. "Tony, do you want to answer that one?"

"Yes," Tony said, getting to his feet. "I'd like you to rest your eyes while I go talk to him."

13

After the door had closed behind them, I shut my eyes and sighed. This wasn't how my life was supposed to play out. The length of my natural hair color told me it had been at least three months since that man took my phone—and apparently my eyes—in the Wal-Mart parking lot.

I'd not only missed the end of the fall term at the university, but I had missed the registration dates for the spring term, too. My scholarship would've gone to someone else. My stomach sank as I realized I'd probably been set back a year. Thank God Paul still had another three years on his enlistment.

Paul.

My heart constricted. He'd been forced to hear that psycho say I was about to die.

"Hey," I yelled, struggling to sit up. "Please come back."

When Tony didn't return fast enough to suit me, I tried again. "I need to talk to you."

The distance between us didn't lessen the snap to his voice. "I really need to talk to Marco. I'll be there in a minute."

I twisted the edge of the sheet in my hands but had to stop because it made my joints ache. The bioscanner thingy was beeping faster now, and I hated it for telegraphing what I was feeling.

Tony opened the door and rushed across the room. He read the screen impatiently. "Mira, I really would appreciate it if you could calm down for a couple of minutes. I really need to talk to Marco."

"I'm sorry. I just need to know if you reached my husband yet."

"There's a problem," Marco told me from the doorway. "Be patient while we sort it out."

"A problem? That's what we're calling it?" Tony asked. The bioscanner screamed my distress, and his finger stabbed at the controls. "Mira," he snapped, "it would help a lot if you at least tried to calm down."

"I'm sorry. I'm trying. I just want my husband."

"He's dead!" he yelled. "Your husband is dead. Your family, your friends, your dog, and even the psychopath who took your eyes are all dead and gone, don't you get it?"

Marco evicted Tony from the room.

"I want out of here," I said. "Now."

"Who can blame you?" Marco asked mildly.

Both the response and the tone derailed me, and I studied him for a sign of how to proceed.

Marco was at least my age, but no older than thirty. Slightly more compact than his uncle, he nevertheless moved with an enviable athletic grace as he sat in the chair near the bed. Other than that, I couldn't get a read on him.

"I just want to know what's going on," I told him. "That's normal, isn't it?"

He nodded. "After you were shot in the head and had your eyes cut out, you were placed in suspended animation for a hundred and five years. Cryopreserved, possibly. Probably."

Probably.

Right.

"Well," I said, "that explains it."

He frowned, the motion a slight, economical bend of the mouth. "It's the best guess we have."

"I'm not disagreeing with you."

"You could at least have the common courtesy to tell me that I'm full of crap."

It should've made me laugh, but nothing was funny about my situation. "Why aren't I in a hospital?"

"For the same reason I don't take an injured woman to the hospital when I suspect her husband beat her."

"What would that be?"

"I doubt your condition is the result of informed consent, so my first impulse is to hide you while you get your bearings. You're safe, your condition's stable, Tony's a doctor, and we're minutes away from an emergency room if your condition gets worse. But if you want to take your chances at the hospital, I'll take you."

"I need a few minutes to think about this."

He nodded. "Call out when you decide. But I do need you to understand nothing was legal about your flight, the people who flew it, or the human experimentation we suspect you were a part of."

"So how does that factor in?"

"I don't know. That's my point."

"But you guys are hiding me anyway? Why?"

"Because it's the ethical thing to do," he said. "It would be a lot easier for the authorities to assume you're a liar, a crazy, or a spy than to deal with the repercussions of believing you're telling the truth. But it's your decision now. Just understand that if you reveal yourself to the authorities, there's no guarantee we can or will help you if things go wrong."

"Why wouldn't you help me? You just said protecting me was the right thing to do."

"It's ethical to protect a storm-tossed stranger who doesn't know which way is up. But if you choose to announce your presence to the people who probably caused your trauma to begin with, well, why should I risk myself for you again?"

"Fair enough."

He stepped out of the room.

Cryo. What a load of crap.

But I had to admit something did seem off. No, it was a million little somethings that were off. The style and fabric of their clothes was a bit odd. The casual spelling of *thru* for *through* on the IV bag was unexpected. The presence of a bioscanner was slightly surprising despite what I had read about scientists developing them.

The minute differences extended beyond the room I was in, too. The high-pitched sound of passing cars wasn't quite right. The window framed predictable architecture in the nearby domiciles, but the odd roofing changed color when a cloud passed overhead. Even the skyline looked ordinary and strange at the same time.

Something was wrong.

It just couldn't be what they said it was.

CHAPTER 3

IGNORANCE

Sheltered by the Little San Bernardino Mountains to the east, Tony's neighborhood was a small enclave of identical houses with identical fan palms in the front yard. Perhaps the backyards beyond Tony's six-foot privacy fence were another story. As I sat in my wheelchair on Tony's patio a month after my rescue, I spent my allotted fifteen minutes of sunshine imagining candy-colored decks and outrageous attempts at individualism. Sadly, Tony's self-expression was limited to a lopsided terra cotta chiminea and a drab bistro set.

"Hey, golden eyes," Red said as he stepped onto the patio.

Subtly shifting in my wheelchair, I managed a smile for Red to show I was making an effort to develop a sense of humor about my new, piss-colored eyes.

He darted forward and yanked the paper and pencil out from under my thigh.

"Cheat notes?" he teased. "I wasn't going to quiz you on—" His eyebrows creased when he saw what I had written on the sheet. "What's a chronology protection conjecture?"

Heat flooding my face, I grabbed the paper and crumpled it in my fist. "It's nothing," I said, failing to manufacture a good lie.

He pried the wadded paper from my hand and flattened it out, stepping out of range so I couldn't get it back.

Shopping list. Why couldn't I have folded it up and said it was a shopping list instead of bungling a sleight of hand that only drew attention to the very thing I wanted to hide?

As he read it, I said, "I convinced myself I could rule out time travel as an explanation for my presence in the future. Cryo might not have been the sole possibility. It's normal to wonder how I got here, isn't it?"

"Who cares if it's normal or not? Why hide this? Why be ashamed of being smart?"

"I'm proud of my academic record," I snapped.

"Why? Because a flawless score gives an accurate measure of who you are or does it only show you perfected conforming to a standard? Even a full genome evaluation indicates the components of your divine spark, not all you could do with it."

"That would mean more coming from a man who didn't bomb his recertification exams," I said. "Why should I trust you as a medic if you can't prove you meet the minimums?"

He snickered and returned the paper. "You have me there. But even though I'm no longer qualified to ask it, I'm going to anyway: why are you still in Tony's old clothes? Prevention of heat injuries is a priority here in the desert."

"The clothes you bought me fit too snugly."

19

"For them to both cool you and recapture lost moisture, they have to touch your skin," he said.

"I'm fine with sweating, thanks."

"But you don't have to," he said with a pointed look at the wet patches at my armpits. "Is this a self-image problem? I'm sorry, but baggy clothes still show that you're skin and bones."

"Health before modesty," I sighed, biting my hangnail. "And I'm sorry about the crack about your credentials. I know you'll do well on the retest."

He shot me an exasperated look for not saying I trusted him even without a renewed certification, and I grinned at him.

But it was a tired smile.

"We don't have to have a history lesson today if you don't want," he offered.

"So now you want to be nice? You wanted to throw me to the wolves before."

He colored. "Look, I helped him smuggle you out of the hospital we landed at, didn't I? I'm trying to catch you up on the knowledge any modern child has, aren't I?"

"You're doing this for Marco because it bores him," I retorted. "You're not doing it for me."

"Let's just get started."

He launched into a condensed version of the history of the new world, but the lecture highlighting the reasons behind America's decline saddened me. It was inevitable that governments fall, but my homeland had been only a few hundred years old before it collapsed into clans that fought amongst themselves as much as they resisted assimilation by the dominant players in world politics.

I inhaled the desert scents, reminded that I wasn't sitting on a deck a couple of miles outside Palm Springs in Southern California. Instead, I sat on a deck a couple of kilometers inside the capital city of Rancho Hernandez, deep in the center of the Hernandez Clan. The Hernandez family ruled what had been the southwest part of the U.S., and while it was one of the biggest of the seventeen territories, it had more than its share of wasteland.

It struck me how surreal the situation was when Red spoke of our neighbor to the east.

I chuckled. "The glorious Republic of Texas always considered itself apart from the union anyway. Does it still use that red, white, and blue flag with the single star on it?" I asked, enchanted by the idea.

He nodded, and my smile became bittersweet. Why couldn't I have been born Texan? At least I could've kept my cultural identity.

He looked to the east, the curve of his mouth wistful. "Tell me about all the places you've been. Outside the clan borders, I mean."

"Red, I warned you," Marco said from the doorway. "We never mention her past. Ever. As far as you're concerned, she was born under a pinyon pine in the Providence Mountains that day."

"It's just that—"

"You're done," Marco said, the muscle flexing in his cheek warning of his mood.

Red slunk off with his tail between his legs.

Marco turned his obsidian eyes my way. "If you walk and talk Hernandez, you will pass for Hernandez. Don't get distracted from that goal."

"I wasn't the one who brought it up."

"I understand that, but he's not the one who will live with the consequences if you stand out to the wrong person."

It was easy for Marco to tell us all to ignore the past, but I still had trouble accepting this as the present.

That evening, I studied the artifacts in the living room for the hundredth time, searching for proof this was all a twisted joke they were playing on me or I was playing on myself. Nothing changed.

A framed poster promoted the play *Blue World*, which had shown at the Grand Theater from August 15, 2096, through March 15, 2097. Instead of being a blank, conventional window shade, the one over the large window facing the street showed a dark sky full of twinkling stars over a lush tropical island. When I sat in Tony's chair, the scanner immediately located areas of tension in my back and massaged them.

No flying cars though. No other jaw-dropping technological advancements either. There had been too many economic collapses and wars while I slept for technology to progress to the flying car point.

"You still don't believe it, do you?" Tony asked, pushing my wheelchair toward my room.

"The brain allows this manifestation of reality as the truth, but the soul doesn't. Not yet anyway."

As the bed registered my weight, Big Blue rolled across the room.

"Is that still necessary?" I asked with a nod toward the bioscanner, whose blue-white scanning light had been my first sight when the bandages came off. As I settled in, its arm darted around, its sensor locking on my navel. Once I was still, it signaled the start of its one-second sweeps. "I'm feeling better every day."

"Blue's monitoring the areas that aren't recovering as quickly as the rest of you, such as your kidneys."

"How damaged are they?"

"Well, you have to understand I don't have any references for stasis experiments. The unidentifiable drugs alongside the load of designer antibiotics are interfering with your body's usual cellular toxin removal. I'm afraid to run your blood through the cleaners in case those drugs are keeping you alive. Until either I've identified those floaters or your kidneys start to fail, I would like Blue to watch over you."

Suddenly, I was grateful for my medical watchdog's constant presence.

"You are getting better," he assured me. "Faster than any of us predicted."

"Once I'm healthy, what's the plan?"

"For now, just concentrate on healing."

"Marco says the same thing. Maybe hiding and healing was enough of a goal the first few weeks, but I'm ready to face my future. Can't you understand I don't want to spend each day of the upcoming decades wondering where I'm going to get the money to eat? I'm used to having a plan. I'm thinking about turning myself in."

"No."

"I've figured out what to say so I don't implicate any of you."

"You have no idea what you're getting yourself into. This clan doesn't deal well with foreigners to begin with, and without an affiliation to any nation, you've got no rights protecting you."

"You know how Marco says I have to hide out of sight and be able to hide in plain sight, too? How feasible is it to hide in a technologically advanced society?"

"I would like you to try. Is it so terrible living here?"

Well, no, it wasn't. It was safe and quiet, for one. Having the internet also meant I had endless access to reading material and movies while I recovered. It was an introvert's dream. So why did it seem so wrong?

I said, "Now that I'm stronger, I want to do some of the cooking and cleaning."

He grimaced. "I'm picky. Let's say that I'll be doing the cooking and cleaning for a while, and if we're both comfortable with it later on you'll do some of it."

Again, it was an arrangement straight out of a fantasy. If he added a sexy, blond cabana boy, I would've hit the trifecta.

Still, I felt my frown deepen. "Tony, you must realize that the longer I stay here, the riskier it is for you."

Would the reminder be enough for him to come to his senses and evict me?

His expression didn't change. "We're not going to be discovered, Mira."

"Well, let's take it one step at a time," I hedged. "How about we assess the situation after I've been here ninety days? I'd also like Marco to be in on the discussion."

"We've already discussed it. We're in total agreement," he assured me. "Good night."

Humming, he walked off, shutting the door behind him before I could get another word in. I didn't know what more I would've said anyway. Asserting myself was rarely within my comfort range.

I swallowed and swallowed again, struggling to lose the lump in my throat.

Why exist if there was no purpose or structure? And to live such an aimless life at such cost to another? How could this be the best solution?

Feeling smothered, I pushed off the covers, exposing my sweaty skin to the air conditioner's chilly drafts. These four walls. Hiding within these four walls wanting for nothing, but doing nothing. I would be confined to a cage whether I stayed here or turned myself in.

No, that couldn't be right. Marco had offered to take me to the hospital the day I woke up. Their apprehension was simply based on the fact that they didn't know how I would be treated.

Any government agent would spend thirty seconds interviewing me before realizing I lacked the poker face needed to be a spy. Given that I lacked the physical signs that definitively pointed to being frozen for a century, no modern scientist would cackle maniacally at the idea of cutting me up to see how I worked.

I'd also been all over the former United States and couldn't think of a place I'd mind being deported to if the Hernandez Clan tossed me out.

So what was the worst that could happen?

I sneaked out as soon as I heard Tony's soft snores.

CHAPTER 4

UNBELIEVABLE

The urgent care clinic was a beacon in the darkness of the sleeping city streets. It would be even cleaner than Tony's house, and the personnel would be helpful and efficient. It would be a prime example of how awe-inspiring and modern the world now was.

If only.

At a diagnostics station with a sticky floor, I was given a glancing examination before I was ushered out to a cramped waiting room to stand alongside dozens of people who jockeyed for position when one of the unbroken plastic seats became available.

Jesus, why did everyone have to stare at me? Why wasn't their attention on the man covered in tattoos and bandages or the purple-faced, screaming child? I knew I was a pale, yellow-eyed, skeletal freak, but their persistent, unsettling stares made me wonder if they thought I came from another planet.

I could run. It's not too late. I could stumble out the door like a drunk and...

And...

My vision was full of stars. I panted too rapidly, too shallowly. The man beside me erupted into a coughing fit, and I clamped my hands over my nose and mouth. It was too late. My weakened immune system guaranteed I would get the modern version of the plague in a germ-infested pseudo-hospital long before any government agent got to me.

Someone whimpered.

It was me.

I couldn't breathe. I had to get out of there. I had left the wheelchair at Tony's so my spindly legs had to bear my weight as I staggered toward the door, twisting awkwardly to avoid touching any of the plague-infected people.

I couldn't leave. I read the ideograms on the panel again, but I still got them wrong because the door wouldn't open. Someone spoke to me, the Spanish so quick and accented I couldn't make out a single word.

I turned away, searching for another exit.

I caught my foot on someone's bag and fell into the arms of a security guard. I pushed at him, trying not to inhale his diseases, but I ended up hyperventilating. The tip of my nose tingled, and my heart fluttered until individual beats couldn't be counted.

I was dying.

Someone scooped me up and rushed into an empty bay in the diagnostics room. Strong hands pinned me to a chair.

"Breathe, Mira, breathe."

I knew him.

"With me. Inhale deeply," the man said, gesturing at the expansion of his chest. "Fill your lungs. Now exhale. Slowly. And again."

"I'm dying," I croaked.

"No, you're not, but I'd like it if you tried to calm down."

Tony. His name was Tony. No one else spoke like that.

"My heart."

"Breathe with me. In—"

"Dr. Rainer?"

"She's having a panic attack."

"We'll take care of her. They need you in administration. Now."

Tony stiffened, paling as he took the first steps away from me.

Were they going to arrest him for helping me? I tried to tell him I was sorry, but I couldn't breathe. I batted at the hands assisting me. I felt the sting of a needle in my shoulder, and a big, black blanket dragged me under.

I resurfaced to the sound of Tony's grunt as he shifted my weight from a wheelchair to his arms. "Watch your head."

I hit it on the car's doorframe anyway, but I was so groggy and worn out by that point it barely hurt.

"Where are we going?" I asked as I fumbled with the seatbelt.

His hands brushed mine aside, and the metallic click promised me I wouldn't launch through the windshield.

"Home," he told me.

"What about being a rat in a cage?"

"We'll speak in the morning."

Tony was silent as he drove down the empty streets.

"Tony?"

He jumped. "Oh, you're awake."

"What about the rat cage?" I mumbled.

"They didn't believe you. You got lucky, but you didn't get away clean." He swallowed hard and whispered without looking at me, "Why? Why did you have to turn yourself in? We were protecting you."

I pretended I'd fallen asleep.

My skull was fracturing, the sharp pieces piercing my brain. I fumbled for the button on the bioscanner, but the sound of swift footsteps meant Blue had already tattled my condition.

"Shh," Tony murmured, catching my chin in his hand and shining his penlight into each eye. "I'm here."

He stuck a syringe in my arm, and I winced at the hot burn of the fluid. He gave me a pair of tablets and held a glass of water steady so I could drink.

After ten or fifteen minutes, the jagged pain eased.

"How do you feel?" he asked.

"Better," I croaked. "Thanks."

I was home. Thank God.

I ignored his helping hand, deciding that if I made it to the medical clinic, then I was capable of making it to the bathroom.

"I'll prep your breakfast," he said.

When I emerged from the bathroom, a battered cane lay on the bed. I snorted but took it in hand and made my way to the kitchen.

Tony asked, "Have you had panic attacks before?"

With hot humiliation staining my cheeks, I said, "No, that was the first one. The final one, too, if I have anything to say about it. What happened last night?"

"I would like you to start that story," he said, eyes narrowed.

I dug my fingernail into the groove of an old knife cut on the tabletop. "I snuck out, flagged a driver, and told him I needed to go to the hospital."

"After I told you how dangerous it was to go to the authorities?"

"Well, I'm here, aren't I? It wasn't the end of the world after all."

His mouth flattened into a line.

A chill touched my spine. "Tony?"

"You don't remember?"

"Bits and pieces."

I should've guessed what they would say at the clinic. They said I undeniably survived some kind of trauma event that jumbled the contents of my skull and produced panic attacks, amnesia—

"Amnesia? I told them I remember everything. That's not amnesia," I said.

"You couldn't get the door open, and it's the most common type of latch in North America. You couldn't even work the stylus right, and you weren't even close to what year it is. Blue didn't report you had the physiology of a liar, so they made natural assumptions."

I snorted in disgust.

"It's 2119," he said.

"Wonderful."

"When you didn't appear in the system as a Hernandez national, they ran a partial DNA sample to make sure you weren't a fugitive from another clan. Then that segment was posted on a secure website where other clans check for their missing members. Legally, that's all they could do for you."

I finished the nutritious, cardboard-flavored shake, and he slipped me bits of scrambled egg for not complaining about the taste. I wolfed down the solid food and pressed against my heaving stomach, refusing to allow anything to come back up. The back of my throat burned, and I reached for my water.

"So that's it?" I asked. "You and Marco had me convinced I'd be subjected to an alien autopsy, but your clan authorities don't seem to care."

"They care. You've got a PDT implanted in your hip-bone now so they can track you. Personal Data Transmitter," he explained before I could ask.

My hand went to my butt and found the small bandage. I pressed it, and pain radiated deep in my flesh. It took me a minute to find my voice. "I didn't consent to that."

"Most people have one, so I don't want you to take it personally."

"In my day, that would've been considered a massive invasion of my privacy."

"Consider it an ID card you can't lose. You're more than welcome to try and dig it out, but I should warn you that yours has a poison core."

"Are you kidding me? What if I'm in a car accident and it shatters?"

"The chances of that are remote. More people die from having theirs popped during an illegal border crossing."

My eyes bugged. "The cops can detonate it remotely? Nice clan."

"And we want to keep it that way," he said. "It's a measure used for felons, Mira. And apparently the occasional stranger like you. Once you're a permanent resident, I'm sure they'll swap it for an ordinary one."

I anticipated more revelations about the previous night, but he cleared the table and left the room.

31

"I can go out and get a job and go to school now?"

"What?"

"My future," I called out. "Since I'm not in jail, a psych ward, or a medical laboratory, I can go out and have a normal life?"

"What? No, I'm afraid not," he said, rejoining me. "Now that the clan knows you exist, you have to come up with a reason why they should let you stay."

"How do I do that?"

"From what the testing office told me this morning, it's different for everybody, but they all start with a preliminary psychological exam to make sure you're not dangerously unstable. A blood draw and DNA analysis will show if you've got a rare blood type or any other anomalies the clan considers favorable. If you're not crazy and not biologically or genetically unique, then they'll find out if you've got skills or aptitude in a needed area. From there, you'll get a formal offer. Perform well and that contracted visa could turn into citizenship."

"Despite my not having a past anyone can verify?"

"You should be happy you've got amnesia as far as the clan is concerned. You've been given official permission not to remember anything before you woke up at my house. I have to admit this all turned out way better than I expected. There are nasty rumors out there about the way strangers are treated," he confessed. "But still, I would like you to keep the truth to yourself from now on."

"No one believes me anyway."

Satisfied, he tried changing the subject, but I wasn't done.

I asked, "What if they can't find a reason to keep me?"

"I'm sure they'll find one."

"Thanks for the vote of confidence, but I need an answer. If they can't find a reason for me to stay, or if my skills are in a saturated field, then I have to leave the clan, right? To go where?"

"No idea. I'm sure they'll find a reason."

"I need to start making a list of what I'm good at," I decided.

"It should show up in their testing tomorrow," he said. He took a step toward his multi-charger and snapped his fingers. "That's what I wanted to ask you. Did you use my computer?"

"I'm sorry, I thought you said I could."

"You can. I wondered why it was low on charge. And you left the page open, but I didn't know if you forgot to close it or if you still needed to learn more about Channing Tatum."

With horrified laughter, I said, "Don't tell Marco."

"Don't tell him what?"

"That I frequently look up how noteworthy people from my era had died or how my favorite TV series ended."

He looked sad. "You looked up your family, too, didn't you? Did you find anything?"

Energy drained out of me, leaving an echo of stunned grief behind.

He said, "Even if they lived in this part of California, most information on public servers was lost during the Clan Wars either because the tech became obsolete or because of physical damage."

"Even if America was intact, historians would've considered my kin too ordinary to comment on. But if nothing else, despite what the man who shot me said, I didn't make history either. None of the search engines lit on my name at all, let alone my disappearance. Granted, it's not much of a victory over a dead guy, but I'm glad he didn't get his way."

He managed a smile, but he couldn't hide his sadness about my being alone.

Before it got to me, I changed the subject. "So what's on my agenda today?"

"Nothing. I would like you to take it easy so you're fresh for your tests in the morning."

My hands clenched at the reminder of the examinations that would choose my fate among the Hernandez.

"DNA analysis," Tony said, savoring the idea. "I wish I could have that done. I mean one of those thorough government ones you're getting, not the lame commercial ones that only look for a couple of common genes."

Before, he'd made it seem like a fast and dirty hunt for a few specific genes, but now it sounded like the government would examine my entire strand to see which genes were coded there.

"It's being stripped naked and being judged by an audience," I said.

"I promise you'll still have plenty of secrets left." Stars in his eyes, he sighed. "Think about what could be learned from it. A person usually has to learn about their strengths and weaknesses through years of trial and error, but how much time would they be able to save if they got a peek at God's design for them? Someday they might analyze everyone at birth so people can be guided along the paths they have the talents for so their full potential can be developed."

"You just made all the free will philosophers roll over in their graves."

He laughed. "Optional guidance, of course."

CHAPTER 5

TESTING 1, 2, 3

"Stop yelling at me," I snapped at the shower fixture that warned I was about to exceed the three drops of water allotted for my wash.

When I dropped into my chair for breakfast, Tony told me, "I would like you to stop overriding the water controls."

"I still have shampoo in my hair and soap on my skin. How is a person supposed to get clean around here?"

"I don't know what to tell you. No one else has difficulty getting it done," he said as he selected another blueberry to be macerated in my shake. "There's no need for you to be anxious today anyway. Even though your third-year university programs are probably the equivalent of our high school or even junior high classes, I'm sure the first test will be generous. Well, no, I don't know that. Never met anyone who had to go through it. I would like to think they make it challenging. That way—"

"Please stop trying to reassure me."

Wrapped in my own thoughts, I missed most of the drive into the center of the capital, but when a ring of iridescent, black towers enclosed us, I couldn't help but take notice.

"Beautiful, aren't they?" Tony asked. "These are the government buildings."

Given how unclean I felt, I wasn't in the mood to be charitable about anything, and the buildings resembled a gaping maw of rotten teeth.

The interior of the testing building was so spacious it was as if they had spent so much on the structure they didn't have enough money left to furnish it. When I saw how far we had to walk to get to the reception desk, I raised an eyebrow at Tony. It had been our mutual decision to leave my wheelchair behind so I didn't appear any weaker than I already did, but I wasn't expecting this.

"Can you do it?" he murmured, regret twisting his features as he regarded the expanse of slick white tiles.

I straightened, tightening my hand on my cane. "I have to."

The first test was the blood draw for the genetic mapping. Tony watched the preparations for the event with rapt attention, but I couldn't shake the sensation that we were attempting to trespass in a house that had been locked up tight for a good reason.

"How long until the results are in?" I asked, repulsed by the contrast between my paper-white skin and the bright red fluid filling the transparent tube.

"We draw the sample and send it to the lab, ma'am. Nothing more."

Tony's shoulders rounded forward, and his features fell in a comical show of disappointment. I bit back a laugh.

The next test was held on the second floor in a giant bay full of slanted tables. The room stank of nervous sweat, and in my perversity, I associated the scent with my past academic victories.

One of the proctors directed me to a distant row of tables, and once I walked within range, a table lit up in recognition, having received the signal from my PDT.

Winded, I sank into the plastic chair and wiped the moisture off my face with a trembling hand. I closed my eyes and willed my lungs to fill deeply and then empty fully to ease the pounding in my head from the exertion. Too much walking too soon. Way too much.

People filled the tables around me quickly. Because the center provided most of the major academic and occupational evaluations, I would have the pleasure of working without having to hide my answers from my neighbors. It was unlikely anyone else in that room was taking this particular test.

It wasn't until I sensed a marked alertness in the other test takers that I opened my eyes. My tabletop touch screen was covered in text. The examination had begun.

The multiple-choice exam used hundreds of questions to cover general knowledge and fundamental problem-solving skills, so it was disappointingly easy. As soon as I pressed the button to mark all my answers as final, a new screen asked if I was ready for the next trial or if I wanted a fifteen-minute recess.

I rolled my shoulders and stretched my back to ease the strain but kept on testing. The second examination was math and science with no multiple choice options, and my cheeks ached from the smile that wouldn't fade. My brain flexed and sighed with delight at being useful again.

Afterward, I crossed the hall and stood at the entrance to the snack bar, searching for Tony. He was in the corner, as far from the other patrons as possible. He wasn't a people person, which is why he retreated into his home to do research evaluation instead of applying his MD to a laboratory or a medical office setting. Given his idea of a pep talk, that was just as well.

He glanced my way and scooped up the disposable wipes he'd used to clean the table. Striding toward me, he said, "People ran out of there crying."

"I enjoyed it. The second one anyway."

Troubled, he said, "I hate to say it, but that means you didn't do it right."

"I prefer to believe I'm a genius."

"I'm sure you do," he muttered, making me laugh.

Filled with dreamy pleasure, I missed everything he said on the way home. Thank God I hadn't chosen to live as a rat in Tony's gilded cage. I would've died from boredom.

After dinner, Tony received notification I was scheduled for an oral exam the following day.

"What does that even mean?" I asked Marco in the morning. Tony was at a meeting with his boss, so I would be taking the train for the first time.

"Spoken," he said coldly.

"I know what *oral* means. I'm asking what they meant by an oral test. Are they going over my results with me or is it a job interview?"

"I don't know."

"Well, should I be worried?"

"Is worrying going to solve anything?"

Was that a trick question? "No?"

He gave me a disgusted look and strode away.

"Turning myself in was the right decision," I yelled after him. "Stop being so pissed about it."

"You don't have enough information to make the right decision yet," he snapped, heels loud on the floor as he returned. "How are we supposed to protect you now? You put yourself at the mercy of the system. You might as well have put a target on your back. And ours."

"Blame Tony. He tracked me down and brought me back."

"Don't you dare say your decision was his fault. That nanotech chip embedded in your carotid artery to measure the decay of your antibiotics without having to resort to a twice daily blood draw is registered to him. They called him."

"You guys really need to tell me things like that are inside me."

His teeth gnashed. "Go to your test. Thanks to you, I have to figure out a way for at least some of us to escape jail for helping you."

"Don't be so pessimistic. You have to allow for the possibility that everything's going to work out fine."

"Not in this clan," he muttered, turning away.

Cane in hand, I hobbled out the front door. A penny from the old American coinage lay on the sidewalk in front of the house, and I picked it up, delighted. The metal warmed in my hand.

"Lucky me."

I arrived at the testing office comfortably early for my appointment. When I told the cheerful man behind the reception desk my name, he gave me a puzzled look.

"You from up north, ma'am?" At my questioning look, he explained as he scanned for my PDT, "I can't place your accent."

I didn't respond, but I didn't have to. With that poison core PDT showing up, he knew I was either a foreigner or a felon.

"Why the clan bothers to evaluate your kind is beyond me. We don't need your kind here."

I tried not to react, but I felt the blood leave my face. People turned to stare, and the hair lifted on the back of my neck. The women in Salem must've felt this unease when the first girl regarded her with a malicious eye and took a deep breath as if to speak.

"Process her," his co-worker said, breaking the tension. "Or call security. Get the line moving either way."

The receptionist called up my information. His mouth twisted with hostility, he told me, "Fifth floor. Conference Room Two."

"Thank you," I said, shock robbing my voice of its strength. I'd never been the victim of such prejudice in my life, and I had no defenses against it. If it had escalated into violence, would anyone have come forward to help me?

Worry about it later. If you can't get yourself together for this test you might as well throw yourself in the pyre and save that dick the trouble.

In the conference room's antechamber, I was distracted out of my wariness when the proctor explained the unique testing format. A panel of five people would pose questions covering physics, mechanics, math, and other related fields. There was neither a set number of questions nor a time limit for me to solve each problem. The trial would end on my third incorrect answer.

Cane thumping on the thin carpet, I walked through an arched door to where the panel sat, their chairs facing a lone empty seat. Two-thirds of the overhead lights were off, bringing relief to my light-sensitive eyes. I set my cane on the floor beside my chair even though I would've preferred to keep it clasped in front of me to put some separation between the committee and me.

A trickle of sweat rolled down the side of my face, and I brushed it away, wiping my hand on my pants, embarrassed.

Without warning, a woman asked the first question.

I glanced around, confused. "Where's the touchpad I'm supposed to use?"

"No aids are allowed," the woman told me.

My jaw dropped, and my stomach shriveled into a hard knot. "You expect me to do these equations in my head?"

"You are permitted to count on your fingers," an old man told me without a trace of humor.

"Thank you," I said, hoping I didn't sound sarcastic. "Will you please repeat the question?"

Furious, I assumed the test would be over in minutes. Even though I could do nothing to prep for a DNA analysis—no way to get a different result no matter how frequently I took it—it still felt fairer than what was going on in this room.

I was about to give them an answer to the propulsion question, any answer to get through with the ordeal, but the evaluators' expressions showed nothing but curiosity and patience.

Well, why not try to solve it without the usual scholastic crutches?

I sat back in my chair and pondered the question. Soon I was able to give them a response I was comfortable with.

Without confirmation or comment, the man looked to the next person down the line, who immediately presented me with a thought-provoking question about molecular adhesion. My unnatural appreciation for the challenge must've shown on my face because they looked startled.

Before long, I drew in the air in front of me to keep track of equations and three-dimensional models. The man with the pronounced drawl asked me a question that took me twenty minutes and half a room's worth of air drawings to solve.

It was exhilarating.

Four hours and six minutes after I started, I failed to understand a question let alone have the capacity to produce an answer.

An appreciative groan came from the panel. "And that concludes our test," the thin man said.

I felt like I was reaching for the last piece of candy only to discover I had already eaten it.

"Sir?"

"It was your third wrong answer," the old man said.

My gaze went to the one person who still looked fresh, the urbane Latino with the drawl. One of them had called him Chavez. He nodded, confirming the end of the trial with an emotion akin to regret.

"We're done. It's done. I'm definitely done," the blonde women snapped, struggling to stand with petrifying muscles. "Go home and eat a cheeseburger, Ms. Donovan."

Puzzled, I looked again to Chavez, and his gaze dropped briefly to my body.

His eyes on the unfamiliar skeleton where my plump figure used to be made me shoot to my feet, blushing. Light-headed, I stumbled and dropped back into the chair, grasping for my cane.

Chavez said to me, "I'm curious. Which military aircraft interests you?"

"I'm sorry, sir?"

"Well," he drawled, "it's not an unreasonable question for someone seeking admission into the military flight school."

"The what? No, I'm sorry, but that's not why I'm here at all."

I had everyone's attention then.

"I'm going through the basic tests to qualify for a visa," I explained.

The blonde woman strode to the wall and moved a panel to reveal a computer. Her fingers flew over the screen, and my file popped into place.

She stabbed her finger at my appointment data. "Third floor. You were supposed to go to the third floor, not the fifth."

"This isn't my fault," I protested. "I went where that sphincter at the reception desk told me to. Why didn't you know I wasn't the person you were supposed to be evaluating?"

"Because our PDT reader is down."

The thin man pointed to the terminal. "Here's our candidate. Ten minutes after the evaluation was supposed to begin, she petitioned to reschedule due to her grandmother's death."

The panel made a few callous snorts, and the thin man smiled at my dismay. "A surprising number of family members succumb to lethal disease when the candidate isn't ready."

I snorted, and he chuckled.

"This isn't funny," the blonde woman snapped. To me, she demanded, "Why didn't you tell us you suspected you were in the wrong place? We could've stopped the exam and moved you over to the correct one if you'd let us know."

"It was just more math and science," I said, wide-eyed at the accusation. "The second exam was an expansion of the math and science introduced in the first one."

"The aerodynamics questions didn't seem odd?" the old man asked.

"I thought the breadth of my knowledge base was being challenged. So you said I need to go to the third floor?"

The blonde shook her head. "Since you finished this test in its entirety, the results were automatically uploaded to the secure servers."

"I didn't hit the button to finalize my solutions."

"Voice command," the thin man explained, pointing at a black bar around the top of the room. "When one of us says the test is over in a specific way, it's the upload command. You could petition for its removal, but it's unlikely they'll give it to you since you tested for a field with a critical shortage."

Dazed, I shifted my gaze from face to face, looking for sympathy and understanding. "I can't be a military aviator." But with a burst of relief, I loosened the white-knuckled grip on my cane. "I'm requesting this be stricken. Not that it's necessary, but I prefer to cover my bases."

"Why isn't it necessary?"

"I lasted only four hours."

"Only?" the old man repeated, eyebrows shooting up.

I grimaced. "Embarrassing, I know. My lack of health combined with my lackluster performance here promises there's no chance I'll end up in a military flight school. For what it's worth, I'm sorry I wasted your time."

"Don't be," Chavez said. "You didn't."

It was late afternoon by the time I limped through the door to Tony's house, and I ignored both Marco and Tony as I wiped away tears of frustration.

"Mira, where have you been?" Tony asked, following me to my bedroom. "They gave you a no-show for your test."

"No-show? Oh, of course."

"This was important," Marco said.

"Tell that to the bastard who sent me to the wrong test, something none of us realized until after it was uploaded. He said he told me the correct floor, so of course they took his word for it. They rejected my petition to strike the results, and they aren't letting me take the test I missed because I've already got an oral in the system."

"You're so pale. Are you well?" Tony asked as I wiped my cheeks and blew my nose.

"Yes. No. Yes. I don't know. With luck I'll get deported to a place with more water to shower with," I said with a smile that didn't reach my eyes. "I have to tell you that I'm not impressed with Hernandez bureaucracy so far."

"It was your choice to become subject to it," Marco reminded me.

My temper was close to its flashpoint, but Tony got between us before I took more than one menacing step toward the younger Rainer. "When was the last time you ate?"

"Before I left."

"That's what I suspected. Why don't you let me make you dinner?"

"I want real food."

Thrusting a new palm-sized computer at me, Marco said, "You'll get shakes and your own palmer with an alarm that reminds you to eat."

"And I would like it if you got a purse to carry a couple of premade shakes and snacks," Tony added. "You shouldn't miss meals, Mira."

"Go eat," Marco said. "Now. If they send someone to take you off our lands, I don't know when you'll get to eat again. Next time, write down the location of the testing room instead of blaming someone else for your mistake."

I lunged at Marco, but my nails didn't reach his eyes before Tony seized me and pointed me toward the kitchen.

"I'll make you a shake and a light meal. While you eat, Marco and I will pack you a bag with a few essentials, but I'm sure there's nothing to worry about."

What a lie. His hands shook as much as his voice did.

CHAPTER 6

MAKE ME AN OFFER

Late that night, someone hammered on Tony's front door.

I jerked upright, clutching the sheet to my neck. It was past midnight. That couldn't be good. If I grabbed my bag and went out the window, how soon would it be before they apprehended me?

As Tony opened my door, the headlights of a passing car glinted off his tousled hair like a muzzle flash. He knotted the belt of his robe, saying, "I don't want you to panic."

"Amateur," I snapped. "This is the perfect time to panic."

"Will you please stay there?"

I dressed quickly, my eyes darting to the window. I could hear voices at the front door, but not the tone or the words. How long could Tony stall them?

Marco appeared in my doorway. "Don't even think about it."

"What are you doing here this late?"

"Waiting to see what happened."

The front door closed, and Tony's bare feet thudded on the hardwood floors as he yelled, "It was a messenger." When he reached us, he waved a thick envelope at us, his eyes bright. "It's your offers."

"A midnight visit for that?" I snapped, hurling my pajamas at the laundry basket. "Why couldn't it wait until morning?"

Both men looked at me in surprise. "Because this is important," Marco said.

"I'm going back to bed."

It wasn't ten minutes before I sighed and joined them in the kitchen. I poured myself a glass of water, muttering, "I still don't see why this came now."

"They assumed you'd want to know as soon as possible," Tony said. "I know I did."

I snorted and sat down. "So my genetic blueprint is good? Where are the results?" I wanted them locked away before the men saw them. It already unsettled me they knew my body better than I did.

"No, there's nothing in here about that at all," Tony said, crestfallen. "How long could it take to process a specimen?"

"The offers?" Marco prompted.

"Right. One from the Ministry of Science and Technology for an engineering job—"

I pulled the glass away from my mouth so hastily water shot across the table.

"Engineering?" I repeated. When Tony nodded, I danced in my chair. "How do I sign for that?"

"Read the details of both before you decide," Marco said.

"I don't need to. I was nearly done with my electrical engineering degree in my old life, and I know it suits

48

me." I grinned and clapped my hands like I was the fresh incarnation of some demented monkey toy. "I'm going to be an engineer."

"Try to look at these as means to an end," Tony suggested. "You may love engineering, but there's much less of a need for it, so there's no signing bonus and the visa's only good for nine months. That may not be time to impress them enough to get papers."

"They're offering me a job in the field I want."

Marco asked, "What's the difference in the medical coverage between the two offers?"

Tony grimaced. "None. It must be standard. It's nearly nothing, merely a pre-approval to be treated for anything communicable."

I said, "So I can get treated for anything that might affect the clan but nothing that affects me solely. Great."

"It's better than nothing," Marco said. "What field is the other offer in?"

Tony said, "The MoD is offering a slot in the military flight academy."

"Is that the test you took by mistake?" Marco asked me.

I nodded. "I failed it though. Why did they offer?"

"They didn't just offer," Tony said. "There's a fat signing bonus and a significantly higher chance of citizenship."

"A fat bonus for it means it's a crappy job," I said.

"It's a critical field. They get a lot of applicants, but few meet all of the qualifications."

"I don't," I retorted. "Look at me."

Tony said, "Don't reject the possibility so hastily. Their doctors say there's no reason you can't improve your fitness to the minimum level by the time you'd be in the air. It's the sole benchmark you don't meet."

"No more," Marco told Tony, tossing the courier's packet in front of me. "We did our part. If she wants to be careless with her future yet again by refusing to read both offers, that's her problem."

"Marco," Tony sighed.

"No, she needs to understand how serious this is. If you'd better explained the consequences, she wouldn't have put us all at risk by leaving our protection and going straight to the authorities behind your back as soon as she was ambulatory." Marco directed his piercing gaze at me. "Pretend for one second that you're prepping for the fight for your life. You're given two boxes, a weapon in each. I bet you'd take both boxes seriously then, wouldn't you?"

I snatched up the offers and retreated to my bedroom before he could take another chunk out of me.

In the morning, Tony knocked until I crawled out of bed and opened the door a crack.

"What?" I asked crossly.

"You got another notification."

"I already have the offer I want. I'm not taking any more tests," I said, pleased that my morning breath was so rank it forced him to retreat a step. I needed to come up with a sentence full of h's so he'd retreat down the hall and let me go back to sleep.

"It's a mandatory invitation," he told me. "Not a test."

"It's a contradiction."

"Go ahead and mention that to the MoD when you get there."

"M-o-what?"

"MoD. Ministry of Defense," he reminded me. "The military."

My mandatory invitation was located at an air show. It was a blatant ploy, but an air show was as good a reason as any to leave the house and enjoy the sunny day.

The scent of sweet, fried food made my mouth water. With a furtive glance around to ensure neither Tony nor Marco fought the crowds to offer me moral support, I rushed toward unhealthy festival food nirvana. I felt the sugar rush of the first churro even before I arrived at the information tent to wait for my appointment. God, if the first sugar I'd ingested in a hundred years felt this good, I could hardly wait for caffeine.

A B-52 pushed the air out of its way over the spectators. Where on earth did they find an airworthy bomber that old? It even had that gorgeous, body-shaking thrum. If nothing else, that revealed the length of the runway. Paul had been stationed at a base that had once housed B-52s, and people flocked to the air shows there because it was one of the few places with a runway long enough to launch the historical bomber.

Paul.

This environment contained too many reminders of him. I gave in to the compulsion to look down to the end of the static displays where a space shuttle sat in the sun, and I could feel Paul's hand tugging me toward it.

I missed him, but I felt a funny disconnect about his death, too. I wasn't dealing with his stuff, seeing the grief when I crossed paths with his friends, and filing the paperwork proving to the government and the insurance companies that he was dead. I'd simply been dropped into a strange world where he didn't exist.

What were the last words I'd said to him? I hoped it had been that I loved him.

The gap in my memory still bothered me, and not only because I couldn't remember what I said to Paul. I had lost the entire month before the shooting, even though I had recovered memories of the shooting itself.

My hand went to the scar of its own volition, and my gratitude swelled that a month of memories was all I had lost. My recall of details, my ability to work math, and my other engineering skills remained.

Granules of sugar under my fingertips made me drop my hand and curse the churros. Paul would've chuckled as he came to my rescue and brushed off all the cinnamon sugar he could see.

And without his guidance, I would choose the comfortable option, even if it wasn't the appropriate one.

But I'd be a good engineer. I wanted it, too, that endless string of puzzles that needed to be solved with math and science.

Movies couldn't have been accurate in describing military aviators as arrogant asses, but I was reasonably confident they had different personalities than the engineering students I'd spent term after term learning to relate to in my old life.

It made sense. All the way across the board, it made sense.

I knew the kind of people I'd be working with.

I knew the kind of tasks.

I already had some of the training.

I already knew I had the aptitude for it.

I was an engineer.

There. It was settled.

However, according to the MoD packet, there weren't many people better suited to aircrew duties than me. For Paul, the collective's need would've held more weight than anything else.

"Miranda Donovan?"

The voice came from a tiny woman in a flight suit sitting in a golf cart. According to her name tape, she was called Luft.

"Yes?"

She glanced at my cane, raised her eyebrows at me, and shrugged. "Get in."

The silence was awkward as we left the public area and headed for an over-sized, windowless building set well away from the flight line. She motioned for me to follow her through a plain metal door. The structure had no sign and nothing in the cream-colored hallway told me where I was.

It was a trap. It had to be.

They know about me. They're going to cut me up. Alien autopsy.

Alarm dumped adrenaline in my system to mix riotously with the sugar. Gripping my cane like a baseball bat, I turned and ran for the exit.

"Hey, stop. Are you going to be sick? The bathroom is this way."

I whirled at Luft, heart crashing against my rib cage. "What is this?" My voice was high and shrill, shamefully full of panic.

"Well, I was supposed to take you on an incentive flight," Luft said. "No offense, but I doubt you're physically up for that."

"My doctor would agree with you."

"Right," she sighed. "Well, I can dial it down to zero in these simulators."

Resentful that she didn't bother telling me what the hell was going on before I was about to die of fright, I said, "I've had enough fun. I'm going home."

"Boss's orders. You're experiencing an Axe."

"Axe?"

"Harbinger-Ellis MPJ-88 Battle Axe," she said, giving me a dark look, probably for not knowing that. "The *MPJ* stands for *Multi-Purpose Jet*, so different shades of fighter, light bomber, and recon. The only thing all seventeen clans agree on is the Axes are worth their weight in gold."

Before long, she had me bundled in an olive drab flight suit that seemed to have wires woven in the fabric.

"Biomedical sensors," she explained. "Not that they'll help. You're too skinny for the suit to lie against your skin. I guess we'll have to do it old school: you'll have to tell me if you're dizzy, sick to your stomach, or whatever."

The simulator was an actual cockpit mounted on a giant gyro in a dark room lined with measures for suppressing the sound. A subterranean rumble from the next bay hinted at the latent power of the machine before me.

"Sweet," I said. "I expected a virtual simulation."

"For certain airplanes, that's enough. Park your cane here." She turned to the man standing at the controls of a six-screen computer array. "Lolly, give her a hand, will you?"

Beside the fuselage, Lolly launched me skyward, and I squealed in alarm.

"Whoa. Sorry, lady. You're a lot lighter than I expected."

"Does that count as my incentive flight?" I asked breathlessly, making him chuckle.

As I settled into the rear seat of the cockpit, he braced himself against the canopy and edge of the cockpit. After he showed me how to fasten the harness and put on the helmet, he plugged my wires into the cockpit. I heard static and then the sound of Lutz's exhalation along with mine.

"I assumed it would be a snugger fit in here," I said.

"It would be if you had all the gear on," Luft said. "I doubted you could handle the weight. The gunnery is on computer control for this flight so don't worry if you bump anything. Sit back and enjoy the ride."

"Have fun," Lolly told me before sealing us in.

In the blink of an eye, the view through the canopy went from pitch black to sunny blue skies. As the instruments came alive with a barrage of chirps and lights, my body fizzed with excitement. This was going to be awesome.

I brooded on the train home, unable to be soothed by the rhythmic sway of the cars.

Stupid incentive flight. Stupid, amazing, three-dimensional dogfighting, ground targeting, and refueling puzzles in the sky. Stupid Battle Axes. Stupid, awesome Axes.

Stupid, sadistic MoD making me do a flight in a plane I would never get to fly. It would take years to get fit enough to fly that plane, and I didn't have years. The paperwork indicated they wanted me in a cargo plane anyway, so why hadn't they given me an incentive flight or simulation in a cargo plane?

Because it would've been lame, and it wouldn't have been enough to make me seriously reconsider becoming an engineer.

But the Axe? Well, that airplane changed everything.

CHAPTER 7

SCHOOL GIRL

The next morning, I approached the cracked walkway in front of the tiny old house, wondering what I was going to tell Marco. He was a hard man I respected more than I liked, and I didn't relish speaking to him without Tony there as a buffer.

Marco stepped back to let me cross the threshold, and I saw comfortable, mismatched furniture around a coffee table with a small, partially built engine on it. Did he know one of the parts was bolted on backward?

"I signed for my offer," I told Marco.

"I know," he said, crossing to the kitchen table to retrieve an envelope stamped with the flight academy logo. "Messenger brought it."

I flushed. "Sorry. I forgot Tony's address but had yours because Tony said you had a room to rent, and I wanted to check out the neighborhood before asking you about it." His obsidian stare for my inability to recall basic contact information didn't stop me from asking, "How much for the room?"

"My roommate is the one who owns the house. I told him you were low on funds, and he said he's fine with you doing some housework instead of paying rent. Or you can pay. Or some of both. He's flexible."

"Nice."

The welcome letter from the academy came with a disc, and when I figured out how to load the disc in my palmer, a list of supplies appeared on the screen.

He tipped the screen so he could read it. "We should set up your stipend account and buy some of this today while we're out."

"We? You're going to help me? You said I learned more by doing it on my own."

"With the Christmas traffic, I doubt you'll get it done in time on your own."

"It's Christmas already?"

He couldn't tell if I was joking or not, and I wasn't in a mood to enlighten him. I was a grown woman, and I didn't appreciate the way he and Tony made so many decisions about my life without including me in the conversation.

"You're killing me," he said.

Marco and I did the most critical items first, and the crowd at the uniform place made me glad we didn't wait a day or two.

The tailors and I argued far more than necessary. I emphasized my increasing weight meant I needed plenty of room to grow into, but they were only willing to bump up my measurements by one size. Another argument ensued when I refused to accept the bill for summer whites because I expected to eat my way through at least two sizes in my trousers by June.

Alterations came next, and after I got hemmed and sleeved, we left with nothing more than a receipt and a promise that the uniforms would be ready in two days. The tailor and I were still growling at each other as Marco pushed me from the shop.

As we escaped the frenetic crowd of my future class-mates, Marco said, "You look sickly."

"I've markedly improved since we met, thank you."

"But compared to these pups, you look sickly," he said, drawing my attention to the virile cadets. "We can't do anything more about how skinny you are, but do you know how to wear cosmetics?"

"To create a radiant glow with modern product? I doubt it. I'm getting a haircut and a treatment to give it a healthy shine. I'll visit the cosmetics counter after that. I'm about at the end of my reserves for today, so it'll have to be tomorrow," I said.

We went to his house, and he introduced me to Zack, who was about as tall as a person can get without being considered a freak. I basked in the novelty of seeming dainty as I stood beside my new roommate.

"What happened to your head?" he asked, pushing a shock of mud-colored hair out of his eyes.

"Got knifed," I said, looking way up at him.

"Shot," Marco told him.

"Isn't that what I said?" I asked. I told Zack, "Thanks for renting a room to me."

"Yeah, it's over here," he said, motioning for me to follow him.

The west-facing room was tiny and empty, but it came with a bathroom.

He handed me a pillow and a folded blanket, and as an afterthought, he added a towel.

"You'll have to buy some stuff," he said. "I don't have extras."

Zack left for work, and I paced the tiled floor, deciding where I would spread my bedroll. I checked the locks on the window with each lap, but I forced myself to stop. Given Marco's comfort with his sidearm, it seemed safer here than at Tony's.

"You surprised me," Marco told me, and I jumped at the sound of his voice.

"I'm not convinced engineering was the worse choice. The MoD gives me another bonus if I choose to fly a cargo plane, so I should be set for money for a while, but it's still a military aircraft. Not exactly the normal life I was hoping for."

"And having a normal life saved you from a bullet once before, right?"

Everyone stared at me on the first day of flight school. I could hear my mother's voice promising it only *felt* like everyone was staring at me and they all had better things to do than notice me, but she was full of it this time. I was anorexic and yellow-eyed. They were staring at me.

Pretending I didn't notice, I took a seat in the shadows in the back of the room and scrolled through the text loaded on my writing pad as I waited for the lecture to start. At least they'd started the term at the beginning of January. I preferred to start the year productively. I hoped there wasn't going to be a quiz on what year it actually was. I still got that wrong more often than not.

Detecting the unwavering stare of the olive-skinned, dark-haired woman who sat in front of me, I lifted my gaze.

She gestured at my face. "You've got something in your eye."

I blinked. "I don't feel anything."

"Are you sure? From here, it's obvious you've got a 24-karat lump of gold in that left one," she said, snickering.

"I'll help you," the broad-shouldered man-child to my left told me. At my confusion, he indicated the woman seated in front of me. "Burying Nidra in your backyard. She's a big girl. It'll take both of us."

A horrified giggle escaped me.

His smile came easily, lubricated from frequent use. "I'm Dante," he said. "And you are?"

The devil in her eye, Nidra was about to respond, but she was prevented from further witticisms by the arrival of the uniformed man with an instructor emblem on the pocket. I wouldn't have recognized him if he hadn't nodded and said in that drawl, "Ms. Donovan," as he walked past me.

It was Chavez, the man from the oral test.

At the end of the lecture, I wanted to thank him. I wasn't certain how much he influenced the generosity of my MoD offer as one of my evaluators, but I did know they weren't reading questions off a list, so if I did well, it was due to what he chose to ask.

Unfortunately, he was surrounded by students vying for his attention. I had other tasks to complete, so I had to delay thanking him.

"Crazy, huh?" Dante asked, glancing back at the crowd.

"What's that about? They didn't do that with the other instructors."

He gave me a strange look. "He's a Chavez. He's from that legendary flying family in Texas. How does he know you?"

I shrugged it off. "I met him at the testing office. We barely said two words to each other."

His shoulders slumped, and he dropped the subject.

The campus was larger than it needed to be, with a handful of structures scattered around a huge quad that suggested there were going to be drilling practices. I was already winded getting from the classroom building to the study hall building, so I added a reminder to my palmer to get a doctor's note from Tony excusing me from any marching in formation.

Study hall was held in a building with as much wasted space as the testing office's vestibule. Desks with touch screen tabletops were placed in loose chevrons, and clusters of seats were placed around sizable coffee tables for group work. The library was at the far end.

I claimed the desk closest to the door, my PDT causing the table to emit a soft chime to confirm I'd arrived as scheduled. Mouth set, I tried to let go of the reminder I was constantly monitored, and I practiced connecting my palmer to the desk. Two girls at a nearby table complained about their delay to get into the flight academy, and I resented having to listen to them. The sign beside them indicated this was a quiet zone.

"That guy there said he got in the year he applied."

"No way. It's always at least a two-year wait to get in this campus."

My head snapped up, and I frowned at them. Two years? All these people waited two years? I had tested two weeks ago.

The man sitting at the next desk regarded me with a penetrating, knowing look, and I dropped my gaze back down to my text.

At the end of the school day, I again delayed thanking Mr. Chavez in person, this time because I couldn't let him see how disappointed I was. According to the syllabus, the first three months of flight school barely covered more than basic flight theory, and my twenty-first century education went far beyond that. I was bored already.

"There have been some advancements in technology," Marco pointed out that evening. "And you heard them say it's a tough program."

"It is, but not for the course work. The program is six days a week, ten hours a day, each with almost eight hours of lecture or structured learning. There are two breaks, a short lunch, and a monitored independent study hall."

"Can you can handle it?"

"For at least the next three months? Without a doubt."

"Three months?"

"Then there's a massive written test and an obstacle course, and if you pass both of those, you tell them what you want to fly. If you fail to pass both tests, you're out. There are no appeals, no excuses. I have to admit it's both beautiful and terrible in its simplicity. There's usually a seventy-five percent change in the number of cadets as a result."

"They lose a quarter of their students in one day?"

I grinned. "Three-quarters."

"Someone should've disclosed that with your offer."

"I agree. They offer personal trainers, so that'll help me with the physical end. And while we're on the subject of my corporeal being, does the community center have self-defense programs? You said I set myself up to be a victim, and I want to change that."

"You'll get that in school in your survival course, but I'll get you started."

"No rush. I need time to figure out who to model."

Marco gave me a blank look.

"Is it not a good idea to figure out who the MoD favors, why they are favored, and how I can copy some of that to improve my chances of being favored?"

"It's a great idea. I'm glad you're taking it seriously."
He stood up, saying, "Change into pajamas without any
metal or synthetics. I'll run Blue over you to get a base-
line."

"Tony ran a bioscan weekly on Sunday mornings
after I fasted for twelve hours."

"Sounds good."

But he was still standing there, frowning.

"What's on your mind?" I asked.

"Three months isn't a lot of time to get you in shape."

"You think I don't know that?"

He studied me. "Still, you're more adaptable than I
expected. Not only have you been healing faster than I
would've thought possible, but I expected you to be more
shell-shocked. Not that you went through the Clan Wars
or anything, but still, this was a massive change for you."

"Since birth I've moved every few years, so it was
always new places, new people, new schools, and then
when I got the hang of a place, it was time to move on. People used to tell me that would bother them, but I always
pitied them for having to live in the same place their whole
lives. Getting admitted to this clan is something I have to
do, not something I want to do because there's a giant
hole in me at the idea of not having a home."

"That's the last time you say that out loud," he
warned. "As far as the Hernandez know, you want this to
be your home more than life itself."

"I know what to say," I yawned. I refused to take my
cane to school, and the effort to walk straight without it
drained me. "They have to give me the chance to say it."

"Three months until you're confronted by a military-
grade obstacle course," he said, glancing over me. "Jesus."

CHAPTER 8

BEAT DOWN

Less than a month into the term, I edged down the narrow shadow of the spacious, sunlit corridor of the instructor wing with as smooth a gait as possible so my heel beats wouldn't echo on the polished floor.

"Donovan."

I straightened and pasted on a polite expression for the very man I was trying to avoid. Mr. Yoshimura had mastered the art of making me doubt myself within the first few days.

Without preamble, the toad shoved a hardcopy test in my face. "What is this crap?"

I felt my cheeks heat as he continued to level his scornful visage at me.

Belatedly realizing he did want an explanation, I said, "I calculated how much fuel would be needed to get within two kilometers of the runway, knowing I could glide in without power. From there it was a matter of adding the amount of fuel in the lines to the tank capacity and—"

"Yoshi, really," Mr. Chavez called out. "I have work to do."

"I'm not out here because I enjoy having a conversation with her. It was a simple fuel utilization equation, and she knew it." He whirled back on me. "Pushing your calculations will get you killed in the real world. More to the point, they will get other people killed. Is anything I'm saying getting through that thick skull of yours?"

"Aye, sir," I managed to say around the lump in my throat.

He slammed his door in my face.

Without giving Mr. Chavez a chance to comment, I fled.

But at home, Yoshi's comments about conforming to expectations left me unable to concentrate on my homework. I tore into the engine of Zack's car with a vengeance to keep my hands busy while I figured out how I was going to fit in. I had given my parents and my husband what they wanted, and they had loved me well for it. However, past attempts at blending in with my peers often left me embarrassed and more confused about human behavior than ever.

I glimpsed movement out of the corner of my eye and sensed a familiar presence. I could've asked Paul for advice, but he was an outgoing man who'd never had any trouble relating to people. Sometimes he learned about issues I'd had at school before I got home, which was quite a feat for a man who didn't even go to my university.

"Please don't start," I pleaded as I wrenched off a bolt. Why did they have to make it so damned difficult to get to the oil filter? "I had a rotten day, but I don't want to talk about it. I'll finish this and start dinner."

I didn't want to see his disappointment, so when I looked at him it was the briefest of glances. His mouth moved, but no words came out.

"Don't worry about it, Paul. I slipped, but I know I can pass for normal as soon as I can determine what's normal for these people."

When he didn't respond, I wiped the sweat-soaked hair off my forehead with a greasy hand and turned to give him my full attention.

No one was there.

Goosebumps broke out across my skin even as the denial burst forth in my mind. Someone had been there. My husband had been standing right there telling me something.

But what?

Six weeks into the term, I was finishing my second set of pull-ups on the academy's chinning bar as the sky started to lighten over the aging track behind the enormous simulator bays. My spoiled classmates clung to their treadmills and other indoor equipment, but I loved the solitude and simplicity of the outside track and static calisthenics stations.

I flexed my hands. Three more pull-ups and I could start my laps. Maybe today I could exhaust myself so much I wouldn't be haunted by Paul's accusing face when I slept. Did he assume I ran out on him when I didn't come home that night?

Three... Two... And one.

I dropped to the ground and rubbed my sore hands.

"Those last two were sloppy," Mr. Chavez said, making me jump. He jogged in place on the nearby track. "Do ten more, five in front and five in back."

Ten more, my ass. I was only up to five pull-ups for my whole workout, and I barely squeezed out the final two even if they were sloppy.

I reached for the cold metal chinning bar, grateful for a reason to avoid looking at him. Out of his severe uniform and still all morning-tousled, he smoldered. I smothered the traitorous thought.

I surprised myself by managing another two in strong form, but the third one was kicking my ass. A pair of hands on my waist gave me enough boost to get it done. I let go of the bar and backed away from him, flesh burning where he had touched me.

"Seven more," he demanded.

"Don't help me. It doesn't count if I can't do it on my own."

I needed his help with every single one. It was three or four parts his strength to one of mine.

Cheeks burning at my failure, I dropped to my feet and turned away.

"Next time, use the pull-up station in the gym," he told me. "It uses fractional body weight. Didn't the trainers give you a personalized workout to follow at the beginning of the term?"

"If I followed their plan, I wouldn't even be up to doing pull-ups yet."

"Don't exaggerate."

Mouth agape, I didn't know how to respond. Did he just call me a liar?

For all the patience he'd shown in the oral, he was actually the most demanding, uncompromising instructor in the flight academy, which of course made him the most hated. He easily thinned the after-class herd around his desk in the first few days by asking penetrating questions from the coursework that had students squirming to get away from him before they had to admit they didn't know the answer.

The funny thing was that if they tried to answer and showed they understood at least some of the material, he would've guided them toward the solution. He did that with Nidra, the woman who kept joking about the color of my eyes even though my expression always indicated I didn't enjoy it.

Mr. Chavez watched me shake out my arms and said, "Do a lap with me before school starts."

I didn't want to run with him anymore than I'd wanted to do his stupid pull-ups, but I complied.

He eased his pace when he realized my trouble staying with him. "Since Yoshi yelled at you, your coursework has become pedestrian."

"I'm staying out of trouble, sir. If my instructors want the minimum, that's all they'll get."

"You won't be the best with that attitude."

A sharp bark of laughter escaped me. "The best? Like I'm competing with my classmates for the number one spot? Why would I?"

He looked at me like I had said the most ridiculous and unexpected thing in the world. "Your instructors are still evaluating your expanded solutions, even if they complain. The sole limitation on how much you learn here is you, Miranda."

His jaw snapped shut on whatever else he'd been about to say, and then he nodded at me before sprinting away.

I grinned after him.

The best. What a crock. I worked to get a perfect score and to master everything I needed to master. I didn't care what the person sitting beside me got on his test.

I agreed that I was the only limitation as far as learning went, but I still meant to surrender the freedom of playing with the questions in order to give them the conventional answer. Being myself wasn't worth the trouble it caused, a lesson I thought I had learned to the bone in my childhood.

I staggered toward the locker room at the gym after the rest of my run, but Mr. Chavez plotted an intercept route as he came from the other direction. Fresh from his shower and flawlessly groomed, he wore the uniform better than anyone else there, and he knew it, too.

"I meant to ask you about your Decision," he told me.

I sat on a nearby bench, easing the strain in my lower back. Why couldn't he have stopped me after I iced my muscles and downed my painkillers?

"The Plough," I told him.

"You can't seriously want to fly that after looking over everything else in the arsenal."

"We're not supposed to get biased information from any of you."

"That applies as long as remarkable cadets aren't making misguided Decisions."

I stiffened. "Are you going to veto me?"

"Not if you don't make me."

I sucked in a breath at the threat. When I pushed past him, he blocked me with his body.

"Hear me out," he said. "Miranda, you can't waste your potential on the easiest, slowest military aircraft out there when your skill set makes you capable of flying the fastest and most challenging. Is your fear of physical weakness holding you back? You've already improved since the day of the oral despite the terrible advice from the personal trainers here. There's no reason why you shouldn't choose to pilot a Battle Axe."

As we ate supper, I told Marco about the threat Mr. Chavez made, but he wasn't concerned.

"Axe crews fare better in crashes," he nevertheless added, with the knowledge of a man who saw plenty of downed airplanes firsthand.

"Hey," Zack complained. "You told me I couldn't try to get her to choose the Axe, but you can?"

Zack was an Axe crew chief and believed aviation history started the day the first Axe rolled off the assembly line at Harbinger-Ellis.

"You don't shut up," Marco said. "I gave one opinion and shut my cake hole."

I burst out laughing. Thanks to me, all sorts of stupid descriptors such as *cake hole* were making it back into rotation.

Zack opened his mouth, but I held up my hand. "After dinner."

He took off for his room, which guaranteed there would be visual aids now that he was allowed to brief me.

While I massaged the knot in my hamstring, Marco's gaze rested on my face. "I wish the MoD gave you more options."

"Me, too, but Chavez called it the least demanding to fly so they may doubt I can handle any other. Not in time, anyway. The obstacle course minimum time for the Plough is relatively generous. Speaking of which, the personal trainer I was assigned is sabotaging me."

"Not everyone is out to get you, Mira. Go tell her you recover faster than normal, so you progress faster than normal."

"Why does everyone make such a big deal about that? I've read the studies about how to care for my body. I visualize repairs, I ice and heat, I track my progress, and I adjust."

"You visualize?" he asked, his mouth twitching.

"Don't disparage my method. One experiment I read confirms cancer patients respond better when they visualize their bodies attacking cancer cells, so I envision in microscopic detail what my body needs to do to repair itself, and I eat carefully to make certain it has the nutrients it needs to do so. It's a valid tool."

Red rolled in, teasing me in a way that was a compromise between being friendly like he wanted, but still keeping a distance like Marco wanted. Red had told me Marco's precautions were dumb since the clan was clearly being so reasonable about my presence. I hadn't forgotten Red's desire to abandon me after Marco had rescued me from that forest floor, so I was satisfied with Marco setting that boundary between us.

Marco left his chair and jammed his palmer in his pocket. "Chavez has no reason to block you, Mira. But if you're still worried, I don't see any harm in telling him the terms of your visa."

I grimaced. I didn't want to remind anyone of my outsider status.

"Don't drink so much," I called after them. "You drunken bastards woke me up last time."

"That wasn't us," Red protested, but he snickered as he said it. "You should've seen your face when we—"

Marco pushed Red out the door, ready to get their Saturday night started.

I sensed Zack's hopeful, patient gaze.

"All right," I sighed, knowing that humoring him was only going to make me dissatisfied with the cargo plane I needed to choose. "Tell me about the Battle Axe."

CHAPTER 9

OBSTACLE

At the downtown testing center, I returned to the room where I'd done my first placement exam and found my table for the academy's test on three months of course-work. It was difficult to comprehend that most of the massive cadet loss would occur in this room. My classmates knew it, too. The sniffs of the runny-nosed weepers were already annoying.

"People like us don't need to worry about this test."

The cadet standing in front of me had the build of a long-distance runner and the feral, unblinking stare of a predator. I recognized him from the first day in study hall.

"I'm not worried."

His smile revealed short, white teeth. "Good."

I flagged Dante on the way to his seat. "Who's that?"

"Kairo Ashton," he said, grateful to have a topic to talk about other than the test. "Your sole competition academically."

The test was long and mind-numbing, but I went through it twice to ensure my responses were the boring, expected ones. Someone passed my table, having finished before I did, and I looked up in surprise.

Kairo Ashton.

I saw him again after lunch as students meandered toward the obstacle course attached to the track.

"I almost aced it," Kairo told me. "Only missed five. How did you do?"

"I don't know. I was comfortable with my answers, though," I said, deliberately vague. I didn't want a daily showdown with a grade point average junkie.

"Of course you were."

Unsettled, I watched him weave around throngs of students to get to the starting blocks. I might get lucky. Maybe he would go into the Battle Axe program instead of the Plough's so my coursework and his were incomparable.

"Who's next?"

Ten more students stepped forward, and I thanked God for them. My classmates had stressed about the morning's exams to the point of stupid snappish fights among each other, but now they swapped teasing insults before taking on the obstacle course.

Typically I would've gone first so I could get on with the rest of my day, but I needed time to evaluate the course and see how everyone else was running it.

Nidra stuck her heel in the ground and stretched her calf, readying herself for a leisurely Sunday run in the park. Now that the test anxiety was behind her, I expected her one-a-day comment about my yellow eyes, but she said, "Relax. You're making me nervous."

I tried to smile, mostly because I read that it helped calm a person down. I hadn't suffered a third panic attack, but I didn't take that for granted.

She smiled back with the kind of dimples that would linger well after the baby fat was gone.

Dante trotted up, his grin changing as he saw Nidra with me. He stood beside her, chest lifted, in case she forgot he was a virile eighteen-year-old with great pecs.

She told him in a fake whisper, "She's worried."

"Do you want me to run with you?" he asked me.

"Thanks, but no."

They left in the next wave. Dante tripped coming out of the starting blocks and knocked into Nidra. He burst out laughing, which made her try to pinch him.

"Go," I yelled, waving my arms. "They're still timing you."

I watched them in case they found a way to shave off seconds, but the ways to ascend bleachers or traverse a length of rotating pipe were limited. And frankly, Dante couldn't disguise his desire to hold back to do the trial with Nidra.

When a handful of us were left, no one volunteered for the shame to come. The instructor picked the three strongest-looking slackers for the upcoming round. I tried to look pitiful and weak so he wouldn't pick me until the end, but I was chagrined when he did.

I fought to keep up with the others, and my thighs burned and quivered from the strain as I sucked air.

Was I going to make it in time?

No, I wasn't.

Keeping my eyes on the top of the bleachers, I hopped from the concrete risers onto the metal seats.

"Get a flag," the nearest instructor yelled, pointing to the few remaining ribbons on the rail. I veered away from him and headed for the end flag.

"You're wasting time you haven't got, cadet."

The flag came away without a hitch, and I planted my foot on the spot I'd taken it from before launching myself over the rail.

"Jesus," he yelled as I plummeted through the air.

I seized hold of the light post with one arm and hung on in terror as my body whipped around the pole. I slid down at an alarming rate, ripping open skin on my arms and legs on bolts and the rough-edged service panel.

My feet hit the ground, the impact to my ankles and knees making my cry out in agony. I lurched forward, stumbled, and righted myself, before forcing my legs into a run again.

Harder. Push harder.

I passed the finish line and lurched to a stop, gasping and coughing. I couldn't have said what part of me hurt the most, so I didn't know what to favor as I waited for the timekeeper to reveal my results.

The woman looked to her companion. "Well?"

"You're the one with the timer. Did she come in under time or not?"

"She passed the time for all of the programs including the Axe, but does it matter? She didn't stay within the boundaries of the course."

"Given the way the instructions were worded, technically that was within bounds," I choked out, sucking in sharp, agonizing breaths that didn't even begin to ease the hammering in my head.

"We'll have to consult the dean, so go to the infirmary to get your arms looked at."

I made it a couple steps before I caught part of the conversation behind me.

"...cheated so I hope they bounce her."

Shocked speechless, I dropped my arms.

"Go to the infirmary," the man instructed.

The medic had finished cleaning my gashes and stepped out to get suture tape when Mr. Chavez appeared in the doorway. "I heard," he said, turning my arm so he could examine the damage from the pole. With a distasteful look at the mess, he released my arm.

"Do you believe I cheated, too?"

"Can I?" he asked with a strange half-smile. "In my lectures, I emphasize finding ways to compensate for your disadvantages in a situation."

"I must've missed that."

"I doubt that. However it does appear in the syllabus at some point." He opened the cabinets until he found gauze. He handed me a pad. "Your cosmetics are smeared."

"I'll fix my appearance after I get finished here."

"Fix it? Your heavy hand makes you appear older, and your clumsy technique fails to accentuate your best features. How is that fixing it? No cosmetics are going to hide that scar either, so if you're self-conscious about it, see a dermatologist."

My cheeks heated with embarrassment, and I was grateful when a woman who dripped authority stepped in the room and asked Mr. Chavez to leave.

After the dean told me I did the course within time and the pole slide was within the mapped boundaries according to the computer, she added, "The complication is that accepting this condones an unsafe act. Other students will read of it or hear of it, and they will try to reproduce it."

And sue them when they got injured.

She said, "Your time was automatically entered into the system the moment you crossed the finish line. Legally, we can't expel you after you passed both halves of the tests, but there's no doubt you would be unable to complete the course in time if you ran it the expected route, so there is weight to the cheating charge leveled against you."

My hands balled into fists, and I forced them to flatten against my legs.

"In short, you've created a dilemma," she told me, her expression indicating she didn't appreciate that. In fact, I was positive she had the lawyers looking for a loophole so she could reject me.

"Ma'am, how long is it going to take for this to get resolved?" Mr. Chavez asked from the doorway.

"What are you still doing here?" she asked, whirling.

"I forgot my water bottle," he said, reaching for mine. When I opened my mouth, he shot me a sharp look. "However, since I'm here, I want to know if I should prep for her Decision tomorrow."

"Her instructors will be briefed when a ruling is made."

She excused herself, and he followed her out, speaking to her low and fast.

By the time the suturing and bandaging was done, I was woozy and shaky. Outside the infirmary, Mr. Chavez handed me a T-shirt and sweatpants marked with the flight academy logo.

"You can't wear those," he said, indicating my bloody clothes. "Get changed, and then come to my office."

After I changed and checked my messages, I slumped into the chair in front of his meticulously organized desk. The sleek, modern workspace suited him.

Ignoring the feeling that I was a dirty sock thrown in the middle of a polished floor, I dug through my bag for my emergency shake and a double dose of painkillers.

I was about to speak when he made a show of tapping a placard on the desk that revealed his office was under surveillance.

"I'm Texan," he explained. "A foreigner."

I slammed the pills and chugged the shake, wiping at the trickles that ran out of the corners of my mouth. "Sorry," I said, leaning back with my eyes closed. A black buzzing in my head made me hope immediate action wouldn't be required of me because I doubted I was capable of it. "I used everything I had. What did you need to discuss?"

"Take a moment."

I willed the shake to get into my system more rapidly, but instead, my stomach heaved, and I staggered out of his office. I threw up in my mouth but kept my lips sealed and nose clamped until I got to a toilet in the women's room.

"I wondered if you would do that," he commented, having followed me into the bathroom. "You should've sipped. I do like that you vomit in a very tidy way though."

I could've chosen from a list of rude comments at that point, but I settled for a banal question. "Sir, what did you need me for?"

"If I didn't tell you when you sat in my office, why would a more opportune time be when you're kneeling with a death grip on the commode?"

I flushed the toilet, and he stepped aside so I could leave the stall. I would've liked to wash out my mouth, but they had a waterless hand-cleaning system.

I used the wall to hold myself upright and sensed his critical gaze on me.

"I didn't reapply my cosmetics," I acknowledged. "It's the least of my worries at the moment."

"I agree with the latter but see no reason why you couldn't do the former. But that wasn't why I was reading your face. You're looking worse. You should go. You'll get a message when the ruling is official."

"And if it doesn't come by morning?"

"Stay home. However, we need to proceed with the assumption that you'll be giving your Decision tomorrow. You met the minimum to get into the Battle Axe's pilot program. It's your best choice."

"My MoD paperwork says I need to choose the Plough."

"I want you in an Axe."

He should've known his wishes meant nothing compared to the MoD's, but I knew what to say to earn my release from Mr. Chavez's presence.

"I understand."

On the train home, I checked my palmer ten or fifteen times, so certain it chimed, but it was silent.

Marco shot to his feet when I shuffled in the door.

"You're late," he told me.

"For?"

"Getting home. I was afraid they deported you already."

I told him about the obstacle course.

He sank into his chair, eyes closing briefly. "Oh, Mira," he said helplessly.

"I'm sorry," I said. "I doubted I was going to get across that finish line in the time I needed for the Plough any other way. If they'd let me do a practice lap, I would've had a better gauge of time and known I was within range."

I spilled the shake I was mixing, and he brushed me out of the way. Instead of sitting with any grace, I fell onto the chair as my trembling legs gave out.

"Well, no one can say you didn't give it everything you've got," he said, mixing me a new drink.

"Trust me, I feel worse than I look," I said, dropping my head into my hands. "Chavez is pressuring me about the Axe again."

"You're the one who has to risk your life in that plane," he said, surprising me because I expected him to tell me to do what the MoD wanted. But if he was fully obedient, he would've handed me over to the authorities as soon as he snagged me from that airplane crash. "If you had no idea what the MoD wanted, what would you pick?"

"The Axe. It's durable, safe, and flexible, and it has an expansive support network. From what I've read, the highest grossing aviators in this clan are Axe pilots, too, which tells me the MoD favors them the most. I want to be in a position that the MoD values over the long term."

"Good. You chose. Now go to sleep."

He had to know it wasn't that easy, but I went to my room to worry in private about what the MoD would do to me if I chose wrong. At least it wouldn't take me long to pack if I was deported. I slept on a bedroll in my closet where I felt safe, clothes forming my pillow. I studied on a low table made of a stack of books. Other than the uniforms and academy paraphernalia, everything I owned fit into a backpack.

My bathroom was another story. The counter was lined with bottles of pills, supplements, liniments, and all the other signs of my struggle to build a sturdy body. I averted my gaze from the pill bottles on the cracked lacquer tray. They were hardcore ones for when I couldn't shut down enough to sleep for two or three days or when the anxiety shook me so much my teeth chattered.

One bottle was particularly nasty, and I'd marked it with a skull and crossbones to remind me to return them to Tony. My jumpiness, sleeplessness, and compulsion to check the locks worsened until he put me on pills for hyper-awareness, but the side effects—such as the hallucinations about Paul—had been so horrible that Marco and I agreed I had to stop taking them.

I reached past them for the analgesics and my muscle rub. I didn't want to be limping in to make my Decision with a weakness that made them question my right to be there.

CHAPTER 10

THE DECISION

The next morning, I cried out with the agony of getting out of my blankets and onto my feet.

Zack was sitting at the kitchen table staring off into space when I dragged myself out of my room.

"You look exhausted," I said.

"You wasted your money on those rented legs again, didn't you?" he teased. "Want a ride to school?"

"No, thanks. Walking will flush out some of the damage. Is Marco up yet?"

He shook his head, sending a cascade of brown hair across his face. "He's probably passed out at Red's."

"Must've been some party."

He slid a penny across the table toward me. "Found this by your chair on the deck."

I wrote a note in my palmer to check my clothes for holes in the pockets, and I dropped the penny in the dish with the others. I definitely had a knack for finding them, and maybe that indicated a reluctance to let go of the past, but I wasn't about to ignore a lucky penny on the ground when I needed it.

When it was time to leave for school, there were still no messages from the flight academy. Supposing they had the wrong contact information for me, I went anyway, but since I hadn't been given a schedule for the day, I didn't know where to report. I didn't see anybody.

Mr. Chavez looked annoyed when he opened his office door to my knock, and he greeted me by saying, "I haven't heard anything either."

"What should I do?"

He motioned for me to sit down and keep my mouth shut while he tabbed the comm on his desk. "If she hasn't been given official notice that she's out, then we have to put her name back on the roster for the Decision."

"You can't," Mr. Yoshimura told him. "Once she makes the Decision, she's in a different accounting system, and the school loses the right to formally charge her for anything she did prior."

"Can she withdraw from the program?" he asked, holding up his hand when I was about to protest. "Or can we release her? I hear the MoST engineering people wanted her."

I beamed. I never did see the results from my genetic testing, but given how well I performed academically I doubted I had ever needed the genetic mapping to get anyone's attention.

"No, of course not," Yoshi snapped. "All cadets are under contract."

"She saw a solution no one else did, and her reward is that she can't stay, but she can't leave. Yoshi, this is intolerable."

"Agreed, but there's nothing I can do about it. Are we done?"

"Did I say goodbye? Look, do you think she cheated?"

There was a hesitation on the other end, making it clear he hadn't expected to be asked that. "It's more important that we recognize she exposes a flaw to our methodology. This isn't the first time we've lost a promising student because of a demanding physical exam so early in the program."

"We haven't lost her yet, and you didn't answer my question."

"There isn't any honor in her using a technicality to pass, but no, she didn't cheat. She just doesn't see the same boundaries most people do. I'm done with this conversation."

After he clicked off, I whispered, "I'm sorry. I do try to think like a normal person when I remember."

Mr. Chavez laughed.

"It's not funny," I said. "These kinds of problems jeopardize everything."

"That risk may have earned you a future at this academy."

The loud, determined clacking sound in the hall was accompanied by an angry voice. "Chavez? Why aren't you in the conference room? We can't begin until you get there. I don't appreciate this prima donna crap."

She'd reached his office by then, and her expression turned sour.

"Oh. Ms. Donovan," the dean said. "It's you. You were told to wait at home for notification."

"Where does she stand?" Mr. Chavez demanded.

Pretending she didn't hear him, she turned away.

What a bitch. She meant to stall me until it was too late for me to have a Decision entered in the computer.

Mr. Chavez's narrowed eyes showed he was equally impressed with her amateur machinations.

He asked me, "Who's your liaison at the MoD?"

"Stop," the dean snapped, whirling. "Chavez, go to the conference room. I'll handle this."

"Go to the study hall with the others," Mr. Chavez told me as he ushered me down the hall. Knives stabbed my legs as I fought to stay upright at the pace he set. "Give the impression there was never any doubt about you staying, and don't mention the obstacle course at all."

"Are you certain?"

"Am I confident she can get the job done? Not even remotely. I'm calling the MoD."

"Thank you."

"I'm doing this for me, not you. I hate my workload being held up by petty bureaucrats."

In study hall, I couldn't concentrate on the website I was reading, so I watched the first student leave to make the Decision. He returned ten minutes later to signal to his friends that the deed was done and to let them know where he was starting the party. We were getting three days off while the school changed gears, and I was the only one who didn't mean to spend the vacation drunk and naked.

Since my surname started with a D, I got called soon.

Thank you, Mr. Chavez.

When I walked into the room with my back ramrod straight and chin high, I knew none of them could tell how much it hurt to walk so proudly.

Ms. Chenier said, "Ms. Donovan, since you're choosing the Plough, this won't take long."

"My MoD paperwork doesn't prohibit me from choosing something else. It says I'll get a bonus if I choose it."

Mr. Yoshimura's eyes narrowed. "It's not a choice, Donovan. After the predicament with your obstacle course run, you more than ever need to prove you can do what's expected of you." He glanced at the clerk. "She'll take the Plough."

The clerk looked at me, and I pressed my lips together, refusing to confirm it.

Mr. Yoshimura sighed. "I'm trying to save you a lot of ass pain here."

"Understood and appreciated, sir."

Mr. Chavez pushed away from the table. "Call the next student. I want a word with Ms. Donovan."

"Well, imagine that," Mr. Johnston said over muffled snickers.

What the hell was that all about?

Mr. Chavez directed a cold look their way before steering me out of the room.

"What's going on in that head of yours?" he asked once we reached the end of the corridor.

To avoid looking at him, I stared out the window, looking across the palm trees and beyond the Spanish colonial styled structures of the old end of campus. Focusing on the pattern the traffic made on the highway, I said, "What if I don't choose the way the MoD wants me to?"

He jerked his head away, a smile lifting the corner of his mouth. "You're considering the Axe."

"Sir, perhaps you haven't noticed, but year in and year out Axe pilot is the most popular option because everyone and their dog wants to drive a fighter jet. That doesn't mean it's the appropriate choice for them. Are you confident I'm capable of completing the Battle Axe pilot program to the satisfaction of the Hernandez? Because I can't afford to fail."

His gaze was direct, uncompromising. "Capable? Definitely. I could add that you're particularly well-suited for it, but I don't want you to assume that will make the program easy for you. There isn't a more challenging warbird to drive. However, a more pressing issue is that it's a physically demanding plane to fly. You'll have to pass a full combat physical at the end of the year."

Knowing the goal would be difficult to achieve shouldn't have made me want it more, but it did. I was so tired of being bored.

"Wait a minute," I said, eyes narrowing. "This isn't about the results of my genetic testing, is it?"

He made a face at that. "As far as I'm concerned, those tests are only good for proving paternity. Is that screening the reason you're here?"

"What? No, of course not. I never even received the results."

"Didn't you? Your records say you've got a hereditary gift for handling g-force acceleration."

My lips pressed together.

"G-force acceleration is—"

"I know what it is," I said. "Is my bra size in my records, too?"

"Don't interrupt me. And no, it isn't. Is your bra size in any way relevant to your ability to fly?"

If he was trying to tease me into a better mood, well, it worked.

"Miranda, I'm Texan, and I haven't lived here long. I don't know the Hernandez MoD well enough to predict it."

"Well, getting my papers will come down to my ability to impress them, and try as I might, I can't imagine a way I could impress them in a cargo plane. So there's one reason to choose the Plough and at least eight to choose the Axe."

I strode into the conference room and gave them my Decision.

Ms. Chenier broke the tense silence by asking, "Did Mr. Chavez coerce or bribe or in any other way influence your decision, Ms. Donovan?"

"No, ma'am," I blurted. The lie was instinctive, and it surprised me as much as the question had.

She said, "Whatever your reasons are for choosing this, I must warn you that once it's entered, there's no turning back." When I showed no sign of changing my mind, she told the man behind the computer, "Enter it. Miranda Elena Donovan, Battle Axe pilot."

When I turned to walk away, Mr. Chavez passed through the doors, took one glance at his colleagues and then grinned at me. "You chose Axe pilot, didn't you?"

I eyed him hatefully. Something was going on in that room. The knowing looks, the sudden chill in the air, and the tightened mouths all told me I had committed a cardinal sin.

I turned back to Ms. Chenier, and she gave me a look of mixed anger and sympathy. "Your Decision has been made. Please leave the room so we can send for the next student."

Back straight, I nodded and strode out of the room. The moment the doors slid shut behind me, voices rose in anger as if the floodgates had been thrown open. I paused, but I couldn't make out distinct words, so I walked toward the stairs.

Sharp footfalls behind me made me glance back up the staircase.

Mr. Chavez's satisfaction with me showed in his smile. His manicured hand lifted toward me. "I'm not offering you a poisoned apple, Miranda. They were remiss in providing your revised schedule and the list of texts you need to download."

I plugged the disc in my palmer and glanced over the agenda so I didn't have to look at him. "It's just as well you're not my instructor anymore, sir."

"Why is that?" he asked, sounding wounded.

"Because you've been calling me by my given name, and if you ever did it in class, I'm not certain I could cover your ass like I apparently did in that conference room," I said.

Shocked, he said, "Ms. Donovan, I never meant—"

"Sir, for—"

"Don't interrupt me."

"—some reason, I lied to my instructors about your involvement in my Decision, and I don't feel good about that, especially since I don't understand what was going on in there. If you won't offer an explanation, then, no offense, I don't want to listen to what you have to say."

His mouth was drawn tight again, and since he showed no sign of admitting what he knew, I walked away.

How greatly did I damage my chances by protecting him, siding with him, or whatever I'd done? And why him? There were kinder instructors. Easier ones, too. Ones who weren't distrusted foreigners. I owed him, but I didn't owe him that much.

But what was I worried about? It wasn't personal. Mr. Chavez hadn't suggested I take what he taught for the rest of the year.

Maybe that was it. Now that I appeared to be high maintenance, they thought he made sure I wouldn't end up in any of his classes.

Wanting chocolate pudding to take with my painkillers, I went to the cafeteria in the main building. It was empty except for lounging permanent party personnel between their rounds in the simulators.

The goo I sucked off the spoon a few minutes later was cold, sweet, creamy, and brown, but I had the nagging suspicion they'd invented new flavors while I was asleep because it wasn't chocolate. I couldn't decide if I enjoyed the dessert or not, but I did resent the false advertising.

I was an Axe pilot.

The thought came from nowhere and was replaced by the mental image of tumbling through the sky as I forced my way through the stratosphere with both hands on the control stick.

I held up my hands, imagining such an expensive tool being controlled by the pale, bony things at the end of my arms. Unfortunately, the days of my left hand being a vestigial accessory for wearing a wedding ring were over, so I'd need to figure out dexterity and targeting exercises for it.

I struggled to eat the final dregs of my pudding with the spoon in my left hand when Dante and Nidra rushed in, whooping and hollering about being Axe pilots.

"Great," I said sarcastically, but I was smiling when I said it. "Stuck with you yahoos for the rest of the year."

CHAPTER 11

CRUCIBLE

Walking through the flight academy campus the first day after classes resumed gave me the strange sensation I was walking through a town after a natural disaster struck. So many people were gone. There was no laughter or casual conversation in the few who remained, just a powerful sense of purpose.

Dante fell into step beside me. "This is weird," he muttered. "Creepy weird."

The classroom for our first lecture was a sunken bowl with three rings of desks around a flat screen that came down from the ceiling. The desks were different, too, curving around the student to the elbow. Twenty desks were placed on the upper tier, fifteen on the middle, and ten on the bottom. The back side of the dimly lit room was roped off, halving the number of available seats.

"Awesome," Dante said, pausing to take it in. "Reminds me of gears."

As I went down the staircase, my footfalls were deadened by the sound-absorbing carpet and wall panels. When I spotted the air conditioning vents, I chose a seat far away from them. Without much meat on my bones, I got cold easily.

Conflicted, Dante looked between me and Nidra, who was sitting front and center in the lowermost ring. I motioned for him to sit near her. He made a face at me for not sucking it up and moving to where we could all sit together, and then he claimed the desk attached to hers.

"Welcome to the crucible," Mr. Yoshimura said as he took the stairs down to the pit. "What you see around you is the entirety of this year's Axe pilot class. Every single one of you is smart and driven, but that's not enough. Not even close. It's time for us to apply pressure to see what you're truly made of."

Fire ripped through my veins, burning away the dust that had accumulated through the months of tedious coursework. I hadn't felt this awake since the oral.

He continued. "The Axe has a crew of two, and most of you are used to working alone. Most of you are control freaks, too. Teamwork, people. Learn to trust that your partner is doing his job. Learn to accept primary responsibility for the outcome of that aircraft. Do you hear what I'm saying? Dante."

"I am responsible for my gunner's life," Dante said.

"Exactly. Donovan, what do you think this program is designed to teach you?"

I didn't hesitate. "To make rapid, ethical, mission-essential life or death decisions while under pressure."

"You forgot to mention learning how to fly the Axe," he said, making everyone laugh.

I pulled at my collar, looking away.

"But you're correct," Yoshi said. "More than you know. There's a reason we don't use computers to fight our battles for us. For the rest of class, we're going to watch vids and discuss why that is."

As soon as I left campus at the end of the day, I was accosted by a former classmate.

"How can you live with yourself?" she demanded. "You didn't earn the right to be there."

Stunned, I didn't know what to say.

Dante approached, snapping, "They weren't limiting the number of cadets who could move on. All you had to do was pass both tests to be in."

"She didn't," she snarled, pointing at me.

"Were you there? Because I remember you being in the cafeteria at the time she was running the obstacle course. And if you weren't there, all you've got is second-hand information. In other words, gossip. If you want to argue about how accurate gossip is, we can start with what people say you did at Mike's party."

She colored. Looking past him at me, she said, "Burn in hell, bitch."

"Grow up," Dante yelled at her back as she stormed off. Seeing my white-knuckled grip on my bag, he pointed out the security guy going after her. "Don't worry about it. They increase security for the two weeks after the Decision for this very reason. This morning I got attacked by Doug's grandmother. I mean, what do you say to someone's grandmother? You can't yell back. It was horrible."

He nudged me toward the station, and on trembling legs, I complied. Never before so conscious of the uniform I wore, I constantly looked over my shoulder to see if the girl was following me.

A week after the Decision, the MoD had not sent a response that suggested they were displeased with my official choice of being an Axe pilot. Nevertheless, I was still jumpy, reacting to every sharp sound or sudden movement. Was the MoD that understanding and that accommodating? Or were they dealing with more important affairs and simply hadn't gotten around to finding out if I had complied?

Starting a new program with a bunch of instructors who thought I was a high-maintenance cheat didn't help any.

But as the weeks turned into months, I settled into the intense, challenging routine with real satisfaction. Not only was my dedication to my fitness routine paying off, but the more I learned about the Axe, the more I wanted to fly it. The controls were set up how I expected them, and systems were clean and programmed in a way that made sense to me on an elemental level. The aircraft had been designed with me in mind.

And while my instructors never warmed up to me, their treatment never worsened, so I would've said I was content.

For the most part.

Flicking an unwilling glance toward my ex-instructor out in the cafeteria at lunchtime one day toward the end of August, I sighed. Despite my best intentions, I still found myself looking Mr. Chavez's way when he entered the cafeteria or when I passed him on the way to class. He offered me nothing more than a formally polite greeting, but when he looked my way, I felt a spotlight on me.

My awareness of him was prickly. Every time I saw him, my thumb folded across my palm to touch where my wedding ring used to be. My ring's absence cost me that warm, secure feeling that banished any stray thoughts about another man.

Doing my best not to look at Mr. Chavez when I passed him, I bumped into someone else.

"What's wrong, Dante?"

I followed his morose gaze and saw Nidra giggling with her friends.

"Ask her out," I said, exasperated.

"So you didn't know either? She's got a boyfriend."

"Why didn't you tell her how you felt about her before you knew that?"

"It's complicated."

I followed him. "No, Dante, it's not."

He whirled at me and gritted out, "Hexadactyly." At my blank look, he said, "Supernumerary digit."

I blinked, glancing at his hands. His grip on his bag was so tight his fingers were white, but I could still count them.

"On my left foot," he gritted out.

I couldn't help it. I smiled. "All this fuss over an extra toe? If it bothers you, why not have it removed?"

"It doesn't bother me," he snapped. "It's fully functional, looks completely normal. My favorite aunt has it, too."

"I assumed it was normal since the more childish guys in the locker room didn't notice it and tell everyone. If it's that innocuous, what's the issue?"

"It bothers people once they find out about it."

"It doesn't," I assured him.

He leaned in, holding my eyes. "It does."

"You're not giving yourself or Nidra enough credit."

"It doesn't matter. She's got a boyfriend," he reminded me.

As he stalked away, I couldn't help looking down at his left foot. An extra toe? It must've sucked to find shoes.

"Stop looking at it," he snapped without turning around.

CHAPTER 12

One Gin & Tonic, Hold the Roofies

The cream and silver nightclub flashed with strobe lights reflecting off faceted glass sculptures. The live music was loud and throbbing, penetrating me deliciously with a rumble that teased me with fantasies of my jet.

Thanks to Dante, I was in a sea of young, energetic, oversexed people who partied together regularly. His argument was that Axe pilot cadets were statistically likely to be paired with Axe gunner cadets from the current class instead of an established gunner. He suggested we extend invitations to the gunner cadets so we could feel out potential partners.

Having met whom I wanted to meet, this would be my last time at the club. I was tired of spending my one day off a week catching up on my homework, my sleep, and my workouts. Staying home would also spare me Marco's lectures about abusing my liver despite my promises I stayed away from alcohol.

"Who knew?" Nidra asked, bumping into me at the bar and gesturing at the dance floor. "Dante's got a pair of hips and isn't afraid to use them. Do you think he's that good in bed?"

"He won't be interested in a threesome with your boyfriend."

"I meant for you. Don't you think he's looking sexy tonight?"

My eyebrows shot to my hairline.

"Or are you into women?" she asked.

"Men."

"You can like both. I mean, when you see a woman like that, how can you not consider switching sides?" she said, indicating a buxom, raven-haired beauty gyrating on the dance floor.

My eyes widened. "What is Profit Carlisle doing here?"

"That's the legendary bitch?"

"Well, I don't know about the bitch part, but she could definitely write the book on social and political climbing," I said. "She's also the number one Axe pilot in the clan rankings right now."

Nidra whistled. "What I wouldn't give to get her as a mentor."

"Mentor? Is there a program for that?"

Please let there be an essay question on the application form that asks why Profit should pick me. I rock those.

She shook her head. "Not even an informal one."

I made a face. "There's no modeling that, either."

"Modeling?"

"Walking in her footsteps in the hopes it will lead to the same destination. But she was born with money, connections, and perfect looks. Everyone's always fighting each other for the chance to tutor her after any misstep she makes, so she would've had to work hard not to be in the top three."

"You got me talking about school again. This is what happens when a person doesn't have enough sex. Go out there and find a guy to grind on before you forget how," she said before she rejoined her friends. They didn't have a man with them, and I wondered if she'd told Dante she was with someone so he wouldn't ask her out.

A booth opened up, and I snagged it, glad I could sit and rest my legs. The strong wind this morning had made a grueling cross-country run even more punishing.

"Rumor is that you solved the Effingham problem," Kairo said as he slid into the booth beside me, his drink sloshing against the glass table. His inner wrist was inked with a glowing white Axe tattoo. "Impressive. I solved the Frankfort."

Ah. The GPA hound was back.

He spoke with such arrogance that I had to say, "So did I."

He smirked. "I did it in one less step than you did."

I paused. He was referring to pre-Decision course-work, and I didn't want to encourage his obsession with beating me, but still, I said, "You have my attention."

He laughed, and we fell into conversation. When he turned to wave at someone, I switched my untouched drink with one of the abandoned glasses on the table. My skillful timing meant that what he saw when his gaze returned was me bringing a nearly empty drink away from my mouth. It was easier than fighting with people when I ordered a sparkling water while everyone else ordered booze.

As the night went on, Kairo showed himself to be aggressive, ambitious, and rude, but he had one hell of a mind. For the first time, I had found someone I'd consider partnering with.

"Congratulations on passing the obstacle course," he said in a sly way that told me he knew about the cheating allegation.

"Finding a legal solution outside the expected one isn't cheating," I said, eyes flashing.

"I agree with you," he said, holding up his hands. "What do you know about the Comp?"

"It's a competition for the best combat air crews on the continent. Seeing as I don't have a competitive bone in my body, I have zero interest in it."

"That makes you useless," he commented before ditching me.

The rejection stung, and my cheeks colored. I'd put in enough of an effort, so I could go home without being challenged. Dante plotted an intercept route when he spotted my escape attempt. Nidra did, too, separating from her friends with a frown.

"You're leaving?" she asked me.

I nodded. "It's getting late."

"If you're taking the train, I'll walk you to the station," Dante told me. "It's safer."

"I'll go with you," Nidra said. "I've got a lot of homework."

I jumped when my arm was grabbed.

"Hey, where are you going?" Kairo asked. "I got us drinks."

"You called me useless, so the conversation was over."

"You're still the best option," he said.

He cursed when someone bumped into him and spilled the drinks, and with black rage, he slammed the glasses on the nearest table and charged after the couple.

"Dante," Nidra said. "He's—"

"Stay here," Dante said, which, of course, meant we all followed him out like fighter jets escorting a big bomber.

In the parking lot, he managed to snag Kairo before he got anywhere near the fighting couple.

Exclamations made me turn to see the woman take another vicious slap.

"Call the cops," Dante told Nidra when the guy raised his hand again.

Nidra was put on hold. Another cadet I didn't know approached the couple and took a terrible blow to the belly for his trouble.

Time stretched. Nidra and both of her friends were all on hold with the cops now.

And the guy continued to beat his girlfriend in the parking lot.

Kairo's rage kept growing. The change in his body revealed the moment he decided the man's actions had provided the ideal excuse to beat him into oblivion for spilling the drink.

I jumped in front of Kairo, my hand on his chest. Muscles leaped beneath my hand. "Don't risk your slot with an alcohol-related incident."

"He's beating her. It has to end."

"I'll end it. You stay here."

Dante swore. "Mira, don't get involved."

"It's all right. I haven't been drinking."

"Mira, no," he said. "Don't do this."

I darted around him and threw myself in between the couple to intercept the punch to the face and turn the tables.

It was my first fight, and it had plenty of surprises.

I learned how much it hurt to hit someone, for one, especially when I connected with the bony parts. My knuckles lit up with pain that radiated up my arm to my shoulder joint.

Emotion never entered into it either. I expected rage or fear but felt nothing but the determination to resolve the situation to my satisfaction.

It was over quickly, too. I'd barely started before the man was on the ground, hands up defensively. He was brawny and more experienced, but he lost. I didn't know what to make of that.

And I didn't expect the woman to yell at me the whole time not to hurt him. She sprawled across him protectively, her crying eyes red and hostile as she told me to get away from him. The blood from her smashed nose and split lip were dripping on the bastard, and she considered *me* the villain.

Most of my fellow cadets praised my skill and my nerve, and Kairo was the most impressed of all. Dante, however, told me it was late and I needed to leave.

"I'm fine," I said, wondering if he was afraid the guy was going to come after me.

Helped by his girlfriend, the man got to his feet, and they stumbled away toward the train station.

"See? It's over."

"So are we going or not?" Nidra asked, looking between me and Dante.

"No, I'm going to stay awhile longer," I said, basking in the adulation. I doubted I'd have to pay for drinks for the rest of the night.

A tall, blond man with a flirtatious smile approached, gesturing to my eye with the cold pack in his hand.

Sucking a bloody knuckle, I sensed the weight of Dante's gaze.

"Mira, you have no idea what you did."

"Lighten up. Fortune favors the bold."

Wow, did I turn out to be wrong about that.

CHAPTER 13

MONEY TROUBLE

On Monday morning, my status was still elevated. As I walked through the cafeteria, the high ceilings bounced people's conversations around until I heard my name being mentioned from every direction. It was sort of unsettling to be so noticed, even if the cadets' tones weren't unflattering.

Before I could get my ice water to take to class, Mr. Chavez strode toward me, eyes narrowed, mouth tight. Eager to avoid being caught in the crossfire, students fled from his path.

So the story had been overhead by the instructor regiment. Great.

I hadn't gone more than a meter toward the nearest escape route before Mr. Chavez bellowed my name. "Don't you dare take another step."

I muttered a curse and turned to face him, hands outstretched in supplication.

His hand shot out and tipped my face into the light, giving him an excellent view of the black eye my cosmetics failed to hide. "It's true? You were brawling?"

I jerked my head out of his grasp. "No, sir, I was not. That man had every opportunity to stop beating his girlfriend. When he didn't, I intervened."

"Intervened? Is that your colorful euphemism for you beating the crap out of someone?"

"I didn't beat the crap out of anyone," I said calmly, hoping he would take the hint to lower his voice. "I only hit him in the places where he hit her. He was conscious and walking under his own power at the end of it."

With a vicious gesture, he snapped, "I don't want to hear it. You provoked and assaulted a drunken man. It was stupid, reckless, and dangerous."

"It was justice!" I roared.

Even as his eyes widened at my outburst, I dropped mine, color flooding my cheeks.

I'd yelled at one of my instructors. In fact, I'd never yelled so loudly and with so much force in my life. The cafeteria was still, and I felt everyone's stare as they anticipated his reaction.

The bells signaled I had two minutes to get to class. I pushed my way through the crowd and left the cafeteria.

Mr. Chavez was on my heels. "I expected better from you."

That hurt more than I anticipated. With as much respect as I could muster, I said, "Sir, you would've been a lot more disappointed in me if I had let him keep hitting her."

He studied my face, letting his brown eyes rest on my blackened one.

Gently, he asked, "Were you ever physically abused?"

"If I were a man and annihilated that dick, would you still be asking that?"

His anger returned at my question. "Do you know what the standard punishment for fighting offenses is?"

"Something tells me I'm about to find out."

When my first lecture was over, I remained in the empty classroom, pissed at myself and everyone else, even Dante. As the most level-headed of us, he should've told me that whether I was drunk or sober, I would still get hammered by the academy if they found out about the fight. During class, I'd received notification of my fine: 100 hours of community service and two months of my pay docked. They'd given me the maximum.

But as my sense of humor surfaced, I had to admit it wasn't a total loss. I'd lost the feeling I owed Mr. Chavez anything. That glimmer of attraction was gone, too.

"It's about time you stopped feeling sorry for yourself, darling."

My head jerked up. A tall, rawboned blond in a flight suit struck a pose against the door frame.

"Ethan?" I asked in disbelief, recognizing him as the man who had brought me a cold pack after the fight outside the club. "You really are a Weapons Control Officer?"

"Want to see me handle my gun?" he asked, grinning. "Hey, did I already use that line on you?"

"It didn't work," I reminded him with a grin of my own. "What are you doing here?"

"Well, I was minding my own business, knocking out my quarterly sims and then enjoying a nice lunch with a hot cadet who thought my gun handling line was funny, unlike you. Then there was this crazy commotion."

"Oh, God. It wasn't me, was it? It was me."

He chuckled. "Even on the permanent party side of the cafeteria, we were all wriggling in our chairs when we saw the look on his face."

"I'll survive," I said as I headed toward my next lecture.

"Hey, don't run away. I wanted you to know if you show them you're flat broke, they'll let you do more community service hours and take less money from you."

A rush of warmth chased away tension I hadn't realized I carried. "First the ice pack for my eye and now that useful bit of info. You sure do come to my rescue. Thanks."

He tipped my chin up so he could look at the eye.

"It's still puffy. I think it needs a kiss to make it better."

I stepped out of his grasp and glanced at the clock tower. "And I think I'm going to be late if I don't haul ass."

After lunch, my stomach growled, and I pressed against it in a vain attempt to silence it.

Dante was ignoring me, angry I had rejected his advice about staying out of that fight. I couldn't stand his determined silence. I never would've admitted it to him, but my dog had shunned me the same way after car rides ended at the veterinarian instead of the lake.

"Nidra said you looked sexy when you were dancing."

Dante's gaze shot to mine.

"Sexy," I repeated.

He beamed, everything right in his world again. "What's with your belly? Are you sick?"

"I know I loaded my cash card on Monday, but it's empty now. I don't have time to figure it out until after school."

"Let me see," he said, considering me book smart and common sense stupid.

Both accounts were empty. "I've been hacked," I said.

He shook his head, expanding the transactions to reveal the MoD withdrawals that had cleaned out my account. The footnote said it was the forfeiture of my initial signing bonus due to a violation of my visa terms. My future paychecks were going to be directed back to the MoD in their entirety until the entire bonus was repaid.

I stared at him, mouth gaping.

"I'm sorry," he said. "I don't have any to give you. I had to get soup today because I'm out of funds."

"No, don't worry about it. I'll figure something out."

Late that afternoon, I stood outside Ms. Roslyn-Jones' office waiting for her to deign to show up for her scheduled office hours. With any luck, she would have a bowl of candy on her desk.

Mr. Chavez stepped out of his office two doors down and glowered at me. "I can hear your stomach all the way over here."

"The MoD stole all my money," I gritted out. "I couldn't buy lunch."

"So they rescinded your signing bonus," Mr. Chavez said. "It's a brutal but effective lesson, isn't it?"

"I've learned I need to hoard money and food once I've got them again," I retorted.

"Then you received two lessons for the price of one."

"Ah, the silver lining," I said, making Mr. Chavez's grin flex. Seeing it, I said, "Sir, this is ridiculous. The MoD said nothing when I chose the Axe over the Plough, something that actually affects the mission in some way, but they're upset about a scuffle that resulted in minor injuries. I wasn't drunk or in uniform, and it didn't have anything to do with the MoD at all. The school gave me the maximum punishment, too. Doesn't this strike you as an extreme response?"

"Perhaps they feel you've exhausted your freebies."

"Do you have any suggestions, sir? Not to be melodramatic, but I need to eat at some point."

"How does your weekly schedule break down?"

I showed him every minute of every day, and he was able to shave off minutes here and there, but not enough to get a job.

"There's no one who'll loan you money?"

"If there's an alternate solution, I would prefer it," I said, my speech becoming more formal in response to his. It was a pleasant change not forcing my speech to be casual. "I've exhausted the generosity of people who didn't deserve to be saddled with a barely functional foreigner."

"Will your needs be met for a few days?" When I nodded, he said, "Perhaps I can find an acceptable solution by the end of the week."

"Thank you, sir."

"Don't thank me. I—No, this is actually really inconvenient for me. I'll accept your thanks."

That evening when I emerged from the bedroom, the gunshots from Marco and Jack's videogame greeted me.

"Oh, hey, Mira," Marco said, pausing the game. I don't know why they were afraid their alien-killing games would give me flashbacks. "Didn't realize you were home."

"They say sleep is a poor man's dinner," I yawned.

"You didn't eat?" he asked sharply.

When I told him about my penalties, his mouth was set tight and he abandoned his game.

Making me a peanut butter sandwich dusted with vitamin powder, he said in a voice below Zack's hearing, "I warned you to be careful."

"You also warned me you wouldn't bail me out of my own stupidity."

"I won't, but Tony will. I wouldn't be surprised if the MoD expects a rule-breaking Hernandez will in effect pay his own penalty by giving his resources to help a foreign jackass."

"What was the appropriate response? Let him hit her?"

"No, you should've done it where there were no witnesses," he said, handing me the sandwich.

"I'm serious."

"So am I," he said, pushing aside my palmer to make room for a plate for my second sandwich. "Would you still have done it if your classmates weren't there to be impressed? Because I didn't teach you how to protect yourself so you could put on a show."

"I need their acceptance."

"Do you want the acceptance of people who're impressed with that?"

Marco was right. If I had been alone, I would've stayed on hold forever, watching the beating unfold with impotent anger, never considering for a moment getting more involved than that.

But I would've carried that guilt with me for a long time. I wasn't pleased with the academy's punishment and I hadn't enjoyed injuring that guy, but I wasn't sorry I did it, either.

When I returned to my bedroom, I spied the dish that held my good luck pennies, the faulty bastards.

"I'm sorry," I told them. "Desperate times call for desperate measures. I have to see if any of you are worth anything."

108

I dumped them into my hand and went out to the kitchen where I'd left my palmer. I turned the pennies with Lincoln facing me so I could read the dates. A few coins of a piddling denomination in a depressingly massive circulation amount probably weren't valuable, but I had to try. If nothing else, the currency value webpage I opened said the copper content pre-1982 was a lot higher.

Seventeen pennies were aligned in a row against the groove on the wooden table where two boards came together, the copper edges touching bread crumbs my hasty swipe hadn't removed.

Seventeen profiles of Lincoln, all pointing to the right. Did they even teach about him in grade schools anymore?

Seventeen coins all in a row, ready to be sorted by... date.

I sat back, looked across the room to reestablish my distance vision, and then focused on the pennies anew. No, I'd been correct the first time.

"That's weird," I muttered. What were the chances? Astronomical. A funny sort of fear settled low on my spine.

"Marco," I squeaked. I tried again, saying the word with a lot more power behind it.

Zack paused his game and hurried toward me. "What's wrong?"

I snatched up the coins. "I saw a bug," I said in a voice that didn't sound like mine. "I want Marco to kill it dead."

"Well, he can't kill it alive, can he?" he teased, tossing aside boots and jackets in the corner I indicated.

Marco came out of the bathroom. "What's going on?"

"Mira saw a bug."

"Mira can kill her own bugs."

"If she had a gun, she would've shot it. She wanted it killed dead."

"I told you we needed to call an exterminator."

"He said the spray won't work on the black widows because spiders don't clean themselves."

"I'm calling one anyway," Marco said, shaking out his boots on the front porch. "Mira, Mira, stop already. I know my name. You don't have to keep saying it. It was a big scary bug, I get it."

"If I had a gun, I would shoot you at this point. Can I please speak to you in private?"

On the back porch, I showed him the pennies.

"Tell me this is nothing," I pleaded. "It could be chance, couldn't it?"

"No."

"It's a far off shot, but it could be a coincidence."

"Nope."

"I didn't think so either," I said, clutching the deck rail so tightly my hands were white.

CHAPTER 14

DIAMOND

Spinning. Whirling, spinning, hair flying in my face, hands tight on the control stick. Flashes of sunlight making me see spots.

Pause. A merciful pause. Dante's face showed as he shouted his encouragement and clapped his hands.

No, I lost it and was again tumbling because I couldn't control the yaw, pitch, and roll of the gyro. Most days it was effortless to balance the three spinning rings until I was stable and upright, but some days I couldn't find my groove.

I had plenty of opportunities to try. To most people the gyro was nothing more than a novelty that illustrated each axis pilots needed to control in flight, and the others grew bored with it and moved on to other simulators. Dante and I used it so frequently we felt the trespass when someone else touched it.

I spat hair out of my mouth. It was no good. I couldn't distance myself from my foul mood long enough to get the job done.

I would have to learn though. The aircraft wouldn't care if I had an awful day. Neither would the pull of gravity.

After another thirty seconds, I had to concede defeat.

"Stop," I groaned.

The gyro jerked as Dante caught the outer ring and locked it down. Soon all three were locked, and I sagged in the harness.

"I might get sick," I said with surprise.

"What?"

"Vomitus eruptus. Barf what I scarfed."

"Oh, hell, no," he said, grabbing at the harness. "Not in the gyro."

I staggered into the nearest women's room and bent over the commode, but despite the frantic clenching, nothing came of it. I still needed the time out though. Without undoing my trousers, I shut the door to the stall, sat on the toilet, and leaned back with my eyes shut.

A pair of women walked into the bathroom, and I wrinkled my nose at the sounds of zippers and urination.

"I don't know why they don't fire him," one woman said to the other. "Not ten minutes after the last reprimand for hacking her records, he was discovered hacking into the dean's files about her. Not ten minutes."

Go away. Or shut up. Either path would give me back my quiet moment.

"You know why they won't get rid of him."

Was that Ms. Chenier?

"They should."

"Should they?" asked maybe-Chenier. "We've never had such a full gunner program before, and it's all because of him. Have you ever sat in on his lectures? He's excellent, and you know how much I hate to admit that."

"I don't care who he is or how good of an instructor he is. You know he's hacking into those files to see if his girlfriend is being treated fairly. The sole reason she made it this far is because he's been changing her scores."

I bit back a sarcastic comment. The centuries changed, but the rumors stayed the same.

"I can't even look at her, she's so skinny," the bitchy one said in disgust. "Women fall into his lap—and a few men do, too—but Chavez chooses Donovan to have sex with?"

My head snapped up.

"The sooner we get rid of the both of them the better," she said, punctuating her sentence with a flush.

I remained in the stall a long time, not wanting to leave the bathroom to see a pair of women walking together and know they were the ones.

What an ugly rumor. I didn't need this. With all those community service hours robbing me of time to do homework, it was already going to be a struggle to improve my reputation. Thank God Tony had floated me money so I could eat, or I'd be totally screwed.

When I emerged, Dante was lingering, my bag at his feet. "You're white as a sheet."

"I need a drink."

"Meet me in the lab later?"

"Of course."

Kairo flagged me down in the cafeteria.

"I got the dean to reduce your sentence to almost nothing," he told me. "I told her we did call the cops, and they said it would be at least an hour before they could send a car. Seeing as you were the only sober one of us, you went in to try and talk the guy down, and he attacked you."

"Truly? Thanks. I was in a real bind."

"I know. Glad I could help," he said magnanimously. However, the glittering speculation in his eyes made me suspect it wasn't an act of altruism, pity, or justice so much as his taking advantage of a chance to make me owe him.

Wondering if my stomach would settle with food, I got a small portion of the daily special. Kairo followed me through the line, piling his plate.

He delayed choosing a seat until I chose mine. He sat beside me, and I wedged my bag between our chairs so he couldn't crowd me anymore than he already had.

"Why are you cutting that with a spoon?" he asked me, scowling.

"Wow, that's all you've got for a lunchtime topic?"

"You're damaging our image." He held out his unused knife like he was doing me a great favor. "Here."

I ignored the proffered implement and stuck the ersatz meat product with my fork, lifting it to my mouth and gnawing off the edge of it.

"You're a humiliation to be seen with. Use the knife."

"No, my stomach's too upset to eat after all," I said, pushing my plate away with distaste.

After school, I saw Mr. Chavez head toward the parking lot. Wishing I had his graceful, long-legged stride, I trotted after him.

"Sir, I wanted to thank you for checking on a way to mitigate my punishment, but Kairo Ashton took care of it."

"He did what?"

"He spoke to the dean and arranged to substantially reduce my punishment."

"He said that?"

"He didn't say it loud enough for anyone else to hear and assume the academy isn't serious about its punishments if that was your concern."

"Yes, I suppose that is exactly what my concern is," he said, amused. When I didn't turn away, he said, "Was there something else?"

I hesitated. "Have you heard any odd rumors about yourself?"

He laughed. "More than I can count."

"I meant linking our names," I said, blushing. "Yours and mine."

"No," he said, brows knitting.

"I overheard a pair of instructors in the bathroom," I explained. "They said you hacked my records because we're seeing each other, and..."

Wow, did I feel stupid.

Puzzled, he said, "Is this a joke? Are you finished accusing me of felony hacking and perpetrating a fraud toward the end of putting a substandard pilot in the air so she can kill herself or others?"

My eyes bugged. "I was explaining why I asked if you heard a rumor."

"You know there's no substance to the gossip, so why are you bothering me with it?" His hand slashing the air, he said, "Just go. You should be prepping for class."

"I was offering an explanation for why you might be being treated unjustly," I said as he got into his car.

"I'm a big boy. I can handle it," he said before slamming the car door.

Mr. Chavez's stinging words stayed with me. I was generally successful in avoiding him to take the wind out of the sails of that rumor, but my grades continued to drop. The more math I worked, the more my understanding slipped until I wasn't certain I could argue which way was up anymore.

By the beginning of September, I had no choice but to head to his office during my study hall.

"Why, *why* are you looking for him?" Mr. Yoshimura asked from his desk. "He's not your instructor anymore."

"I need clarification on a topic both he and Ms. Roslyn-Jones both addressed. There seems to be a significant discrepancy."

"I doubt that."

"I got seven answers wrong yesterday," I told Mr. Yoshimura, sending his white eyebrows skyward. He was still my instructor, but since the Decision, his lectures revolved around combat theory, not equations, so I still performed well there.

I admitted with a grim smile, "I wasn't even close."

For the rest of the hour, we went through the questions, his confusion at my math making me suffer a lot of his sarcasm until he set his stylus down and regarded me.

"What's one plus one?"

"Depends on—"

"No, it doesn't. What's one plus one?"

"Mr. Yoshimura, I don't have time for games."

"Neither do I. You know what the accepted solution is and you know the accepted path to get there. Why can't you give it to me?"

I struggled with the question we'd been working on until I could give him the expected answer.

116

I was sweating bullets by then, my head pounding. Gritting my teeth, I gave into the compulsion to take it further, so much further until my answer wasn't even an integer anymore.

"Something's wrong with you," he told me. "I don't mean that as a complaint so much as an observation of some kind of mental illness. You need to make an appointment with a counselor."

"And say what? I now work in a range of math only dogs can hear?" I asked, pushing my hair back with a shaking hand. "I'm not some kind of idiot savant, am I? Perhaps my math does make sense at a range far beyond your doctorate."

He pointed out one particular part of my work. "Look at this from here to here. This isn't genius, Donovan. It's insanity."

Alarm surged through me. "That's a strong word."

He leaned back and regarded me, spindly arms crossed across his broad chest. "Do you want to complete this program?"

"Yes."

"Why?"

"Accomplishing the program to the clan's satisfaction will lead to the citizenship required for a person to have a home, protection, and legal standing in the modern world."

"What a nice, neat manifesto. How many times have you told yourself that in an attempt to convince yourself?"

I gave him a sharp look. "You're the one who taught me to give answers that are as short and complete as possible."

"You're sabotaging yourself, Donovan. Other times when you've messed up, it was a judgment call on someone else's part to keep you, but you know nothing can save you if you fail fact-based testing."

I clenched the edge of his desk. "I don't accept that. Everything is coming together according to the logical, conventional plan I laid out to meet clan expectations. From fitness to reconciling the killing-in-the-line-of-duty, I'm solid. I've even got a gunner cadet lined up to partner with. There's nothing standing in my way."

"Of course there is. Maybe it's time and pressure turning you into a pile of rubble instead of a diamond. Maybe not. You need to have a conversation with a counselor to determine what emotional malfunction is overriding all your logic."

A counselor?

I banged my head on his desk.

"You'll have limited success with that technique," he said.

An unwilling chuckle escaped me. "I'll consider it."

"No, you won't, but you won't be able to come back and say it wasn't offered to you."

I gathered my palmer and notepads, still detecting his toady eyes on me.

Without looking up, I asked, "Sir, do you know anything about the rumor going around that Mr. Chavez and I have a relationship other than teacher and student?"

He was silent, and when I got up the nerve to gaze at him, he gave me a sardonic look that told me he did. "Shut the door. I want to talk to you."

With dread, I complied.

He said, "He's always been criticized for being too concerned about your welfare, but it's escalated since the Decision. He hacks the secure server all the time to read your files. Just yours. He's never interceded on behalf of any student except you. He's done nothing to suggest he'll stop hacking to read your ratings, and most damning of all, he doesn't bother to deny there's a relationship between you two."

118

I stared at him, cheeks hot.

"Look at all that surprise. Don't you want to tell me that you're innocent?" he asked.

"Of what? Trading sexual favors for a passing grade? I thought I was fairly treated by him in the classroom, so if I chose that method, trust me, he wouldn't have been the one I started with," I retorted.

"Who's been hassling you?"

"Since you've witnessed some of it, I'm certain you know. But for what it's worth, I doubt my instructors are letting their personal opinions affect my grades. I'm capable of failing all on my own. Speaking of which, thanks for the help with my math, Mr. Yoshimura."

"Stop. Did Chavez ask you to become an Axe pilot?"

With an eye on the clock, I said, "I've wanted the Axe since the incentive flight that came with my visa offers. I didn't dwell on it though. Until I met the minimum time for the obstacle course, the Axe was never a possibility."

"That wasn't my question."

"He suggested it."

"I knew it," he said, slapping his hand on the desk. "Get out of here before you're late."

Somehow, I knew less than I had started out with. Either Mr. Yoshimura was lying or Mr. Chavez was when he said there was no substance to what they were saying about him. And if Mr. Yoshimura was telling the truth, what was Mr. Chavez doing in my records? If he was curious about how I was doing in my coursework, he could've asked my instructors. Or me, for that matter.

It didn't make any sense.

CHAPTER 15

JETTISONED

September twentieth, my husband's birthday, closed with me sitting at home in a kitchen chair in the middle of the room so Marco could walk around me and check my movements. Marco took the urine collection cup from me and checked the color before dumping it into the liquids recycler under the kitchen sink. "One more time. I want to step in closer this time."

I'd gone through it five times already, but it was worth my time to perfect. His, too. If I were discovered, it wouldn't be a challenge for them to determine who'd helped me.

I cleaned my hand, then pulled the tip of my thumb away from the fingernail enough to create a larger space. I dipped it in the indicator powder and released the tension, packing powder under the nail. I spread my legs to reveal the missing slats in the chair's seat and set my hands flat on my thighs.

"Show me your hands."

I held them out palm down, then palm up. He handed me the specimen cup reloaded with more stale beer. There was no need to waste drinking water on the experiment.

I put the cup between my legs as if peeing in it and gripped it tightly so the pad of my thumb stayed put while I pushed down, releasing the powder trapped under my nail into the cup. I returned the cup to him.

He stirred it with his finger and then gauged the color change to see if I reached the minimum concentration. "Good. Don't forget, you're going to have to piss as forcefully as you can to get as much of it into the solution as possible before they load the sample into Little Blue. For God's sake, don't swirl it. They know to look for that."

"I've been practicing, but peeing with that kind of pressure causes it to splash back out of the cup."

"A small price to pay for masking the fact that your kidneys aren't quite performing to standards yet," he said, handing me a tiny vial of the real chemical I needed to sway the test. "They're doing a lot better though. I'm hoping you'll be within range for the next one."

"You're not the only one."

Kairo said my name, and I came awake with a gasp. I was in study hall in my usual shadowy corner.

"I had trouble sleeping," I said. The nightmares about getting caught cheating the system had been so horrible I had finally abandoned the idea of sleeping.

I'd managed to appear calm for my piss test, calm and embarrassed about someone watching me pee. My act was wasted, though. The tech was running late and rushed through the evaluation of the sample, barely glancing at the results. I opened my mouth to protest the sloppiness but shut it with a click when she passed me, sanitized the Blue's specimen port, and called for the next person. When I hesitated, doubting it was going to be this easy, she said, "You're authorized to go, Ms. Donovan. Have fun on your flight this afternoon."

Right, the incentive flight. That's what the analysis was clearing me for. How could I have forgotten?

"Mira?"

I focused on Kairo again. "How was the lecture?"

"Voodoo hates me," he snarled. He annoyingly used the instructor's old call sign instead of his name, like they were colleagues. It was because of him that everyone called me Justice. "The dean's still not doing anything because my grades aren't being affected by it. That's what she said anyway."

Tired of his complaints about his instructors, I didn't commiserate.

"How's your average?" he asked. At my smile, a lot of the tension left him. "Good. I knew you could work through it. It was simply a matter of when."

Over the previous month, it had been solely through Herculean effort that I was able to take my answers to the appropriate point and stop there. After every exam, my skull felt like it was going to explode and my hands were knotted from the death grip on the stylus, but at least my grades shot back up.

Good thing, too. I wasn't about to go to a counselor and admit that a couple of my mental malfunctions came from a century-long hiatus that was most likely caused by a faulty cryopreservation experiment.

Kairo looked me up and down with insulting thoroughness.

"I'm not for sale," I said.

"No, when I see how pale and skinny you still are, see how your hands shake, it makes me think your DNA must be as phenomenal as mine. Possibly even better."

I tried to hide my affronted dismay, but I doubted I succeeded. Whether the DNA results favored me or not, I was of the opinion the topic of genetic inheritance shouldn't come up in polite conversation.

He smirked. "You bypassed the waiting list to get admitted here, and the MoD makes the academy keep you every time the dean tries to jettison you."

"I heard someone here was going to bat for me."

"I heard that, too, but do you believe the Hernandez MoD does what a foreign instructor wants them to?"

The dread flooding me was accompanied by the familiar bitterness of denial, but the point he made was too logical to ignore. Reluctantly, I asked, "How did you see your DNA results? I've yet to see mine."

"I paid for my appraisal. One like yours, not that commercial one. You can't imagine what it cost or what I had to do to get them to do it. It was worth it, though. When you get yours, I want to see it."

Did he really think I'd just hand over such personal information?

"If they haven't shown it to me by now, I doubt they ever will."

"I guess it doesn't matter. There's been plenty of confirmation your DNA strand is fantastic. I mean, you're so smart your drug abuse isn't even slowing you down. Your hands shake so much you can't hold a stylus some days, but that big brain of yours continues to fire."

My eyes narrowed at him. "I don't use."

I had quit that new batch of hyperawareness pills from Tony, but they hadn't quit me yet.

"Oh, I know you passed this morning's drug test, but let me remind you that you will have to have a much more thorough physical with the flight surgeon at the end of the year. Think fooling him will be as easy as a dumb tech?"

"I don't use," I snapped.

"You won't when you're my pilot, I promise you that," he said, holding my gaze for a long moment before he left.

It wasn't until he was out of sight that I let out a long, shaky sigh, rubbing my sweaty palms on my trousers.

"It's my opinion that your gene mapping is average and your clumsiness with your stylus is because your left hand still lacks any dexterity," Dante offered without looking up from his work at a nearby table. "I also think you're going to have to lay down some boundaries with him."

"You always say the best things. How can you be so wise at your tender age?"

With Kairo out of sight and my heart rate slowing down, it wasn't long before my exhaustion sneaked up on me again. Why did naps always come so easily when it was so difficult for me to get a good night's sleep?

Mr. Chavez looked up from helping one of the gunner cadets in time to see me bite back another yawn, and as soon as he was free, he approached me. "I understand Sonneburg's deportation upset you, but you can't lose sleep over it."

Dante's head snapped up, and I sensed his shock.

"Deportation?" I asked. I wouldn't have recognized the high, wavering voice as mine if it hadn't come from my mouth. "I thought he was out sick. You're saying he had a visa? Am I next? They said I cheated the obstacle course. I didn't choose the Plough. I got in a fight. He did everything he was supposed to. He was barely behind me in the standings."

"Calm down."

"Did the police show up at his residence? Where do deported people get sent?"

He held up his hands. "I don't know. He's already gone, and his apartment is empty. The academy found out about it after the fact."

"Can you determine where he went?"

"I suppose I could try, but I won't. You need to let it go." He spoke over my protests. "Looking over your shoulder wastes time you need to use looking forward to ensure you're taking the proper steps toward your goal."

How could he be so calm?

"This isn't a mass culling of visa holders," he promised me. "Don't lose sleep over it."

Seeing one of his students trying to get his attention, he nodded a farewell to the two of us and moved on.

I tore my gaze off him to look at Dante.

His frown gave way to a shrug. "I never liked Sonneburg. You didn't care for him either," he reminded me. "He was the dullest human being on Earth."

"That's not the point."

"Fight with me about it later," he said, noticing the first of our classmates to pack up and aim for the exit. "It's time for our flights."

I rolled my eyes at him. "Your flight, you mean. I get to whirl around in a simulator at such a sedate speed that it makes the gyro creak. The train goes faster."

"You don't look like a twig on the verge of being snapped in half by a stiff wind anymore. I'm sure you'll be approved for a real flight this time."

But then he took a good look at me, evaluating me as an outsider would. "You do need to calm down about Sonneburg. There's no color in your face except for the purple around your yellow eyes. Is there any way you can look less poltergeisty before we walk in there?"

"I should forget it," I said.

"You always have to try, Mira."

At the airport, I ducked into the women's room to scrub my cheeks and bite my lips until a healthy pink returned. I caked on the concealer around my eyes, too. When I emerged, Dante approved my efforts.

Soon the color returned to my face for real. Someone had put me down for a ride in a Plough.

With an empathetic smile but merry eyes at my most recent failure to get into an Axe, Dante abandoned me to accompany the Axe pilot out the door.

Rubbing my head, I said, "Yes, I understand my MoD paperwork says I was supposed to fly the Plough, but I'm in the Axe program."

"Ma'am, this isn't a carnival," the woman on the other side of the counter said. "You don't get to pick what you get a ride in. Your paperwork says Plough. If you don't want your flight in the Plough, you can sign here and leave."

"No, I'll take it." I sighed, needing the distraction.

"Well, don't piss your pants with excitement," a man in a flight suit said as he approached. "Let's go. You already made us late."

I explained the predicament as we walked across the tarmac.

He said, "Well, that explains it. We thought all the Plough cadets were down in Diego. Look, do what you're told and stay out of the way, and we'll get along."

My safety belt attached to the inside fuselage in the rear compartment of the Plough, I watched the crew unclip the first cargo pallet and roll it toward the gaping maw while cold air whipped around us. Below us, the Pacific Ocean was gray and angry with frothy white tips frosting the waves, but it was still gorgeous after a year stuck in the desert. I inhaled deeply, hoping to capture the scent of the water, but I smelled metal and dust.

The pallet snagged, and the nearest crewman braced himself and rammed his shoulder into it with an ease born of familiarity. The pallet continued down the rollers, exposing the bent track where it got hung up. When the pallet went out the back, I leaned forward, tracking its path down, wanting to see the parachute deploy. My safety line kept me on a very short leash, though.

I felt a polite tap and pressed myself back to get out of the way again. The second pallet snagged in the same spot. When shouldering it failed to get it moving, he tried again. I could see his strain, see the pallet shift onto his foot.

He started to fall backward, and I unsnapped my safety line and surged forward, shoving the man from behind so the fall with his trapped foot didn't snap his ankle. We both hit the pallet forcefully, and I felt it rock and drop back, now moving freely on the rollers. I got off the crewman, gripping the webbing on the pallet to pull myself upright. The pallet was picking up speed, and I couldn't get my feet under me.

A hand clutched my flight suit and another grabbed my arm. I cried out as the fingers in my left hand bent and twisted, caught in the webbing. Once I was free, the crewman stood me up, got me to the side, and clipped me in. I slumped against the metal, right-hand fingers wrapped around the nearest hook.

Thank you, Jesus.

Once all five pallets were out the rear, they raised the door, closing the back of the plane.

The crewman limped toward me, blood oozing from a scrape on his face. "Baby bird, next time don't try to fly until you've got your wings."

"You were in trouble," I said, cradling my damaged hand.

"You almost went out the rear with that pallet. You have to save yourself before you're in any position to save anyone else. I mean, what was the number one rule?"

"Don't touch my safety line."

"And what did you do?"

"I touched my safety line, but—"

"Ma'am."

I glared at him but shut up.

He smiled at my difficulty and pointed to his own safety belt, which had been connected the whole time. Then he indicated his boots, telling me, "Standard safety boots lined with titanium mesh. My foot was in no danger. In fact, you did more injury to me than my job did."

"Are you going to report me?" I asked, panic tightening my grip.

He burst out laughing, along with the other cargo handlers. "No, but do us all a favor. If they ever offer you another incentive flight with us, say no."

"Agreed," I said, making them laugh again.

As soon as we touched down, I rushed to get to the train station. Marco wasn't taking calls, so I called Tony and told him to dust off his bioscanner because I was on my way.

As he aimed Big Blue over my hand, he read me the results.

"A fracture through the ring finger, pinky dislocated, some bruising and contusions. It shouldn't take long to bounce back from this."

I exhaled noisily, relieved.

"But I'm not seeing the bone density I was hoping for, so I want to up the dosage of some of your meds. I would like to run the numbers after I check your lab values, and I'll get back to you after that."

The brusque tone was accompanied by his hasty clean up.

I asked, "Is that a dismissal?"

He hesitated and then nodded. "Marco will have a fit if I encourage you to stay longer than necessary. He still suspects there's a lot of risk in helping you."

"I'll keep my distance."

CHAPTER 16
LOVE AT FIRST SIGHT

On the last day of September after school, I watched them knock down the final hacienda-style building on campus. It would be replaced with architectural landscaping that complemented the soaring spaces and sleek design of the rest of the flight academy. For me, the loss was a visceral one since it meant Mr. Kim's illegal food truck would no longer be lurking behind the building. He had rarely been chased away by the administration, so I suspected the dean enjoyed Mr. Kim's spring rolls as much as I did.

Needing a change of scenery, I did the two-train pilgrimage to the diner outside the military airfield for dinner.

Ethan, that tall Texan I had met at the club, acknowledged me with a fake leer.

"Looking for me?" Ethan asked.

"That's it," I said.

He grinned. "Seriously, are you meeting anyone here?"

"No. Zack said the food here was cheap and plentiful."

"He said you were having cash flow issues," he said. "Can I buy you dinner?"

"As long as you understand that I'm coldly using you for a meal and that you'll get nothing in return."

He burst out laughing. "Sounds good."

Eying the splint on my left hand, he raised his eyebrows. "Weren't you done fighting?"

"Broke a finger on my incentive flight."

"How did you manage that?"

"At the moment, I'm leaning toward gypsy curse."

When our food arrived, he ate leisurely while I wolfed down home fries and meatloaf.

"Know any good pilots?" I asked him.

"Hmm?"

"I need to study good pilots and do what they do to get what they have. The top three Hernandez pilots have factors to their success I can't hope to duplicate, so I've been trying to find someone normal to model."

"Good luck finding a normal Axe pilot."

"It's not funny. I'm months behind schedule on that. Do you know what I've had to resort to?"

"Tell me."

"Studying hard. That was supposed to be the backbone of my plan, not the plan in its entirety."

He laughed.

"Easy for you to laugh. You have a home," I said. "Check this out." I flexed my forearm. He didn't understand. "Look at it. I've got a rock-climber's forearms because I've been trying so hard to be strong enough to grip a stick for hours on end. Will that be enough?"

"It won't damage your chances."

"But it won't be enough, either," I said. "What I'm doing isn't going to be enough. You know that."

He shook his head. "I don't know. This isn't my clan."

It was obvious he wanted the conversation to revolve around anything but flying, but Sonneburg's deportation scared me.

"You've been flying for a while," I told him. "Surely you've got some secret kung fu that makes you good at this." At his sly, teasing look, I hoped he wasn't going to proposition me again.

He said, "Speaking of secret kung fu, I hear you're doing more than flexing your forearms to get ahead."

I bristled, expecting yet another snide comment about Mr. Chavez.

He smirked. "It seems that with enough glue and cardboard, a person can make a rocket ship."

I froze. There was no way he knew about that.

"Or should I say the front end of the cockpit in her bedroom?" he teased.

"How on earth did you hear about that?"

"Zack."

"It's always the ones you don't consider defending yourself against," I muttered, slumping back against the seat.

"He called it cute. But he understands why someone might think it a smidge extreme, so he asked me not to say anything."

"Yet here you are saying something. It's a tool," I said, fanning my blushing face with my hand. "I use it for muscle memory exercises as well as familiarizing myself with where the controls are."

Inspiration seized me, and I aimed my best smile at him. "Ethan."

"No."

"You haven't even heard my idea."

"Does it involve being naked?" he asked.

"No."

"Then I don't want to hear it."

"Well, can I at least go to the hangar with you?"

"You're not sitting in my warbird," he told me, smiling to take the sting out of his words.

Phooey.

"But," he said with a winsome smile of his own, "I might be willing to renegotiate if you let me see it."

"Oh, all right," I said, scooting out of my seat. "Let's go."

When I let myself in the house, Zack greeted Ethan familiarly.

"My plane is two bays down from the one Zack works on," Ethan explained.

Zack. Why hadn't I asked him?

"Why do you need fifteen bottles of peroxide?" Zack asked me.

"What a deliciously random way to say hello," I said.

"When the exterminator got to your bathroom cabinet, there was a ton of peroxide."

"I've got one or two bottles."

"Try fifteen. I counted."

I eased around the mockup in my bedroom and checked under the sink. "Wow, these bottles could teach bunnies how to multiply."

"You're not a crazy hoarder, are you?"

"No, I'll get rid of them."

"You don't have to get rid of them. Stop buying them."

I nodded, but my frown remained as I shut the cabinet door. "Weird," I muttered.

"Weird? It's *awesome*," Ethan said, running his hand over my cockpit.

"Hey, hey, hey, no touchies," I said. "It's delicate."

"No, it isn't," Zack countered. "If there's an earthquake, we probably could shelter under it."

"Out," I told them.

Of course, they ignored me.

"Threw a football at it to see, and it bounced right off," Zack told Ethan. At my outraged noise, he said, "I helped you build it, Mira. If I smash it, I'll fix it."

Ethan squeezed around the side to climb in the seat, but I blocked him. "You wouldn't let me in yours, so you can't sit in mine."

"You've got to let me drive it," he insisted, holding his palmer out of reach when I blocked him from taking pictures of it. "Mine's an ordinary Axe. This is wicked. I have to tell my roommate."

"I will kill you dead if you tell anyone," I told him.

"Do you sleep in it, too?" he asked. "I mean, it takes up the whole room."

"Of course it does," Zack said, pushing the hair off his face. "It's to scale. She sleeps in the closet."

"Did he need to know that?" I asked. "No, he did not."

Ethan tabbed a switch and laughed with pure delight. "It lights up."

"We were striving for authenticity," Zack said.

"Stop encouraging him," I wailed at him.

"Hey, you're the one who invited him over."

"I hate you so much right now," I told Ethan.

He pointed at the mockup with both hands as he backed out of the room. "This is awesome, Mira."

"Don't you tell anybody," I warned.

He grinned. "Stop your fussing, woman. Let me call over to the hangar and see if they'll let you walk through it with me. When are you available?"

"Now."

After the security guys verified I was an academy student and Ethan took responsibility for me, I got to go through the heavenly gates, through a door propped open with a brick and down into the jet bays.

What a sight. Axes in different configurations sat gleaming and powerful in their bays while men and women tended to their every needs. All my doubts were gone in that instant, and I knew this was where I wanted to be. Wanted? The word wasn't intense enough. I needed to be bound to one of these planes. I needed that surge of pride every time I came close to it. I needed a connection formed from millions of hours of touching it, feeling it respond to me as I responded to it. I needed its strength, its beauty, and its power. In exchange, I would be the aircraft's soul, its unpredictability, and its poetic side. Together we would be whole, both of us, for the first time.

Ethan had to nudge me roughly to get my attention again. "You ready?" he asked, hiding a yawn behind his hand.

"Can't we stay here?" I asked, unable to look away from the nearest Axe. At that point, it didn't matter I wasn't allowed to sit in one.

"You'd rather be with a plane than me?"

I deeply breathed in the scents of jet fuel and hydraulic fluid. "You don't want me to answer that."

Chuckling, he goosed me. "I'm sorry your crazy effort isn't getting you anywhere, but I'm not that skilled of a flyer. However, you could come to my house and take a peek at hardcopy books about flying if it would help."

135

"Real books?" I asked, tearing my gaze off the Axe. "That's a well-baited trap, to be sure."

He tugged me toward the exit. "My roommate is spending the night at his girlfriend's apartment, and you'll have all the books to yourself."

I shook my head, not letting myself be tempted.

"We've got more publications on the Axe than anyone else on the planet. Stuff you can't get here."

"What kind of stuff?" I asked against my better judgment.

As soon as I walked into his house in the high-rent district, I saw massive, overstuffed bookshelves lining the dining room walls floor to ceiling. With so many intriguing titles, I didn't know where to begin.

"See, this is the kind of party I enjoy," I murmured, touching the spines reverently. "Me and a couple hundred of my newest friends."

"It's late," Ethan yawned. "Mind if I go to bed? I know you don't need babysitting, and I doubt you'd pay me any attention if I stayed up with you."

"Do you want me to borrow a few and go?"

"Sorry, but that goldmine stays here."

I pulled a volume off the shelves and sat at the glass-topped dining table.

"Wake me when you want to leave, or you'll set off the security system," he said as he shuffled down the hall. "But stay as long as you want."

I flipped open the book from their library to look for the copyright date and found an inscription on the inside cover.

Voodoo, Not that you need any help in this department, but I thought this would make a great doorstop.

–Bear

"Son of a bitch," I murmured, rereading the note five or six times to make certain I wasn't mistaken.

I was so stupid. This was *his* house. Ethan was *his* roommate. I was sitting at Mr. Chavez's dining table reading *his* books, some of which were from *his* previous partner.

I knew about Running Bear, of course. I'd read the bio on every Comp-winning pilot in the previous ten years, conveniently glossing over any mention of their gunners. There was some mystery as to why Bear had quit at the height of his career.

One of the bookmarks was a reference to another text, and it was written in a bold, confident hand I knew from the notes on my first three months of schoolwork. Out of everything, that one note rammed home how much I was trespassing in the man's life.

If he discovered me, I was screwed. Why hadn't Ethan ever told me who his roommate was? He knew I was a student at the academy.

I scrambled to put the book back exactly the way I found it. I was on the verge of running down the hall to tell Ethan I had to leave, but I couldn't bring myself to walk away from the finest library in the Hernandez Territory. At school, the library was nothing more than a couple of shelves of hardcopy references at the end of the study hall plus a few rooms to watch videos. What I saw in front of me was the real deal.

I eased the book off the shelf, the whisper of it sliding across the wood filling me with pleasure.

Well, Ethan did say his roommate was going to be gone all night.

CHAPTER 17

THAT VOODOO THAT YOU DO

For the rest of the night, I raided the library, taking notes on my palmer long past the point where my hand cramped and my back was sore from being hunched over.

Noticing the rising sun, I closed the books scattered around me, replacing the miscellaneous papers and memorabilia that served as bookmarks.

I hurried down the hall to nudge Ethan awake. "I need you to do me a favor."

"Sure," he said sleepily.

"Don't tell your roommate I was here. He's my instructor. I could get in trouble."

He nodded, eyes closing, hand fumbling on the remote house locks. "You've got thirty seconds to get out the front door. That enough?"

"Plenty. Thanks."

"Call me," he mumbled, burrowing under the covers.

He had to know he was off limits to me now.

I had almost made it through the house when the security tone at the front door sounded. It couldn't have been thirty seconds already. Mr. Chavez must be home.

Panicking, I ran back toward Ethan's room but didn't want him to yell in surprise, so I shot into the guest room and hid behind the door.

Mr. Chavez tapped on Ethan's door. "Did one of the academy students stop by last night?"

I froze. How could he know that?

"Ethan, Miranda was my student for six days a week for three months, and I'm familiar with her scent. I thought I knew her, but if she came here with you, I'm going to have to reevaluate things."

Ethan chuckled. "She didn't come here for me. You should've seen her in the hangar. She fell in love with the first Axe, and I swear to God that love was reciprocated."

"I'm not surprised. Why was she here?"

"I said she could look at some of your books."

Mr. Chavez grunted. "Did she ask you about the rumor about the two of us?"

"What? No, she didn't mention you at all except to tell me not to tell anyone she was here once she figured out whose books she was reading."

Mr. Chavez said, "I want you to stay away from her."

"Obviously she has something you want if you're being so forgiving about her having been here, but you know I'm not going to turn her down, Jayce. I wouldn't turn down your mother."

"That visual just cost you everything in your banking account."

"Stop hacking my account when you're pissed at me," Ethan snapped in a rare show of temper. "I know who your family is, so stop."

"What's that supposed to mean?"

"Since childhood you've tried to build a bigger reputation than your family's so people stop assuming you only got your trophies because you're a Chavez."

"I don't do that."

"You do. Damned if I know why. You've been legendarily evil and legendarily talented since you were fifteen. It's time you got over it already."

"Are you finished?"

"Yeah," Ethan said. "Every time we move, we have to go through this crap with your reputation all over again, and I'm sick of it."

"So am I. Look, I'm serious about you staying away from Miranda. She's a student at my school, and she still consults me. I don't want there to be complications."

"Then don't go around chasing after her smell in other men's bedrooms," Ethan said, unimpressed with the reasoning.

After Mr. Chavez had stalked over to his side of the house, I snuck into Ethan's room and nudged him.

From underneath the covers, he snarled, "Jayce, if you don't let me sleep, I'm going to—"

"Going to what?" I asked. "Tickle me senseless?"

Amused blue eyes peered over the edge of the sheet. "Where were you hiding?"

"Guest room. I don't suppose you could get me out of here without his noticing."

"No."

"What do you mean, no?"

"He means no, you're not going to be able to sneak out of here without me noticing," Mr. Chavez drawled from behind me. "Good morning, Miranda."

Ethan watched the blush creep up my face with interest. "I don't believe she appreciated being snuck up on."

"I don't either," Mr. Chavez said dryly.

140

Without looking at him, I headed for the door.

He followed me down the hallway. "How do you know Ethan?"

"Sir, I'm very uncomfortable about being in my instructor's home, so if you'll excuse me, I need to leave."

"Ex-instructor. An instructor. Not your instructor."

"Seriously?" I said, exasperated because he wouldn't let me pass. "I'm extremely uncomfortable about being in one of my ex-instructors' homes, an instructor's home, not my instructor's home. Are you satisfied now?"

"Yes," he said sincerely.

Before I could help it, I said, "You are the strangest man."

"Because I want you to be accurate?"

"Is it me or is this conversation getting stranger by the second?"

"It's you. Why are you in my house?"

"Not your house. His house," I said, tipping my head toward Ethan's room.

"I paid for it. This is my house."

"His end of your house."

"My books. You did read some of my books, didn't you?"

"Yes," I said. "I'm so sorry."

"You're sorry that you have a desire to be well educated? Why?"

"For intruding."

He made a face. "You're not going to start with honor, morality, or fraternization rules, are you? I don't have the patience for it. Hey, you're not going to cry in front of me, are you?"

"No," I cried.

Swearing, he went to the bookshelves, scanned the titles, and removed a slim volume. He shoved it in my hand. "There."

"I can't," I sobbed. "It's yours."

"Do you want the book?"

I nodded so quickly my hair swung in my face.

"Then take it," he told me. "It's a loan. Well, it's a bribe to get you to stop crying because it's irritating me, but we can call it a loan."

"I can't."

"Of course you can. Simply don't tell anybody where you got it."

My tears stopped as abruptly as they had started. It was a brilliant, elegant solution. "Thanks."

"Don't thank me. I gave you that one because you—"

"You're a Comp champion," I blurted.

"I know I've told you how much I hate being interrupted," he said. "And yes, I'm the champion gunner for 2118. I can't make it through a workday without someone bringing it up, so I don't know how you missed that. Perhaps you should look up from your books every once in a while and see what's right in front of you."

Tired and overwhelmed, I walked out.

Centered at the junction of their walkway and the sidewalk, a penny faced me. Despite the dread, I picked it up and checked the date to confirm it was indeed for me. My fist closed around it, and I looked around wildly. No one was there.

I ran down the street, fear prickling the back of my neck.

A few days later, a broken air conditioner in the study hall building drove Dante and me to the hall of statues to do our homework.

"Voodoo was giving me crap again today," Kairo snarled as he strode through the arch. "He's so jealous of me he can't stand it."

I said without thought, "Dante and I had him for basic theory. He's demanding but fair."

"Are you calling me a liar?" he snarled, lunging at me.

I flinched before I could help it. I hadn't pissed him off this much since I'd told him I wasn't going to call him Apollo, the call sign he arrogantly chose for himself. "No," I said calmly. "I just realized who you've been complaining about, and I'm surprised you're having trouble with him."

"I'm not," he snapped. "He's the one with the problem. He hates me because my DNA is stronger than his. None of his money or degrees or family influence can change that."

Bored, I said, "So if his genetic blueprint is finite, immovable, and unchangeable, could we move on to another topic?"

"Look, I either say it to you guys or I say it to him," he said, tossing his bag against mine as if he wanted them to meld into one. "After graduation, though, I'm going to tell him what I think of him."

"I'm sure there'll be a line," Dante said with a grin.

"I'm going to be first in that line. And probably last, too, because I'm sure I'll have remembered a complaint I missed the first time around," Kairo said, making Dante laugh. Kairo's lips were quivering by that point, and he let go and laughed. It wasn't a pleasant sound.

Kairo noticed my lack of amusement and gave me a penetrating look. "You're having sex with him, aren't you? That's why he's so jealous of me."

Dante sucked in a breath.

Kairo towered over me. "No comment?"

"I'm curious. Did you know he's dating Profit?" I asked him.

"What?"

"Zack is her jet's lead mechanic. He told me. So let me ask you why Chavez would be with me if he's already with the most talented and beautiful woman around."

He glanced over my body, making a face. "He wouldn't, even though she's probably screwing him in the hopes he'll be her gunner. She didn't do very well at last year's Comp, and she didn't get that kind of a call sign for being a romantic."

"You've got great eyes," Dante told me as if to make up for Kairo's blunt assessment of my lack of appeal. "I love that crazy yellow color."

I batted my eyelashes at him.

"They are pretty," Kairo acknowledged. He took my injured hand, and I fought the desire to yank it back. He turned it over, checking through the transparent splints for swelling, discoloration, and any other sign it wasn't healing well. "How does it feel?"

"My other roommate is a medic. He's monitoring the situation. I would've warned you if there was a setback."

I tugged on my hand, and he released it to shut off the alarm on his palmer. "I have to go. Mira, don't forget to meet me in the quad after my meeting with the dean. Fifteen minutes to a half hour?"

I nodded.

Dante delayed until Kairo was out of the hall of statues. "Relax. He's not trying to have sex with you."

"I know."

"Do you? When he comes close to you, you look for the nearest escape route. Are you reconsidering him?"

I shook my head. "There isn't a stronger, faster problem-solver in his class. He's going to be an excellent gunner."

"Well, he's wondering if you're about to bail so you might want to woo him." I must've looked reluctant because he added, "Think about it."

After he left, I crouched in front of the Comp statue and found the name I sought: Jason Alexander Chavez. It had been there all along.

Sensing his presence, I said, "Why is it every time I turn around, you're nearby?"

Mr. Chavez said, "At this point there are almost as many instructors as students. Everyone is bumping into everyone."

"What are you doing here, sir? Come to worship your own statue?" I asked with a nod to the gleaming black sculpture of a pleased gunner standing slightly behind a pilot who lacked any sense of humor.

"Sort of." He reached down and touched Running Bear's name. I noticed the engraved letters were free of the grime that darkened the other names, including Chavez's own. Sounding like his mind was far away, he murmured, "What are you doing here?"

"I'm dodging Kairo Ashton as long as I can. You always put him in a foul mood."

He straightened. "Who?"

I didn't know what to do with that response. It was sort of cold and perfect. Nothing would've disrespected Kairo more than to be regarded as insignificant.

"Well, I'll leave you to pay your respects," I said, stepping back.

"Miranda," he called out. "Did you enjoy the book?"

I hurried back to him so he would lower his voice. "Yes."

145

"Give it back."

"No."

My defiant response seemed to both amuse and satisfy him somehow. When I walked away, he said my name again. I looked over my shoulder at him, refusing to come to heel.

"Happy birthday."

A startled rush of pleasure went through me. I hadn't said anything to anyone about it, and I had no expectation anyone would recall the occasion on their own. It shouldn't have meant so much to me, but it did.

CHAPTER 18

THANKSGIVING

The third week in November, everyone was finalizing plans for Thanksgiving. Tony and Marco were driving north to be with their family, and I was hurt I wasn't invited, but I didn't say anything.

It was a struggle to keep friends when I wouldn't open up about my past, too. Nidra definitely took it as a sign I didn't trust her. I would've lied if I knew I wouldn't be confronted with an inconsistency down the road. Dante alone didn't hold my silence against me.

Three days before Thanksgiving, a bright-eyed Dante ran across the quad to meet up with me as soon as he saw me step through the security station. "Nidra invited me to her family's ranch for Thanksgiving dinner. Well, not just me, but I'm going. I'm going to find a quiet moment and I'm going to tell her."

I whooped. "It's about time. Are you ready?"

"I've been working on how to tell her for a while."

"She's going to want to see it. Do you have crusty man foot?"

The color drained from his face. "I don't think so."

"You need a pedicure," I told him.

He backed away from me.

"Men get pedicures, too," I assured him. At least I suspected they did. I never met one who admitted it, though.

"Go with me," he pleaded.

"What? No, it makes me uncomfortable to be touched by strangers."

He shook his head. "It's too soon to tell her anyway."

"You're getting a pedicure after school. I'll go with you."

At the nail salon, Dante was wary about removing his boots, but after the initial surprise, the technician shrugged it off and approached his anomalous appendage without comment.

I was hypnotized by it, though. Even with the extra toe, his foot looked natural, albeit aesthetically unbalanced since his right foot had five toes. "Does it make you more stable?"

"What are you talking about?"

"Toes are for balance. You're broader across your forefoot, and you've got an extra balance point. Theoretically, it would make you more stable."

"I don't know," he said. "Will you stop looking at it like you're developing some way to confirm your hypothesis?"

Reluctantly, I discarded the experiment that had been forming in my mind.

"You should get some bling for it," I said. "Let them put a happy face on the toenail to make her laugh."

He glared at me. "Death first."

Thanksgiving Day arrived in silence. Marco was gone, and Zack was at work and would go straight to his family's house after that. Alone in the empty house, I drank my morning shake, wishing it was my mother-in-law's breakfast casserole. I missed all of it. Handwashing her grandmother's china with ice in my veins, so afraid to drop a piece. Hollering at the TV when the football game went wrong. Biting my tongue at someone's bratty kids. Dessert negotiations when there was not enough pie and too much gelatin. Holding hands around the table, saying what we were grateful for.

I went to morning services at a local chapel and gave my thanks there. God had heard it all before, but I said it again. I was grateful for my healthy mind, an improving body, friends, food and shelter, and so on. I most emphatically thanked Him for the chance for admittance. With all its limitations, the visa often felt like a noose around my neck, and I so desperately wanted to feel free. Free to learn, free to do, free to *be*.

At the reminder of my purpose, I took the train to the academy, figuring I'd have the library to myself, but Security closed me out at the gate. The campus was closed for the whole four days.

"I thought that was you," Mr. Chavez said as he came through the gate. "What did you forget?"

Out of uniform, his choice was an elegant suit. He looked very comfortable in it, so it was possibly his normal style. It was definitely flattering.

"Nothing. I was going to the library," I said. "I heard they received new books in preparation for the upcoming term."

"New references were added, but not for the Axes. Do you want to borrow one of my books?"

"Yes."

Twenty minutes later my footsteps echoed on the immaculate hardwood flooring in his living room. Now

149

that I knew the men better, I recognized Jason's personality overpowering Ethan's everywhere I looked.

"Is Ethan here? I would like to say hello."

"He returned to Texas for the weekend to be with family."

"Didn't you want to be with your family, too?"

"Very much, but sometimes my volatile family doesn't want to see me."

Was that a polite way of saying his Texan family had disowned him for spending his talent teaching cadets in another clan? A Hernandez family definitely wouldn't have tolerated that.

"Sir, which one might I have?" I asked as I crossed the room to look at the bank of bookshelves. I knew my voice was too sharp, but I was nervous. What had I been thinking coming here?

"You're not impressing me with your speech. Speak plainly."

"I am not in your class, and I will speak how I choose to," I said in irritation. "I read a lot. Research says you become like the five people you spend the most time with, so given what I read I am inextricably becoming like the designers and engineers who created the Battle Axe. Another month or so, I am likely to go past words and speak in equations."

He gave me a big, beautiful smile, and the showy display of delight threatened to leave me blind and senseless.

"I speak equation, too, so communication is assured," he said.

"And the observation that I sometimes communicate like an academic paper being spoken aloud is noted." I chose my next words with more care. "So what's shaking?"

"That was terrible," he said, wrinkling his face.

"I know. I need to watch more television. My speech is passable when I watch a lot of television, but I haven't had time for it."

"You're blushing. Would you rather tell me what it would take to wipe that haunted look off your face for good?"

My gaze shot to his face.

Leaning on the wall nearby, he said, "From the moment we met, I could see something is profoundly wrong in your world, something that goes far beyond a simple lack of citizenship."

I looked back at the books, but I wasn't seeing any of them.

He said, "I know you're supposed to have amnesia, but I don't accept that. The Hernandez government uses it as a convenient excuse when they want someone but don't want to have to explain where they got her."

"Life is full of mysteries, isn't it? No one seems to know why you split with your partner immediately after you won the Comp either."

After a moment, he said, "Running Bear fell in love and was ready to turn in his wings."

A wealth of emotion was wrapped up in the words, and I ached for him.

"I didn't ask. It's none of my business."

Ignoring that, he said, "I convinced him to stay long enough to fly in the Comp. He loved flying, and I doubted he'd be able to quit after facing adversaries that challenged his abilities. However, I underestimated his feelings. I gambled and lost."

The silence stretched uncomfortably after that. Love and loss were not topics I wanted to talk about.

To put space between us, I walked to the giant sliding glass doors that faced a pool.

I knew I should leave, but I wasn't going anywhere without a book. Given how appropriate the previous one had been for my stage of development as a pilot, I wanted him to pick it for me. To spur him toward that end, I snatched a book from the shelf.

He took it from my hand. "The Hernandez don't fly that."

His voice was hypnotic. Even ordinary words became a velvet caress.

I whirled and faced the window.

"What's the matter?" he asked, standing way too close behind me. I could sense his body's heat.

"Nothing," I lied, watching the sunlight shimmer on the water's surface to avoid looking at him.

"So turn around," he said, and when his hot breath stirred my hair, I felt a shiver slide down my spine.

"No, sir," I said, proud and disgusted with myself at the same time. When was the last time I'd been with a man? When was the last time someone touched me at all?

God, it would feel good to kiss him. My lips swelled in anticipation. When was the last time I felt so ripe, so ready?

He tucked my hair behind my ear and drawled into it, "I'm tired of waiting for you to decide who you want me to be. What would it take to get you never to consider me your instructor again, Miranda? If I peeled back the collar of that shirt and gave you the gentlest of bites where your neck slopes toward your shoulder, would that do it?"

My body's quickening was impossible to hide from him.

"What if I ran my hands over your thighs and under your shirt until they were cupping your breasts? Would you stop calling me *sir* then? Or isn't that intimate enough? I've seen you stare at my mouth; is that what

152

you want? Do you want me to explore your hills and val-
leys with my lips? With my tongue?"

"Stop," I whispered. I liked my sex with love, but this
was raw, carnal need.

His response was a husky chuckle that made my
heart skip a beat. "Stop what? Stop wanting you to treat
me as an equal? Or stop wanting you?"

"Stop," I whispered. "I'll call you whatever you want."

"Sugar, I doubt that's going to be enough anymore. I
want to tear down those walls for good. Now turn around."

I loved the skip in his voice. He wanted this as much
as I did. I couldn't resist teasing him.

"No."

He flipped back my collar, and I gasped as I felt
his mouth low on the side of my neck, testing the flesh
slightly with his teeth.

"Turn around," he coaxed, kissing his way up to my
ear.

I didn't want it over too fast, so I stayed put.

He put his hands on my hips. How could his hands
be so hot? His hands traveled, and to halt their progress
I put my hands over them, unable to ignore the heated
fireworks sparkling through me where he touched me.

His hands tightened on me, and I pulled away,
snatching a book off the shelf on the way past him.

"That one is in Italian."

With a muttered curse, I tossed it on the table and
grabbed another before I could take his mouth in a sear-
ing kiss that would reveal my desperate need.

He blocked my retreat. His hands sliding into my
hair, he kissed me with a hunger I'd never experienced
before. His intensity sent waves of heat crashing through
me with shocking force, and nothing on this earth could've

torn me away from him. I had never felt wanted like that, needed like that.

Moments later, we were both naked, and he was on the verge of entering me. Breathing hard, he stopped, holding me still.

"Tell me you want me," he whispered.

"No," I told him breathlessly, grinning.

He gave me a smooth, hard stroke that made me cry out, and then he stopped again. "At least say my name, Miranda. I need to hear you say my name."

"I can't," I told him before kissing him deeply. As his tongue thrust into my mouth, he entered me again, and this time he didn't stop until we'd both cried out like we'd lost our souls.

Afterward, he had the strangest expression on his face. I was probably giving him a similar look, so I glanced away.

My lips still tingled, and my skin still ached to be touched again by the man in front of me.

It was natural for me to remember Paul. I couldn't stop the agony of the weakening bond between my husband and me, a bond that would get even weaker as time went by. At some point, I would have to let go and move on. Was this it?

Not certain where to look or what to do, I pulled away from him and reached for my shirt.

He put his hands around my waist to stop me from buttoning the shirt. When I avoided his gaze, he ducked down and caught my mouth with his, kissing me fiercely.

"Are you sorry? Is that why you won't look at me?" he asked in a wounded voice. "I'm not your instructor any-more. That makes us consenting adults."

I reached for the rest of my clothes, and when he reached over to stop me, I jerked out of his grasp and gave him a sharp look.

"Miranda, I need you to tell me that you're here because you fantasize about being with me, not because you're so desperate for human contact that you had sex with the first person who laid a hand on you."

I didn't know what to say. It wasn't supposed to be this way. And the longer I looked at him, the more certain I was it wasn't supposed to happen with him. But what was I supposed to do, thank him and say good night?

I couldn't even be normal having a one-night stand. No, I had to have sex with my instructor.

Ex-instructor. An instructor.

Great. He had me correcting myself, using a technicality to make this event more palatable.

Shaking his head and sighing, he said, "Feel free to look at my books while I get dressed and consider how to salvage this. I doubt you believe it, but I wasn't planning on having intercourse either."

That comment combined with the ache between my legs made me say with wonder, "You bastard."

He made a long suffering face at that. "What now?"

"You took me without even bothering to see if I was protected," I said, so appalled that I could barely get the words out.

He stood there naked, so shocked his mouth was agape.

Waves of self-hate driving my desperate need to get away, I snatched a book from his shelves and took off running.

CHAPTER 19

STAB WOUND

When school resumed, I trapped Dante as soon as he left the cafeteria line with his green tea. The overcast skies muted the colors around us, leaving his golden hair tarnished and his tan washed out. However, the lack of luster in his blue eyes clearly came from something else entirely.

"Nothing happened," he said, refusing to meet my gaze.

"Because she was supportive and understanding when you revealed yourself?"

"Because I didn't tell her."

"You're killing me, Dante."

"You weren't there," he said. "She was so beautiful, so perfect—"

"She's got flaws."

"Yeah, but they're cute flaws," he sighed. "I'm going to tell her. I want to. It's not time."

A week and a half later, the sun was back to the desert's usual piercing brightness, and I bounced on the balls of my feet, happy to start my day with the Resistance, Evade, and Escape segment. The time away from the Axe-based coursework and the physical activity was what I had needed to clean out the cobwebs before I hunkered down to prepare for finals.

Marco had shown me a lot about unarmed combat over the past year, and my comfort level had set me up to be the sparring partner for the guest instructor, Rabbie, the previous week. Most cadets struggled to cross the line from polite behavior to knocking someone on their ass.

Well-prepared as usual, Kairo had sent me videos of what to expect for this week's knife skills. None of it looked difficult, so we'd moved on to the handgun unit prep. He'd grown up around guns and was surprisingly patient about teaching me how to handle a sidearm very similar to what we'd be issued. After a couple of days at the gun range downtown, he told me I'd be good for next week's pistol course. I was still worried. I rushed targeting.

He was in the classroom now, learning the material that would be presented to my class when we flip-flopped after lunch.

I helped Rabbie carry gear, making him chuckle because what was an easy load for the ex-Marine turned out of be an ass-kicker for me.

"You ready to slice and dice today?" he asked.

"Oh, aye, sir," I said.

Brandishing the wicked blade that was a standard part of an air crew's gear, he showed us the moves and then switched to a neon green dummy knife. He called me forward, and I made a face.

"You shouldn't stand at the end if you don't want to go first," he teased. "Take a blade and come over here."

I picked up a rubber knife with distaste, holding the blade between two fingers.

"Justice, you're killing me. Hold it like this."

My palm curled around the handle. The pressure inside my head made it difficult to listen to him.

His own knife in hand, he took a step toward me.

Everything seized up inside me, and I blacked out. As soon as I came out of my faint, I vomited violently.

What the hell was that all about?

The medic pulled me aside and motioned for Rabbie to continue the lecture without me.

Mr. Yoshimura came trotting up with a bottle of water. "I saw you drop from the window. What happened?"

"No idea, sir," I said, bewildered. "Perhaps I'm coming down with the flu."

"Not according to Blue," the medic said. "Did you eat this morning?"

"Of course. I'm not dehydrated either."

Mr. Yoshimura said, "Donovan, that scar on your temple isn't from a knife, is it?"

I shook my head. "I got shot."

"Are you absolutely, positively sure about that?"

"A large handgun pointed at your head is a memorable event, trust me."

"Maybe you locked your knees. Ready to try it again?"

I nodded and strode toward the group.

Dante was up front, fair hair stirring in the wind. I joined the clapping and cheers of encouragement, but I couldn't resist adding, "You've got enviable stability on your left foot."

He glanced at me, exasperated, but it gave Rabbie an opening. Dante glimpsed the movement out of the corner of his eye and tried evading the half-time strike, but he wasn't quick enough. Rabbie's dummy blade sliced Dante across the gut.

Something broke in me, and I collapsed, unconscious.

I woke in the fetal position surrounded by the smells of the infirmary. I was afraid to open my eyes, though. They showed me such terrible sights.

"...says she was shot, but there must be more to it than that. You know how her records say she has retrograde amnesia? Could it be a big, fat repressed memory?"

"She remembers the temple wound as a shooting," Mr. Yoshimura said. "She refers to it with ease."

"It does look like she was grazed," the flight surgeon agreed. "Her doctor was able to recover residue from the tissue that supports it. Maybe she witnessed a stabbing."

"So what do we do about it?" Mr. Yoshimura asked. "She needs to pass this unit by the end of the week."

"I doubt she can, but maybe her physician can give you a better answer. He's almost here."

"What?"

"Said he was on his way."

"Let me in there," a dark, velvet voice said.

"Chavez, you're adding fuel to the fire," Mr. Yoshimura sighed.

"Chastise me later," Mr. Chavez said. "I've got to find out if it's guns, too, or just knives."

I sensed his presence and inhaled his coffee-scented breath.

"Miranda, look at me."

I risked a peek through my lashes. He was close enough to take up my whole field of vision, so I opened my eyes. "Dante."

"He's well. He's worried about you, but he's fine."

Tony rushed into the room. "Mira."

"My head hurts blackly," I whimpered, my eyes never leaving Mr. Chavez's.

Tony's hand smoothed my hair back. The bright flash of light in each eye showed me the veins in my eyeballs, and then I felt the coolness of an alcohol swab on my shoulder. I barely felt the stick.

"What are you doing here?" I asked as the horrible prickliness at the back of my skull eased.

"Marco asked me to be nearby today. I don't know why," Tony said.

He gave me a pair of tablets to take, holding the glass to my mouth. As he pocketed the bottle, I saw the drugs weren't in his name. Mine, either. Thanks to my need and Tony's money, the Hernandez black market for drugs thrived. No one could write legal prescriptions for a visa holder.

"I'm okay. I just have to get in the shower and change clothes," I said, trying to get up.

Tony pressed me back down. "Shh, Mira, shh. I would like it if you rested here for a couple of minutes."

Energy drained out of me again, leaving me limp.

Mr. Chavez's brown eyes were locked back on mine, his face filling my vision again.

"Why do you need to shower?" he asked.

I was glad his voice was soft. One harsh word would shatter me. "I'm covered in blood," I whispered. "Can't you see it?"

His fingers briefly lit on my scar. "From this?"

"No. I only remember the shooting up until he pulled the trigger. I must've bled, but I don't remember it."

"Then whose blood is on your clothes?"

160

Agony lit up in my skull, obliterating me before the answer could be recovered.

"Hi," Mr. Chavez said, his dark eyes so close to mine.

The room was dimmer and warmer. My cramped muscles protested my attempts to relax them, but I eventually got to a comfortable position lying on my side.

He moved until he took up my whole world again.

"Hi," I said shyly.

"Your doctor tells me you're married." His tone was no different than if he were telling me the cafeteria had pie today. "What's his name?"

"Where is he? Where's Tony?"

"He's close. I wanted less of an audience while we had this conversation. Is it warm enough for you?"

"Better, but I'm still cold."

He took off his suit coat and draped it over me. "What is your husband's name?"

"Paul Frederick Donovan."

"That's quite a mouthful. I would've named him something tidier."

My lips turned up at the edges for a moment.

"Was your husband shot in the head?" he asked me in that ordinary tone.

My brow creased. "No. Is that what you ask all married women?"

"Yes."

"You really are a strange man."

"Miranda, did someone stab your husband?"

Agony lit up in my skull once more, obliterating me.

I felt woozy. I couldn't quite remember where I was, who I was.

Dark brown eyes took up my whole field of vision.

"Stabbed twice," the man said.

"What?"

"Paul's dead."

"I know," I whispered.

"The obituary got it wrong though. They said he was stabbed twice."

"Why would they change it? Was six times too gory?"

"I don't know."

This man preferred accuracy. "Five times."

"Not six?"

"He was stabbed five times. Then his throat was cut. Is that five times or six?"

"I'm starting to see why they didn't know what to write about it. Who killed him?"

"I did," I whispered.

CHAPTER 20

PAUL'S DEATH

Mr. Chavez was speaking to me, his voice low and urgent in the confines of the infirmary room, but I wasn't listening to him anymore.

Paul stood shocked and angry at the foot of the gurney. His mouth moved, but I couldn't hear him.

This time I didn't turn away.

A small tear appeared on his shirt, and blood flowed out. There was another rip and then another, and more of the hot, red fluid spilled down his shirt to soak his jeans. There were four, then five punctures before the slice appeared across his throat. A trickle there, he didn't have much blood pressure left.

Unable to bear that ashy death color of his face, I jerked my gaze away from him.

I gasped. Blood splattered my clothes. My right hand was covered with the blood I had spilled when I stabbed my husband to death two weeks before my fateful trip to Wal-Mart.

Hands tightened on me, and I pushed them away. Stumbling in my haste, I ran to the sink and turned the tap on full. The water splashed back cold and slick, and the force of the déjà vu made me dizzy. The blood diluted but never disappeared as I rubbed my hands together. Why couldn't I get clean? Why couldn't I ever get clean?

"Inverse tangent," I said, looking over at Mr. Chavez in surprise. "Not tangent."

He ended the litany of aerodynamics formulas with a forceful exhale, his relief tangible.

My clothes and face were wet, and I helped myself to the stack of towels on the stainless steel table while I tried to find my way through the maelstrom of confusion in my head.

I had never fought with Paul, so there was no way an argument could've escalated into that kind of violence. But why couldn't I remember the last time I spoke to him? What could I remember from that last month at all?

I hadn't celebrated my birthday on October fifth. Paul had been away, and I had an exam to prep for. I'd taken on too heavy of a workload at 24 credit hours instead of my usual 20, so I had no margin for error.

Pushing past my birthday resulted in a vague, unsettling nothingness.

Paul appeared on the other side of the infirmary again. His mouth moved, but I couldn't hear him. The first tear appeared in his shirt.

I jerked my head away, closing my eyes. Even as I toweled them off, my hands remained as wet as the shirt sticking to me, and my stomach heaved from the scent of punctured bowel.

It wasn't a real memory. It couldn't be. With a jolt of relief, I remembered speaking to Paul the night I got shot. He had been very much alive, wondering why I wasn't home yet. He had said—

Color faded from the memory. It had been Adam on the phone, not Paul. Not knowing what else to do, I had gone to school as if nothing had changed. Adam and Paul had bonded over beer and both being from Pittsburgh, so Adam had watched over me, making certain I made it home from class, that I ate, that our dog ate, that I was around to answer the cops' questions. The police had told Adam there was virtually no chance of an arrest because...

Because...

"Miranda, talk to me," Jason Chavez said. "If not to me, someone else."

It came to me then. The memory of the worst moment of my life finally broke free.

The doorknob of the front door to our townhouse had been cold and slick under my right hand, and Jackson's stiff new collar had cut into my other hand as he barked. A familiar middle-aged man in uniform had stood on the porch beside an elderly woman with a Red Cross volunteer name badge. Jackson hadn't settled down, and embarrassed I couldn't control him, I had used my knee to push the dog inside while I had stepped outside to find out what was going on. Master Sergeant Taylor had looked sad, but that hadn't diminished the First Sergeant's usual aura of strength. He had said helplessly, "Mira, I'm so sorry." He had cleared his throat. "It is my terrible duty to inform you..."

"It's all right," I told Jason, sad that death made it easy to think of him by his first name when sex hadn't. "I remember everything."

"Do you or are you telling me what I want to hear? What happened after your husband was stabbed to death?"

"Nothing. They never apprehended the man who did it. They didn't even make much of an effort because it was a big city and people got mugged all the time. Sometimes people got killed."

"Why did you say you killed Paul?"

"Jason, I understand your curiosity, but it's unwarranted. Sometimes things go wrong."

He frowned. "I'm not a fan of downgrading the death of a loved one."

I cried at that.

"Miranda, whatever you did or didn't do, whatever your involvement in his death, you can talk to me about it," he said. "You'd be surprised at what I can understand."

"My budget said I could take on two courses beyond what my scholarship covered. When Paul made me redo the budget with more realistic, conservative estimates, it proved what he suspected: I needed more money for school. He was so tired of being away from home, but he volunteered for that mission so I could take the courses I wanted when I wanted to take them. It's my fault he was killed in that mugging. My fault." I wiped the tears off my face. "When it's all out in the open, it sounds so banal, doesn't it?"

"It's not banal at all," he said.

"No?"

"No."

"I don't remember the last thing I said to him. It was early morning. He was getting ready to leave for that trip, and he kissed me awake and told me he fed the dog. It was ordinary. I was half-asleep and probably said *thanks* and *bye*. Maybe a casual, mumbled *love you*."

"How were you to know it was the last time you would ever speak to him?" he asked. "You can't treat every conversation with a loved one as the final one. Your farewells would take hours."

"You don't understand."

166

"Well, that, and I'm bored. I was expecting a murder-for-hire so you could use the insurance money for tuition or perhaps a crime of passion where you walked in on him with your French tutor and stabbed him. But you had nothing to do with it."

"Look, simply because I wasn't there, didn't know it was coming, didn't do it, and didn't hire someone to do it—"

"Perhaps you should hold that thought until you're capable of presenting me with a well-reasoned argument because you sound ridiculous claiming responsibility at this point."

Drained, I leaned in his direction, sliding off the edge of the gurney. He caught me and held me close, and without hesitation I put my arms around him, too.

"Miranda," he murmured against my hair. "I know this isn't the greatest timing, but it can't wait any longer."

"You're pregnant?"

For that, I was rewarded with a muffled chuckle and a brief squeeze that wrung the air out of me. "No, but you did remind me how much I want children. What about you? Are you pregnant?"

"No," I said. Why had I mentioned it at all? "And yes, I'm certain."

"So you let me stew on it because you were angry."

I blushed. "No."

"I would've done the same," he told me, making me chuckle despite my effort not to.

I pitied the woman he would marry and have kids with. He was impossible.

"Miranda, I want you to be my pilot."

I pulled back and stared at him.

"I'm going back on active duty," he told me, "and I want you to be my partner."

CHAPTER 21
Your What?

Jason Chavez motioned for me to precede him into the unused simulator bay, and I hesitated, detecting Mr. Yoshimura's gaze as he stood in the hall conversing with a colleague. Given that Jason's office was under surveillance, it was obvious we wanted privacy, and given the rumors about us, I hated to think of what Mr. Yoshimura assumed we were doing.

Then again, given my meltdown over the knife, it was feasible the surprise on his face was because I was still on campus at all.

"Miranda."

I jumped and entered the bay. It was immense and dark, and the depth of the sound-muffling precautions muted my footsteps to the visitors' chairs. Jason turned on a few lights, revealing the simulator sleeping on its gyro, marked with maintenance tags.

My knee bumped into his when I sat, and I flinched.

"Are our worlds colliding too frequently for comfort?" Jason asked. "At least you're not pregnant. Are you carrying protection now? But there is no good answer to that, is there? If you say no because you don't have casual sex, then you look irresponsible in front of the one man who knows for a fact you do have casual sex. If you say yes, you are taking precautions, then it could be interpreted as an invitation or an expectation."

"I notice you aren't taking the question back."

"I'm curious how you'll respond. Would it have been so terrible to have my child?"

"Oh, God."

He laughed and held out a flat packet. I blushed at the foil square and snatched it off the chair before anyone walked in and saw it.

"It's the most reliable brand out there," he told me. "I want children by an amazing woman, but not yet. Research says these are the best."

"Don't top-tier personnel in critical fields have their procreation matings chosen for them? But they don't call it eugenics."

"They refer to it as resource management," he said with a grim smile.

"Nature over nurture," I mused. "I don't understand the modern emphasis on genetics. Having a gene for intelligence is no guarantee it will be applied. I doubt a man relishes being told the probable gene expression of his children is more important than his free will, either. But at least you don't have to have sex with her."

"I'm not having children by anyone I didn't choose," he said, his eyes narrowing.

"Sorry," I said, belatedly recognizing the signs this was a touchy subject for him. I held out the condom to him. "I don't want to leave you without any. I'll get my own."

"I've got three more in my wallet," he admitted, shifting and looking away.

It was my turn to laugh. "Haven't found your amazing woman yet, huh? Won't Profit be disappointed she didn't make the cut?"

"I've found the right woman, but the timing's not good."

"Well, congratulations," I said, embarrassed to be having such a personal conversation with someone I didn't know very well. Discussing clan eugenics policy was one thing, but his offering something from his private life was something else entirely. "So you're coming out of retirement? What prompted that?"

"I didn't retire," he said, straightening.

I was hitting one nerve after another.

"My three-year visa locks me into teaching, but at the end of this term I can return to the cockpit if I find someone I want to partner with."

"Why would you agree to teach when you want to fly?"

"I told you. I broke with my partner. I didn't want to fly with anyone else, and my teaching created a necessary goodwill between the Hernandez and Texas."

"Why don't you rate a high-caliber pilot? Is their prejudice against foreigners that deep?"

"You can't be surprised I chose you. I've known since the obstacle course that I wanted to fly with you. You took a course that had one possible route, and you created a legal alternative that gave you the advantage. Before that, you made teaching more interesting, but that was all. After that, I saw nothing but possibility. I've read every project you wrote and every exam you took here. Now that you know why you've had the compulsion to push the math, you can deal with it, only increasing your aptitude."

"What do you mean?"

"You think you killed your husband with conservative math."

Trying to puzzle that out, I bit my lip but stopped when I saw his gaze drop to my mouth.

His focus returned to my eyes. "The conservative math in your budget made him take the mission that got him killed. Following the budget where you pushed your math all the way to the edge would've prevented his death. The more you've had to contemplate having a partner again, the more you had to wonder if you were going to get your gunner killed by playing it too safe like you did Paul."

"What?"

"I didn't say you were conscious of your attempts to prevent being paired with someone. But you have to concede that if failing your math-heavy coursework wasn't enough to get you thrown out of school, it still would've driven off any sane gunner candidate. How did you not see this?"

"I'll thank you to show some sensitivity. I just remembered the truth about Paul, so I haven't fully explored the repercussions. And as for partnering, I'm sorry, but Kairo and I have been planning to pair up."

"Kairo," he said with a strange smile. "You still want to partner with Kairo."

"What's your issue with him?"

"Mostly it's because he lied and took credit for what I did."

I tried not being amused at the idea. "What could that have been? He can't get published for your research."

"After analysis of your punishment for that fight revealed the depth of your struggle to comply, I paid your penalty in its entirety, and I took care of most of your community service."

I couldn't have heard that right.

He said, "Kairo's appointment with the dean to complain about me yet again was delayed while she and I hammered out the details of our illegal, off-the-books arrangement. You got lucky there. She came from an abusive relationship, so she was sympathetic. She had to enforce it publicly to save face. If you want to check on it, call up the volunteer hours using your student ID number."

The silence stretched while I tried to find my voice.

"Why would you do that for me?" I asked.

He made an elegant motion of his hand that warned he took issue with my conclusion. "I did that for me. My future pilot needed the money to eat and the time to prep for class."

The depths he'd gone to to bring me to this very moment were staggering. I was too surprised to be creeped out or flattered by the single-minded attention.

"The MoD will allow us to be paired," he said. "I fly with and only with whom I want. If you don't want to fly with me, you'll end up wherever it is you would've ended up before we had this conversation, probably with Kairo if you both request it. Keep in mind I need to get my request to the MoD by the end of business on Wednesday, but the sooner, the better."

"This Wednesday?" I asked. "That's less than two days. I would've appreciated more time to make a decision."

"Blame the MoD. They bumped up the date for fixing partner assignments for this school year from December thirtieth to the fifteenth."

I didn't have any further questions, so he released me.

"Thank you," I told him.

"For what?"

It took me a minute or two to find the words. "For asking the right questions this morning."

"This is getting tiresome, Miranda. I can't make it any plainer, but I'll keep trying. I did it for me. My pilot needs to be able to finish her academy coursework, including the REE portion."

"Say that all you want, but I suspect you like me."

He studied me for a moment or two before replying. "That'll come down to how many of the rumors are based on fact. Or perhaps what the flight physical reveals."

"What's that supposed to mean?"

"You do understand that you have to pass a drug test."

"I don't use," I snapped. I undid my chignon and yanked a strand of hair from my scalp complete with root bulb. "Here. Have it evaluated yourself."

He looked at it in distaste. "Keep your biologics to yourself. I have confidence in the medical establishment's ability to perform an analysis when the time comes."

"Keep my biologics to myself? With pleasure," I said, throwing the condom at him and walking off.

"Stop being a child."

Ignoring that, I twisted my hair back up and jabbed in the pins before throwing open the door to the hall.

Yoshi was still there in conversation, and his eyes went to my hair, telling me I hadn't gotten it right without a mirror.

"He wanted a drug test," I snapped. "I gave him hair because spitting in his eye would get me expelled."

"You can't be drug tested off-schedule without a formal request," Yoshi told me.

"I didn't ask," Jason said, annoyed. "I reminded her there would be one. You know, Ms. Donovan, innocent people don't overreact."

173

"They do if they've been persecuted since school started and they had a potentially catastrophic morning," I snapped. "I'm going to the cafeteria to get a snack."

"You don't have time," Yoshi said. "Class starts in ten minutes."

"Well, that's just great."

"Yes, emotional outbursts are such a poor waste of time, aren't they?" Jason asked with an acid smile. "Mint?"

I considered telling him what he could do with his mint no matter who was there and how much it damaged my chances to graduate.

"It's five calories. Five is better than none."

Yoshi grinned at my hesitation. "Would it be any easier taking it from my hand?"

A sharp, unwilling burst of laughter escaped me at my foolishness, and I claimed the spearmint candy from Jason's palm.

After my REE lecture had let out for the day, I went to the library and researched Jason Chavez's previous pilot so I had an idea of what he considered the customary interaction between pilot and gunner. Unfortunately, he was Texan so I could find nothing but footage from their ill-fated Comp.

Running Bear had been defiant and strong in the interviews, but when the vids caught him in the background of other interviews, he looked so different I didn't recognize him at first. The distant stare, the way his arms clutched his body like he felt he was coming apart at the seams, and the way he shook made it seem like everything he believed in had failed him.

I doubt he would've wanted my sympathy, but he had it. It wasn't the first time I'd seen people have to choose between love and duty or love and a career after everyone had promised it was feasible to have it all.

"You're here late," Dante observed.

I shut off the video. "Tell me, what are the rumors?"

"That you got stabbed," he said, pointing to my scar.

"That'll do," I decided. "Between you and me?"

"Yeah," he said, glancing around to be certain.

"I remembered the murder of someone I loved."

He opened his mouth to speak, but there wasn't anything to say to something of that magnitude, so he squeezed my shoulder with his big paw.

I said, "I'm surprised they're giving me another chance tomorrow."

"You want to talk about it?"

I shook my head. "Thanks, but I've got a more pressing issue. Jason Chavez asked me to partner with him. For real. He needs an answer by Wednesday."

His regard turned from sad to thoughtful. "So it is like that after all. Interesting. But you wouldn't mention it unless you were torn between Kairo and him."

Nidra called out to him, and whatever Dante saw when he looked at her made him frown and cross the room to her.

I peered out of the back room. Nidra was mopping up a spate of tears, mascara so smeared she resembled a raccoon. Dante appeared to be saying he couldn't do something for her.

I said, "Dante, we can hash this out later."

Nidra strode over and pulled me into a hug, her potent perfume making my nose twitch. "Oh, Justice, are you okay?"

I nodded, eyes watering. The sneeze burst before I could help it. Did she roll in ragweed?

"Are you?" I asked her, accepting a tissue.

Her dark eyes were shiny and solemn. "Kairo said it had to be a post-traumatic flashback that made you pass out," she said, pretending she didn't hear my question. "Was it recently? Were you horribly cut up?"

"Nee," Dante said. "It's none of our business."

She ignored that and told me, "Yoshi tried to get you a waiver for the knife stuff."

"No, I'll be there tomorrow," I said.

"Good." She looked between us. "And getting you through tomorrow is what you two were talking about. Dante, you need to help her get through this. You've always got the best advice."

Torn, he watched her leave, but as soon as she was out of sight, he said to me, "We shouldn't talk about this here."

"She was weirdly huggy."

His lips were pressed together, but his eyes were bright.

"She broke up with her boyfriend?" I guessed.

"Her long-distance relationship ran out of fuel. How long do I have to wait until I can ask her out?"

"When you're ready to tell her about your dark secret."

Grabbing his bag, he made a face and motioned me forward. "You know I almost told her. It's not my fault her sister walked in. Hey, can I meet you at your house? I want to make sure she's okay to get home."

"Take your time."

On the train home, I called Ethan. "Can I ask you about Jason's reputation?"

"He's earned every bit of his nasty reputation and then some," Ethan told me. His voice held the fond tone of a man describing a dog that does nothing but bite and growl but is nevertheless a part of the family. "He's a petty, manipulative liar who uses people to his own end. He would've told you that himself if you asked him."

"That's not the reputation I'm interested in," I said, understanding why Jason was so annoyed by exaggeration. Everyone lied and had their own goals to pursue. Jason was odd, but he wasn't the man Kairo and all the other prejudiced Hernandez said he was. "Is he as good a gunner as going to the Comp would suggest or was he along for the ride?"

He made an abrupt choking noise like I'd caught him in the middle of taking a drink. He coughed and gasped and coughed more. "Sorry," he croaked.

"No, I am. I didn't realize that was such a loaded question."

"Not loaded. Funny. He's good, Mira. Easily the best in Texas. Why do you ask?"

"Too many inconsistencies in the way people talk about him."

"I wouldn't worry about it too much. I doubt you'll have trouble with him."

After the call ended, I chewed on my lip. Perhaps this wasn't such a crazy idea after all.

Chapter 22

Decisions, Decisions

When I walked into the house, Marco's dark eyes glanced over me more thoroughly than usual.

"How did you know?" I asked him. "How did you know I'd need Tony today?"

"How did I know that you have an aversion to knives? I live with you. If you can't cut it with a butter knife, it doesn't get cut."

"I didn't know that."

He showed rare hesitation. "I know. I'm not a psychologist, Mira. As long as it wasn't hindering you, I let it be."

"The knives, the peroxide, the pennies—how many quirks have you been ignoring while you tell me to be normal, to fit in, to hide in plain sight?"

Dante rapped on the door, making me curse his timing.

"We're not done talking about this," I warned Marco. After I let Dante in, I told Marco about Jason's offer.

He grunted. "It's risky."

"Yeah, I'm saying no, too," Dante said, shifting his weight around to find the sweet spot on Lumpy Couch. "He's foreign. It would make you more foreign."

"He's an experienced flyer and a willing instructor. What I could learn from him could make me a bigger asset."

"It could," Dante allowed. "But is there going to be a test you have to take? How else are you going to show you're worth more for being partnered with him for a short time?"

"How short?" Marco asked.

"He was picked up the day after the Comp, so he'll be leaving here in late April before the next one," Dante replied. "And then she'll have to try to find a Hernandez partner."

Marco's scowl increased. "After having already chosen a Texan over all the Hernandez options?"

"Can I have a few of these?" Dante asked, pointing out the jar of nuts on the coffee table.

Marco nodded.

"Kairo's a dick," I said. "Talented, no doubt, but a dick and a liar. I don't relish the idea of being stuck with that."

"So request to be put in the pool," Dante said. "Kairo will assume your application to partner with him was denied because he's being groomed and they don't want to risk saddling him with a foreigner. You know he believes he's got the DNA of a minor deity."

Marco's eyes flashed at the mention of genetic material. "Mira's MoD paperwork expires halfway through January, which means the simulations can still make or break her chances. Introducing an unknown gunner is the riskiest option." His palmer signaled an emergency responder call, and he collected his gear. Before he left, he told me, "I vote Kairo as long as his crap isn't the kind that sabotages you."

Dante and I tossed it around for few more minutes before I sighed, "But he won a Comp."

"Mira, you've got to let go of that Comp win of his. There's something very weird there. The Texan DM wouldn't split up her best team after their most significant win unless there was a monumental problem."

Put that way, falling in love did seem an inadequate reason. Nero Hernandez definitely wouldn't have accepted it as grounds for one of his air crews splitting up.

Dante's struggle with the almond jar registered. "What are you doing to that poor jar?"

"Got my hand stuck in it," he said matter-of-factly, showing me his encased paw.

"I'm friends with Scooby Doo," I said. "Why didn't you shake some out into your hand?"

"Because it looked big enough to stick my hand in, and I was going to pick out the burned ones." He leaned on his elbows, studying my face. "We all know Kairo is an arrogant, ambitious prick. But he's Hernandez, and he's willing to fly with you."

"I can't take you seriously with your hand in a jar, Dante. Let me help. You're eating all of these nuts, by the way."

"I only wanted the burned ones."

"Your cooties are all over them now."

He and Marco were right. Kairo was the better choice on paper. I opened my mouth to commit to him, but I said, "I suspect Chavez is better."

"Once you've sworn fealty, you will live here permanently. You're being given a chance to blend in better, to become more one of us. Don't waste it."

I told him about the discrepancy between Jason's and Kairo's stories about the reduction of my punishment, and he sat back, thoughtful again.

"You checked your hours?"

I nodded. They supported Jason's story since the number of assigned hours hadn't been reduced at all but had been chipped away week by week until the entire bill was paid off. I had set up the app on my palmer to give me a progress bar that showed my hours picking up trash in the park, but I hadn't bothered to check the numbers.

"I sort of owe him," I said.

"You didn't ask him to do it. You wouldn't have agreed to it if he'd offered."

"Does it matter? He still got me out of a hell of a jam."

He grimaced.

I asked, "Would you partner with Kairo? If I choose Chavez, Kairo will be available."

"Well, no, not if I could help it, but my situation is a lot different. No, I take it back. I would choose Kairo. He's phenomenal, and you'd be lucky to have him."

I chuckled. "Nice try."

He stood up and shoved the jar of nuts into his bag before he slung it over his shoulder. "Kairo's the safer option, Mira. You know he is. He's made stupid mistakes, but he's my age. He'll get past it."

"Thanks for coming over. I'll see you in the morning."

I didn't eat breakfast. Well, I had a shake when I was up at three in the morning, but I didn't eat anything else before I went to my knife skills class. I couldn't talk to anyone. I couldn't even be near them. I focused on Rabbie to learn what I needed to, and I snatched up a dummy knife and pushed between him and his demonstration partner.

He didn't hesitate. We went through the drill at full throttle, my determination making it all but impossible to listen to his corrections.

A brief, intense twenty minutes later, he signed me off.

I hurried off the mats.

"Replace the knife in the bag where you got it," Jason Chavez said, arms crossed and expression stony.

I hurried back and snatched up the knife I had dropped. I wasn't capable of speech yet, but I managed to nod my thanks to Rabbie. After I had returned the knife, I ran to the bathroom and heaved over the toilet but got nothing but mouthfuls of stomach acid for my trouble. Soon, I felt steadier on my feet. With visualization and mindful effort, I would get better at handling knives.

Over lunch, Rabbie and I made up the coursework from the day before, and this time I was able to thank him for not cutting corners with me. I knew at least one instructor would've passed me if I'd tried to meet the requirements after the revelation of some PTSD there wasn't time to fully deal with. Rabbie wasn't about to qualify me before he was satisfied.

"Life and death," he told me without apology. "That's what it all comes down to."

Simple words, but a powerful idea. Suddenly choosing between possible partners was easy.

When I tracked down Jason Chavez after school, he took one look at my face and graced me with one of his devastatingly beautiful smiles.

"Out of morbid curiosity, what sold it?" he asked me.

I hesitated, creating and discarding several expected explanations.

"You can be honest with me," he told me.

I supposed I could. What could I say that would be worse than admitting I'd killed my husband?

I said, "Best case scenario, I will fly. It's a dangerous job, and with brutal practicality I chose the partner who can keep me alive longer."

"I can do a lot more than that. I can make you a legend. Have you ever had a taste of glory?"

"Glory? I just want to fly to the edge of my ability."

"Well, I can help you with that, too."

When I got home, Marco leaned over a computer he'd set up on the kitchen table.

"Come take a look at this security feed," he told me before I could say anything. "I think it shows the guy who's been putting those coins in your path."

I didn't want this. I was settled in this world now, and these pennies tormented me with reminders of a past life and the man who'd ended it.

"This is the guy," he said, pointing out the figure in the shadows across the street. "Do you recognize his build or the way he moves? Anything?"

"How did you even spot that? I see a blob. Why do you suspect it's our guy? Was there another penny?"

Marco motioned for me to watch the feed. The stranger made a throwing motion toward our house before retreating into the shadows altogether. No more movement occurred.

"It's out in the gutter. I didn't check it for the date. He spotted the cameras, so he couldn't place it better without exposing himself. And look at the time stamp."

"Two nights ago. So?"

"So you were in here fighting with Zack at the time because he had the game on so loud you couldn't study. You're not the one leaving the pennies for yourself."

I digested that. Confirmation I wasn't a complete lunatic was a relief, but it meant I had a stalker of sorts, a conclusion that came with its own complications.

"It's been a while since the last one," Marco said. "And he's keeping his distance."

"He's not escalating, you mean. The dates are, but he's not."

The pennies had come in sequential order from the year of my birth, so the one out there was probably 2010.

"We need to get a picture of his face. I'm moving the cameras around. One of them is going to be pointed at your bedroom."

"So don't strip in front of the shade. Got it."

"You chose Chavez, didn't you?" When I told him why I did, he grunted. "I can't argue that, but it will cost you."

CHAPTER 23

Nosey

I woke early the next day, a hard rock in my belly, my palmer in my hand. I checked it, but Kairo still hadn't responded to my message that we needed to speak privately and as soon as possible. It was remotely feasible he heard I was partnering with someone else and was spurning me, but it was more likely he was still working on that snag on his term paper. When he was deep in a project, he would've told God Himself to wait a minute.

It was just as well. I still wasn't certain how to handle it, but I knew he was going to show less maturity than Jason would've if I'd gone the other way. Kairo was going to yell. A lot. Maybe he would escalate to throwing things.

The knot in my belly clenched even more.

Out in the kitchen, Marco saw me take out an egg and then replace it.

"No matter how nervous your stomach is, you're not leaving without eating," he told me, pushing away from the table to make me a shake. "Zack, Mira's having a crappy morning. Do you have an Axe-shaped chocolate or toy to cheer her up?"

Zack burst from his room, radiating child-like excitement.

"So that's a yes?" I teased. "But do me a favor and put on pants first."

Fingers clutching the handle to my bag, I scanned the tables in study hall. "Where is he? Do you see him?"

"None of the gunners are here," Dante noticed, sweeping his hand through his hair self-consciously when he saw Nidra. "They weren't at the cafeteria either. Must be down at the simulators or the jet bays again. Why do they get so many more field trips than we do?"

"I've got to find him."

"I don't want to be anywhere near when he finds out. He's not going to take this well."

"You did."

"Well, I never had a good feeling about Kairo in the first place, so I'm sort of relieved you didn't pick him." His eyebrows rose. "It's going to make the final weeks of school ugly though. Maybe you should delay until after his finals to tell him."

"All the while praying someone doesn't tell him before I do? Or that he doesn't figure it out when he sees Jason Chavez's excitement about returning to the cockpit? Why did he have to be Kairo's instructor?" I tossed my bag on the table nearest the door so I could keep an eye out. "This is a disaster."

After school, I went down to the jet bays to find Zack. We had talked about how jet engines mask their heat signatures all through breakfast, and he'd promised to show me the latest modification to his jet after school.

186

He opened up one of the back panels of his baby and told me to take a look. Since only one of us could fit, he told me what to look for while I wriggled up into his plane.

I said, "It smells acrid."

"Let me in there." After replacing me, he said, "I can't smell it, but that doesn't mean anything," he said. He rifled through the drawers in his wheeled cart. "I'll be back. Go ahead and take another look if you want, but don't stay in there too long."

Holding my breath, I went in for another look, committing to memory the questions that came to mind so I could look them up later.

I felt a forceful tap on my back.

"Just a sec."

Hands on my waist yanked me out of the jet with such force and speed I hit my head and gashed the underside of my chin.

I stared at my tormentor in disbelief. "What was that?"

Profit slapped me.

My cheek stinging, I barely got my hands up in time to deflect the follow-up shot. "Have you lost your mind? Zack's authorized to show me this."

She didn't care. I blocked, deflected, and dodged slaps and scratches, still stunned that she wanted to beat the crap out of me for touching her ride.

"Mira, take her down," Kairo yelled as he ran up. "End it."

Incredulous, I shook my head.

With an impatient sound, Kairo yanked Profit off me and bitch-slapped her to the ground.

He turned to me and repeated the motion.

"What is this sudden aversion to fighting?" he snapped as his foot caught me in the stomach, forcing the breath out of me and making me lock up with agony. "You had no problem laying out that guy in the parking lot." With another kick that nearly made me pass out, he said, "Get up."

It took me a few tries, but I got to my feet, hating him with every fiber. He went to slap me again, but I blocked it.

"Hit me back," he commanded, forcing me to deflect a punch. "One hit to prove you won't stand there like a lamb to be slaughtered if we get shot down and I'm too injured to fight enough for both of us."

"I'm not fighting you," I said, straightening from my defensive stance.

Profit told him, "She doesn't give a crap if you think she's a coward. She signed with Jason Chavez this morning."

Kairo swung around, pinning me with his wide, dark eyes. I'd seen the bulge of his palmer in his pocket. He had to know I hadn't stopped trying to tell him this before someone else could.

Kairo's hand came up, but his intention didn't register until I sat on the concrete seeing stars. Blood poured from my nose. I touched the bridge of my nose gingerly, and fresh waves of splintering agony shot through me. My gorge rose.

He crouched before me, his face rigid with hatred. "After everything I did for you and everything I had to put up with, you sign with him? Why? Because of that Comp win? You know how he got ahead, don't you? Because of his family. Years of clumsy eugenics loaded that family tree with enough flying achievements to make it one of the Texan MoD's favorites, but that line went sour a long time ago."

I spat a mouthful of blood.

"Got you good, didn't I?" he said, smirking. "Broke your nose? Good luck getting all your simulations and your flight checks done before your papers expire. I got to screw both of you with one blow. It's funny how life works out, isn't it?"

Refusing to lie at his feet, I struggled to mine, meeting his gaze squarely.

He threw another punch. I blocked it and brought my knee up between his legs. He dropped with a yelp, but he wasn't willing to stay down any more than I was.

I backed away, dividing my attention between Kairo and Profit. A hand on my shoulder made me spin around, crying out at the stabbing pain at my ribs.

"It's me," Ethan said, holding his hands out wide to show he meant no harm.

"I need a doctor," I told him.

Profit stepped forward, anger and dismay warring on her face, and he pointed at her, shaking his head. "Watch it, bitch. You know I'd love to testify against you."

Kairo was on his feet, but Zack had made it back and stood between us. "Get her out of here."

Ethan scooped me up and rushed out of the hangar. "Damn wolves."

"Pull this bus over. I'm going to throw up."

He hastily set me down.

"What's the point of me teaching you how to defend yourself if you won't?" Marco asked me in the hospital treatment area as he read the scan. He'd been called as my next of kin when I passed out.

"In the first place, I wasn't going to get sucked into a fight when the first one cost me so much. Second, I was naive in assuming he wouldn't hurt me."

189

The nurse hurried in. "I'm sorry, but you have to leave. The administration just found out you're a visa holder who shouldn't have received the medical treatment you did. They sent for security. If they don't catch you, they'll probably drop the matter."

Marco swore. He yanked off his shirt and handed it to me to cover my bloody one. I pulled it on and reached over to stuff the hem of his t-shirt back in the waistband of his jeans and pat down his hair while he wiped the bioscanner's memory.

He stopped me from opening the door. Turning me around, he tore off the brace across the bridge of my nose, apologizing as I cried out. After taking a final glance to see if anything else could be done to make me more inconspicuous, we sneaked out.

As he pulled Zack's car into traffic, I said, "They can't tell if it's going to heal well. I may be out on a medical before I ever make it into the cockpit to prove myself."

I said it matter-of-factly, but we both knew I was on the precipice of being seriously screwed.

He said, "We need to see a specialist before your nose starts healing. It'll hurt, but you'll pass your physical."

"Sounds expensive."

"You want to fly, don't you?"

"Yes," I said without hesitation.

"Well. There it is," he said as if that settled the matter for all time.

"How are we going to get a specialist to see me in the first place? I got lucky with that emergency room team. They knew what I was but treated me anyway."

"I know someone."

"Well, viva la revolution."

By the time Marco and I made it home, I had lost every trace of humor. Despite the analgesics and anti-inflammatories, I was in miserable agony, and both my eyes were swollen shut. To make matters worse, Jason was sitting in the living room in Marco's chair.

Seeing me, he flew out of the chair, face paling. "Oh my God, Miranda, your beautiful face. Profit said you hit the pavement relatively hard when you fell, but I didn't imagine this."

Fell?

My mood blackened.

I knocked his hand away. "You have to leave. I don't want to have to explain to my instructors that I'm not prepared for class because you were keeping me from my homework."

"Will you at least tell me where you were treated? I want to pay the bill."

"Help yourself," I said, figuring he was at least half the reason I got assaulted. He had money to burn, too, according to Ethan. "Marco can give you the details."

My nose throbbing with every heartbeat, I went to my room, shutting the door, shutting him out, shutting them all out.

I stared at my reflection in the bathroom mirror, disgusted. My nose and part of my cheekbones were a monstrosity of stitches and swelling, and both my eyes were bruised beyond recognition. Flecks of the polymer still stuck to my face from the rebuild. Kairo hadn't broken my nose; he'd shattered it along with part of my cheekbones. It hadn't been the power of the punch so much as the fragility of the bone underneath that made the blow so catastrophic.

But I couldn't help marveling at the human body. I would survive this with minimal loss of function. How much could I take before I couldn't make it back from the edge?

"That which does not kill us merely makes us stronger," I muttered to myself, dousing peroxide on the dried blood on my favorite shirt.

Within days, it became clear nothing would come of Profit and Kairo's attack. Of course nothing was going to happen to the gorgeous, talented, favored pilot. That much had been assumed all along. I found it difficult to blame her anyway. Jason was her boyfriend, and she was the clan's best pilot in search of a powerful gunner to help her place better at the upcoming Comp. When his option to choose a pilot came up, she must've been devastated when he didn't choose her. Seeing me in her warbird, too, well, yes, I understood why she drove me away.

And frankly, my younger sister had done more damage to me when we fought as kids. Profit wanted me gone, not broken and dead. Kairo, however, was elated with broken, and I suppressed the possibility he'd feel even more strongly about me dead.

No Hernandez other than Zack backed my story. If I'd been another citizen, one person's witness would've been enough to start formal charges, but everyone but my roommate said that I fell. Ethan wasn't permitted to give a statement, being a foreigner himself.

I was surprised Zack spoke up. When he heard I had chosen against flying with a clansman, the look on his face had been nothing but acute betrayal.

Kairo asked for and was granted a transfer down to the San Diego flight academy to finish out his schoolwork. Dante and I told ourselves the clan was separating us because Kairo couldn't be trusted around me and he couldn't be punished, but neither of us believed that.

I closed my eyes and calmed myself. If there was ever a time for me to heal quickly, this was it.

I envisioned an osteoblast along with a few of his friends synthesizing a mineral-based matrix from the calcium and phosphate that my supplements kept readily available. Microscopic brick by brick, the structure was repaired through an amazing, innate, biological knowledge that was passed down from generation to generation, coded in the DNA.

CHAPTER 24

GRADUATION

I paused just inside the hall of statues, marveling at how beautiful the long hall was with a starry sky presiding over the glass roof and crystal chandeliers suspended from the rafters. Elegant black chairs formed curving rows around a dais in front of the Comp statue.

Dante and I stared at each other in our pilot formals, awed at the transformation.

"You look good."

"That's my line," he said, twirling me around and catching me when I stumbled from the ache in my ribs. "That's a great dress. It shows a lot of leg," he added with a fake leer.

With no ruffles or other fluff to get in the way, this white dress was simple and elegant. In fact, it might have been considered severe if it weren't for the long slit that ran from ankle to mid-thigh. I wore two bands of color on my sleeve: one crimson, one black. Hernandez colors.

In less than an hour, a set of wings would further distinguish it as a formal uniform.

"We finally made it, Mira. Graduation day."

I was lightheaded from elation. The military orders I'd receive tonight would be a strong sign the clan was keeping me. The laws about a clanless person acquiring papers suggested that it came down to the decision of one of the ministry heads, the lieutenant chieftain, or the chieftain. A fealty oath and prenuptial series of paperwork would make it official, of course, but the route to get to that point was maddeningly vague.

After I had watched videos of past graduation ceremonies, I prepared for the event by practicing ascending a short flight of stairs in my dress and heels. No one said anything about my partnership with Jason, so I had practiced what I would say to my classmates when that bomb was dropped, too.

"When are you guys leaving?" I asked Dante, hating that we were parting ways.

"In the morning."

I gave Dante a helpless look. Although I was happy he and Nidra were dating and I understood why he'd followed her lead and asked to be assigned to the base near her family, I was going to miss him. "What am I going to do without you?"

"Work too hard and make more short-sighted decisions, while I go back to being too afraid to go after what I want. I'm going to be calling you a lot."

"Good."

Nidra squealed and rushed in to hug me. Well, air hug me. She wasn't about to risk her immaculate appearance, and using deft swings of her hips and tosses of her head, she managed to avoid Dante's affection.

Dante laced his fingers with hers. "C'mon, they're calling for us to line up."

The graduation ceremony was long and the speeches were full of duty, honor, and anything else President Sung could make up to puff us up. It was verbatim the speech he gave the previous year.

We were called up one by one to receive diplomas, the formal announcement of our partners, and our official assignments, even though most of my classmates knew who they'd fly with and where.

I did my walk across the stage on shaking legs. I was so close to being in. So close.

The president of the academy said to the microphone more than to me, "Ms. Donovan, I'm pleased to announce that you will be flying with…"

Oh, crap, a pause. That wasn't good. They changed their minds. They revoked my security status. They decided I'd instigated the fight with Profit and Kairo or I'd done more than defend myself. I was out.

He wasn't simply pausing; he was checking his palmer, frowning.

How was I supposed to leave the stage with any dignity? I took a step back with the intention of walking away before I burst into tears, but his hand shot out, gesturing for me to stay where I stood.

"I am delighted to announce that Ms. Donovan has completed the scholastic portion of the Battle Axe Pilot program."

Unlike every other cadet in the history of time, I did not have my new partner pin my wings to my uniform as our flight assignment was read aloud. He'd already said as much as he was going to.

After an awkward pause, President Sung stuck out his hand for me to shake. I was released with a practiced double-pump, and I left the stage as serenely as I could.

I took a seat beside the other teams, my gunner seat conspicuously empty. I ignored the looks and whispered

196

comments from Dante and my classmates, hoping I looked bored or otherwise aloof instead of like I was dying inside.

Caught up in the possibilities, I missed the final whoop as the class was dismissed for the final time. The friends and families spilled over into the joyful throng. Zack was working, and Tony didn't do crowds, but Marco had planned to stand in as my family until he got called out. I was glad he wasn't there to witness my anticlimactic stage walk.

I escaped the building, but the number of people walking toward the station convinced me to change direction so I didn't have to listen to anyone's questions about what had happened.

The cold grass under my feet was a pleasant contrast to the confines of my high heels, and the farther away from the buildings I walked, the faster the sounds of the celebration gave way.

No, I was not going to panic.

So what if I didn't get a flight assignment or my wings then and there? The MoD was probably delaying until I finished sims and flight check. It wasn't a rejection but an understandable delay. Still, they let me graduate, so it was confirmed I had completed that hurdle to the MoD satisfaction if nothing else. That was still good news. Everything was fine.

Once I reached the track, I climbed the risers, giving my aching ribs plenty of warning with each movement. When I could go no higher, I stared at the sky for a long time, not even picking out constellations or features on the moon's face like usual. I marveled at the moon's pretty orbit around the earth and the earth's orbit around the sun. What a beautiful balancing act the sun went through: gravity pulling in while thermonuclear fusion forced the release of energy outward. Eventually, the sun would run out of fuel and gravity would win, causing the star to collapse, but not in my lifetime.

Or lifetimes, as the case may be. I smiled at the moon, which looked the same as it had more than a century ago. It felt like I shared a secret with the silvery sphere and the whole universe in general. I wasn't supposed to be here, but I was, and no force of nature was ever going to give me away. I loved that. It made me seem like I was a part of a divine plan larger than all of man's pettiness and ambition.

"Hello, Miranda," Jason said, his drawl as unmistakable as the use of my born name.

Still feeling a part of everything around me, I looked over at him. His attire indicated he'd meant to attend the ceremony, but he'd taken off his tie and undone the first few buttons of his pale shirt, exposing his throat. He looked beautiful and ethereal.

As he shifted, waiting for my response, I saw the tiniest flash of silver. He was wearing his wings. From the Comp videos, I knew Jason's highly polished wings were a gift from the Texas Republic when he won first place. They were a sleek, deco style with a tiny medal suspended from the bird of prey's feet. It was that miniscule disk that reflected the scant light my way.

Realizing he was still waiting for me to speak, I said, "Your wings are beautiful."

He sat beside me, his thigh grazing mine as he leaned back against the riser. "I've never worn them before. My last time in the cockpit was the final day of the Comp I won, and I hadn't received these yet. Last year's graduation, I wore the standard Hernandez issue. This year's graduation was special to me."

"I want my wings," I wailed. "Everyone else got theirs."

"The snot is unacceptable," he said. "You vomit tidily. Why can't you cry tidily?"

"They should've warned me not to get my hopes up. I looked ridiculous up there. Where were you?"

"All this drama over wings you haven't earned yet? Texans don't get theirs until they pass a flight check."

"I want my wings."

"Then come here, you big cheater."

I felt his fingers on my skin as they slid under my lapel, and I shivered from the unfamiliar sensation of another person's body heat. As if he'd done it a dozen times before, he deftly pinned a set of generic Hernandez wings on my dress.

"They're so pretty," I cooed, looking down on them. But the weight of his gaze made me sigh and take them off. "After my flight check."

He smiled his approval. He had such a finely shaped mouth. My hand was halfway to his lips when I gasped and snatched my hand back. I grabbed my shoes and ran down the bleachers.

"Hey." His footfalls were loud behind me. "We need to talk about this. I don't want you to fall in love with me."

I spun around and stared at him. It didn't feel like my husband had been dead very long. Did he assume my rare flickers of desire were more than a healthy, heterosexual woman's recognition of a young, healthy male?

"I'm not in love with you," I said emphatically. "At all."

"Good, because I don't want you to be."

"I'm done," I muttered, walking off. "So tired I can't see straight. Not that I'll get any sleep tonight thanks to the way my stupid nose hurts. No wings. No flight assignment. Nothing but Jason Chavez positive I'm in love because I stare at his tonguable mouth."

Falling in step beside me, he said, "I need you to be more accurate."

"My tongue, your mouth. That's sufficiently descriptive, isn't it?"

199

"I'm pointing at your nose, not your mouth," he gritted out.

"The throbbing behind my eyes is so forceful I feel it in the bridge of my nose, and I have a tension headache. I'm also on the verge of tears."

"From emotion?"

"Frustration and emotion. You didn't need to know all that. Your penchant for accuracy makes conversations continue longer than they have to."

"It's a good habit to get in. You have to be able to explain an issue with the jet in a concise, complete way. Learn to say *three* instead of *a few*. Learn to estimate to percentages instead of using the word *some*. Say *grinding* instead of *noise*. Use Spanish if you can't find the most descriptive word in English."

"I understood you with the first example," I said. "So, are we a flight team?"

"Yes."

"To be stationed where?"

"All foreigners are stationed here at the capital."

"Why didn't the president say that?"

"Because someone was hacking the file and changing it while he read it. You asked me where I was. I was attempting to correct your file. He gave up and said the one thing he knew for a fact, which was that you graduated the academic portion."

"Why was someone hacking it?"

"Because you are hated, Miranda," he said. "Humiliating you in front of a room full of people was the goal."

"Mission accomplished."

"I doubt it was to their satisfaction. Don't brood on it. The better you are, the more people will launch such cowardly attacks. The trick is to prevent them from seeing that it bothers you. It would be even better if it didn't actually bother you."

"How do you stop it from bothering you?"

He grinned. "I see it as a compliment. They're admitting they can't beat me in a fair fight."

Chapter 25

Simulations

After midnight on January first, more than a week ahead of schedule, Jason and I had our first simulation together.

Forrester, the sims boss, checked my harness with a yank. I was afraid she was going to pat my helmet and send the facemask crashing against the bridge of my nose, but she didn't. Theoretically, the polymer matrix was as sturdy as the bone growing on it, but I didn't want to risk it.

"Stop looking so worried," she told me. "If you weren't ready for this, you wouldn't be here."

I wasn't concerned about the simulation as much as disappointing the Comp champion in my back seat, but I just nodded at her before she sealed us in. Like Luft had promised me during the incentive flight, with all my gear, it was a far snugger fit. I reached for controls and when I realized the limitations to my range of motion, I inwardly cursed the designers for not making the cockpit bigger.

"Anytime you're ready, Whiskey 4-5," Danny said over the comm link.

"Aye, control," I said, surprised at how calm my voice sounded. "You ready, Voodoo?"

"Aye, Justice." Jason's voice was smooth and confident in my ear.

Reassured by his confidence, I said. "Start her up on my mark. Three. Two. One. Mark."

We flipped the switches to bring the jet online in perfect synchronicity, and my heart skipped a beat as the panel in front of me came to life in a blaze of colored lights.

When the jet was prepared for launch and all my boards were green, I said, "How say you, gunner?"

"Locked, cocked, and ready to rock, boss."

The joy of finally being in the cockpit made my cheeks sore because I just couldn't stop smiling as I took off, made a wide circle around the valley, landed, taxied to the hangar, and powered down most of my systems so the tug could attach for berthing. It was probably the most boring simulation in the arsenal, but I loved it.

"Good," Forrester said. "Do it again."

Sometimes she gave me a landing gear fault or winds so heavy we nearly came in sideways, but it was variations on a theme. She gave me a sweet engine issue that raised my blood pressure for a couple of minutes, but in the end I set the jet down nice and easy like I had been born of this metal cocoon instead of a womb.

When Forrester popped the seal after the simulation ended, I regarded her dreamily. "I'm not getting out of this cockpit."

"You are. We have to swap out a couple of panels so you can train in the D series, too," she said.

When my feet hit the deck, I struggled with my head-gear until another set of hands worked the clasps with an ease born of familiarity.

"You can handle a jet with ease but can't get your helmet off by yourself?" Jason teased as he removed the offensive contraption, careful not to pull my hair.

"Consider it a character flaw," I said, examining the helmet to see what the snag had been. I wasn't autho-rized to wear my own set of flight gear until I passed the first twenty-five hours in the simulator, so the ill-fitting helmet had to do.

Of course, Jason's gear made him look like a fashion plate. His helmet was in Texas's colors of red, white, and blue instead of the darker crimson red, white, and black of the Hernandez clan, and I saw the Hernandez send dark looks his way.

By the third sim of the day, I was up to in-flight interaction. Refueling was easy enough, matching speeds with the tanker and catching the end of the boom, but the bomb restocking was a challenge. For that, I had to flip the aircraft on its back while using my instruments instead of my eyesight to line us up with our aerial arms dealer. Then Jason could navigate the acceptance and securing of the weapons. It was tricky and dangerous, and sweat poured off me as we attempted the maneuver. I was dying to take off my helmet to get more breathing room in the cockpit, but I was afraid to even pull my hand off the stick long enough to wipe my face.

"Easy, Justice, easy," Jason murmured as I fought against the buffeting to inch us closer to the belly of the big jet above us. I had waved off, and he'd settled me down twice before this, scarcely getting a single missile each time instead of loading up. I concentrated on fight-ing the panic that rose up every time I lost sight of the jet carrying a whopping arsenal in its belly.

An alarm klaxon sounded, and I jerked away from the arms dealer without checking to see where Jason was during the ordinance transfer. I knew that was wrong, and I filed that away for future reference as I scanned my displays. Two bogeys were headed our way.

"Forrester, back down," Jason snapped.

The bogies kept coming, and he hit the ejection sequence to end the sim.

Even before the gyro stopped spinning, he vaulted out of the cockpit to get in Forrester's face. I hoped I wasn't supposed to react, too. I wasn't exactly sure what had gone wrong.

"It was her third sim. It's her first day," he said, yanking off his helmet. How could his hair still be perfect? "We shouldn't have been doing bomb transfers until the end of the week, let alone dogfighting."

"She showed proficiency in the fundamentals so fast the computer automatically jacked her up to the next logical level: defending herself."

"No one can learn it all in one day. If you keep rushing her through her coursework, I'll continue to punch out the instant the situation gets out of hand like it did today." He reached across her and snatched out the disc. "We're done for today."

"You can't do that," Forrester said with the satisfaction of someone who got to hammer a thorn into a lion's paw. "You prevent her from fulfilling her contract, the Defense Minister will pass her to someone else so fast you won't have time to blink."

"The DM knows I turn pilots into champions, so go ahead and see where your interference gets you. She and I won't be setting foot in this place until the day after tomorrow."

He took my arm and escorted me to his car.

"Wait here while I get your bag from the locker room."

We were silent on the way to my house. The way his jaw muscle kept tensing made me want to save my questions until he calmed down. Was he disappointed in how I flew? What about Forrester? Was she going to report noncompliance on my part?

He followed me inside, carrying my bag. Examining my face, he said, "Eat a big meal, take a hot shower, and then get at least eight hours of rest. Promise me you'll do that."

"Eat, hot shower, rest. I promise."

The tight lines of his face eased. "I expected you to fight me on that. You'll feel better tomorrow. Don't brood about that third sim. I want to discuss it but need time to take the edge off my temper and come up with a new training plan. I'll be here in the morning."

I nodded.

His hand lifted and gently touched either side of the bridge of my nose, searching for swelling. "How's it doing?"

I peeled off the adhesive strip that held my nares fully open.

"There's discomfort," I said, "but no pain. I'll have Marco check it in case I need anti-inflammatories or anything."

"And your ribs?"

"They're holding. I'll still be sleeping upright."

"Don't overuse the anti-inflammatories. Inflammation serves a purpose in the healing cycle."

"I know."

Thanks to Jason's prescription, I fell asleep easily. Nevertheless, I woke full of stiffness from the new use of old muscles, so I took Marco up on his offer of joining him for tai chi on the patio.

"Pretend you're moving through water," Marco murmured. "Pace me. Keep the moves calm and liquid."

I kept his words at the front of my mind. I didn't have that inherent cat-grace and apparent serenity he had, but I could at least fake it for minutes at a time.

"Good morning."

Glancing toward the sound, I nodded a greeting to Jason. He was in a suit again, so at ease I suspected wearing a uniform was dressing down for him. Most of his salary must've gone to dry cleaners and grooming supplies. The rising sun made his thick, dark hair shine like a fur pelt. I itched to touch it.

A smile reached my lips as I looked past him to see Zack stumbling through the kitchen. Unlike the demigods out on the deck with me, Zack woke groggy and wild-haired from thrashing around all night, just like I did.

I asked Jason, "Why didn't you want me to focus on that third simulation?"

"It was an unrealistic sim. If we'd been in the air, we would've been the wingman of a more experienced pilot who would've made the call when the bogeys showed. The arms dealer would've had its own protection, too. Forrester let the computer amp it up because it would've amused her to watch us go down."

"So why were you so angry at me?" I asked. "It wasn't my fault the sim got out of hand."

"Of course it was. Your comfort with the technical end masked how green you are. When you attempted the bomb transfer simulation, I assumed you'd prepped for it, but it became apparent you went in there unprepared. Did you assume you could simply figure it out on your own?"

"Forgive me for trusting you were there to instruct me in that learning environment."

"In the air, I'm your gunner, not your pilot instructor. If you sit your ass in that cockpit, I expect you to be prepared for what comes next. When we're on the ground, I'll mentor any way I can, but in the cockpit, it is your responsibility to lead. I know Yoshi taught you that."

"Perhaps you should've mentioned the expectations before we started."

"Maybe you should tell me why you drove yourself past the point where you normally would've asked for clarification about a task."

He was more astute than I gave him credit for. "It was in the news that a visa holder was murdered. A human rights legal analyst was outraged because no one seems to care enough to look into it."

Marco turned to look at me, his expression tight with surprise. His news feed must not have carried that story. Most didn't. No one cared what happened to someone in my position.

Jason said, "You need to stop worrying about what's happening to others."

"No, what happens to them is germane, whether you see that or not."

"Do you understand why they are so unforgiving of outsiders? Not the rhetoric, but the reality?"

"Because I'm different, and I'll bring different ideas to the masses that will start a revolution?"

Eyes crinkling with humor, he said, "Well, that, too. The rhetoric is that if you're barely getting food on the table for your family, you don't welcome guests, especially if they don't contribute."

"I understand that."

"What they don't say is that all visa holders are treated monstrously even if they do everything to the letter, and most withdraw their petition and try again in another clan like the Hernandez want. Not only do these former visa holders stop being a drain on the local economy, but their complaints about this place spread the legend of the Hernandez throughout the other clans. This isn't the biggest clan, but it is without a doubt the most feared."

"I can apply to other clans?"

"Well, your situation is problematic," he allowed. "You've got no ties to another clan and no history for anyone to check. You'd have a better chance applying to a nation outside the Confederacy. But let me finish. I checked on people who ran the gauntlet here, and unlike other clans, once you are formally accepted here, you receive all the rights of a born Hernandez. For example, I know my clan restricts voting and job opportunities to outsiders who become citizens. Here you get everything."

"Or nothing."

"More than nothing, Miranda. You graduated from a Hernandez military flight academy, and you're being personally trained by a Comp champion. Don't take their apparent callousness to mean they aren't interested, but understand they aren't going to give it away for free."

After he left, I returned to Marco's side.

"You're worried about Kairo, aren't you?" Marco asked me. "I could hear it in your voice when you mentioned the murdered man."

"Kairo can try to kill me, and there's nothing the police would do about it. If he does manage to kill me, he'll get away with it."

"You know it wouldn't be that simple for him," he said with a ghost of a smile. "Legally, sure, but not in real life. Personally, I won't hesitate to shoot an intruder during a home invasion. He's running out of time to act anyway. You'll get your papers in two weeks."

"Two weeks is plenty of time for him to kill me."

Chapter 26

Tailspin

After dinner the next day, the front door slammed, signaling the departure of Zack and his foul mood. Marco and I exchanged weary smiles.

The house was blissfully quiet. After finishing the four long simulations, I was far too tired to do anything more than digest my pasta.

"Do you want to do your physical now or wait until you've had some sleep?" he asked.

"Another one? My nose is okay. It's not at all beautiful, but it works."

"It's been months since you had a full body scan," he responded, yawning behind his hand. "You can feel good and still have a significant malfunction brewing."

The doorbell rang, and I motioned for Marco to stay seated. I opened the door, yawning.

"Well, hello to you, too," Jason said. "How does that doorbell not bother you? The first tone is flat and the second is sharp. Why not have a wailing banshee instead? It'd be easier on the ears."

"Look, I'm exhausted. I'll meet you early, but I'm done tonight. As soon as I muster up the energy to brush my teeth, I'm going to bed."

"That reminds me," Marco said. "You got packages. I put them on your bedroll."

"You could've left them out here."

"Zack assumed they were his birthday presents and was going to open them as soon as I turned my back. He can't reach your closet."

I went into my bedroom, edging around my cockpit mockup to the stack of boxes on my blankets. I unpacked the first box. It was my helmet, done up in proud Hernandez colors in a custom design based on my call sign, which was lettered across the front. This had to have come from the MoD.

Elated, I felt so light I could float all the way to heaven. "Marco, look. Isn't it beautiful?"

He may have responded; I wasn't paying attention. I reverently unwrapped another piece of my gear, inspecting it at length, cooing and fussing before nestling it back in its box to go on to the next item.

"What the hell?" Jason asked in a strangled voice. "Miranda, you've got the front end of an Axe cockpit in your bedroom."

Hugging my flight gear boxes, I said, "I never had such lovely stuff in my whole life."

"Miranda, this is an accurate model of an E series mod four Interceptor."

Exasperated, I said, "Yes, Jason, there is an accurate mockup in my bedroom. Why wouldn't there be?"

His jaw dropped.

"Why is this weird?" I demanded. "I've known what I was going to fly for months, so I built my own cockpit. Why do you think I'm so comfortable with the controls in the simulator? I've been flying my faux Axe for months, so my muscle memory is rock solid."

It took him time to find his voice again. "This can't be here."

"And yet here it is."

"No, I mean anyone could walk in and see how the inside of an active duty combat jet is laid out. This can't be here."

I took hold of the edge and tore a chunk off. It wasn't much of a chunk. My mockup was built well. "I should've known better. At least the controls face the closet instead of the window," I sighed, tossing the piece on the seat.

Jason took the crumpled bit out of the seat and pressed it back in place. He sank into my seat and looked around. "It's so beautiful," he said. "However, it does compromise security. It has to go."

"I'm in the simulators now, so I don't need it anymore," I said. "It'll be nice to have room in here again. I need a place to put my gear."

Marco frowned at my cockpit, probably realizing that since he was home, he was going to be stuck helping me tear it apart.

I told him, "If you wouldn't mind sharpening the handsaw, I'll get the utility knife and start separating the biggest chunks."

Jason looked at us like we were about to dissect his firstborn.

Exasperated, I told him, "There's a hangar full of the real deal less than ten kilometers from here."

His hands curled protectively around as much of the cockpit as he could reach, and he said, "Simply make it less accurate."

"Less accurate?" I teased, pretending to be scandalized. "This from you?"

"I can't watch this," he muttered, striding away.

"That's sweet," I said, unwillingly touched.

"The man loves his airplanes," Marco said, looking at my stack of flight gear.

I rushed out the door to catch Jason before he left. He wouldn't have stopped by without a reason.

"Your nose is swollen," he said when he saw me approach.

"We're monitoring it," I promised him. "Kairo tried his best to keep me out of the simulators, but his best wasn't good enough."

He got out of the car with so much haste he lost his balance. Clutching the door for support, he said, "You *fell*. You and Kairo argued about his desire to be stationed in San Diego, and when you stomped away, you tripped and fell."

"That's what they all said," I agreed, lip curling.

He stood there pale-faced, two beads of sweat rolling down from his temple, and he kept swallowing like he was throwing up in his mouth.

In a creaky voice, he said, "That bastard tried to kill you because you chose me."

Alarmed at the way his eyes rolled back into his head, I leaped to his side, grasping his elbow. "Breathe, Jason. That step may not look it, but it's damn comfortable."

He wobbled precariously and collapsed into a heap on the front porch.

I pushed his head between his knees. Rubbing his back in circles, I said, "Kairo's an impulsive brat, not a killer. He's gone now, so everything's fine."

I felt him tense. I never was much of a liar.

His voice cold, he said, "Everything is not fine. Everything is so mixed up it's going to take years for everything to be fine again."

"Listen to the drama king," I said, withdrawing my hand.

"Did I tell you to stop? You're the one who made me feel like this. The least you could do is keep rubbing my back until I feel better," he said, crossing his arms on his knees and pressing his forehead to them.

"If you're yelling at me, you're no longer that miserable."

"Rub my back," he demanded, but there was a hitch in his voice, so I rubbed the Drama King's back, now consciously aware of the sensation of his taut back under my hand. It gave me a funny ache inside. I missed all the casual, affectionate gestures that had been a part of my marriage: rubbing Paul's back, caressing his cheek on my way by, and hugging him from behind when he was brushing his teeth.

I stared off into the distance, locking onto the distinctly modern-looking spires on one of the buildings downtown to remind myself that the world Paul and I shared had crumbled under the weight of its failures decades ago.

Jason's lingering tremors made me sigh mentally. I wanted to go inside, but I couldn't leave him. Marco had to have a sedative I could give Jason. Promising I'd be back, I entered the house.

Marco was still in my doorway looking at my presents. "You know that flight gear is from him. It's custom."

I stumbled. "No, you're wrong."

"I've seen all kinds of flight gear," he reminded me. "This is expensive stuff. Custom. It's from Chavez."

Closing my eyes, I leaned against the door frame. "I don't know why I keep getting my hopes up."

"Because they have to know you're worth keeping by now."

"They've forgotten I exist. There hasn't been any sign of them since I got in that fight at the club." I pushed the flight gear in the seat well of my Axe mockup and turned my back to it.

The light tapping at the front door reminded me Jason was waiting. He still looked chalky, but he was clear-eyed and steady on his feet.

He said, "I need to go home. I'll see you at six tomorrow morning."

"I'll be there."

After he left, I pushed past Marco to get to my bed.

"Mira, are you sure he doesn't have feelings for you?"

I shut the door in his face and curled up on my bedroll. If I had money to burn, I would buy my partner quality equipment, too. It didn't mean anything. It wasn't like Jason was ignorant of my fresh sorrow for Paul.

I was on the verge of sleep when Nidra's ringtone chimed on my palmer. Reaching for it, I muttered, "Please, nothing terrible."

As soon as I opened the connection, she complained, "Dante won't have sex with me."

"What?"

"That's exactly what I said."

"Did you ask him why?"

"He said he doesn't want to risk losing me as a friend. We haven't even done it once. Here. Talk to him."

I listened to them fighting over whether or not he was going to talk to me, and then I heard his voice, embarrassed and sullen. "Hi."

"You're going to have your shoes off in front of her at some point," I said.

"I have. A couple of times."

"And she didn't notice your feet," I guessed. "You're spending way too much time worrying about this, Dante. Are your feet clean? Man pretty?"

"Yeah."

"Then let her kiss you up and down. If you suspected she'd be shallow and crappy about your anomaly, you wouldn't be attracted to her in the first place. If you love her, trust her with this. If you don't love her, then do it doggy style or delay until dark to have sex with her so she doesn't see them."

"Why does it make sense when you say it?"

"No idea. I don't know what I'm doing."

He laughed.

"Thanks, Mira," Nidra called out, and the line went dead.

Shaking my head, I had to smile. I missed those two. I didn't laugh half as much without them around.

I'd barely put my palmer down when it rang again, this time with the imperious ringtone of my partner.

"Hi. This is me not thanking you for my flight gear," I told him. "Sorry it took me so long. I assumed it was from the clan."

"I'm glad you're not thanking me because I did it for me. Seeing you in ugly, old, ill-fitting flight gear made my eyes bleed. The reason I stopped by earlier was to tell you your flight check is on the morning of the fifteenth."

I held the palmer in a death grip. "That's the day my papers expire. What if there's a weather alert that prevents the flight? I've got to get in there sooner."

"I'm working on it. I know you're tired, but try on that flight gear tonight to make sure it fits. Keep your mockup in place for now, but remove all the weapons controls, including countermeasures."

"All the displays are gone already. Just the frame remains."

"Pity," he said. "Miranda, about Kairo. You don't have to worry about him. I took care of it."

"I'm done talking about him. Like Marco said, once I'm a citizen I won't be such an easy target."

"He won't lay a hand on you," he promised. "And as for your flight check, I'm researching the cause for the delay. It's too close to the edge for my comfort as well."

CHAPTER 27

SURPRISE, SURPRISE

The next morning, Jason dismounted the simulator after our second dogfighting simulation and held up his hand to help me down. "What a ride. Sugar, you are something else."

"I notice you don't say what," I teased, buoyed by his good mood. Every day, my comfort increased in the cockpit until I was confident I could learn the final few tasks required of me before I took a real Axe into the air for my flight check. All my preparations had been worth it.

The simulation bosses reviewed the sim on the big screen, the sound turned low. I sat in the visitors' seats, watching the cold, unhesitating annihilation of the three targets. That couldn't be me. It looked like any other simulation I'd seen during training. But wasn't that what I wanted? To look just like them?

"Look at this part again," Wild Child was telling Danny. "It's an aggressive, definitive strike. It's like one of—"

I left without a word and pushed through the locker room doors.

A penny was centered on the floor in front of my locker.

I felt the helmet slip from numb fingers as I stared at Lincoln's copper profile. I bent down and picked it up with a shaking hand, ever surprised at the coolness of the metal against my skin. 2011. And a tiny 'D' for Denver, where it had been minted.

Getting closer.

I didn't know what would occur when the 2014 penny arrived. Perhaps it would end with a gun being fired at me like in the year 2014. And for him to get access to a secure building inside a secured campus was a brand new level of suckiness.

"Why can't you let me be?" I whispered to my tormentor.

"I wanted to see if you were okay," Jason said.

Giving him an exasperated glance, I said, "This is a women's locker room, and I can personally vouch for the fact that you're not a woman."

"You looked upset," he said, picking my helmet off the floor and holding it against his chest like I'd seen him do with his.

"Thank you, but I'm fine," I said, the penny still clenched in my hand as I opened my locker and snatched up my bag.

"You don't look fine," he said, fingers wrapping around my arm. "Is it something I did? I know I needed extra seconds on the bomb run because of that relay fault, but I compensated for that."

"First, you don't believe you did anything wrong, so don't pretend you have a doubt about your end. Second, I can't find fault with your performance, today or ever. I'm worn out. I'll see you later."

"I'm not letting you go until you tell me what's wrong," he warned, blocking my path.

Surprising us both, I shoved him back, yelling, "Stay away from me. There are things about me that you'll never understand, one of them obviously being that I need some damn privacy."

My bag had been knocked from my hand when I pushed him, and I snatched up what had spilled out so I could throw it back in the bag and get away from him.

Ignoring my outburst, he bent down and picked up what had fallen out of my hand. Looking at the penny, he said, "2011? That's one of my favorite years. At my blank expression, he explained, "Miles January was born. I can't imagine modern aviation without him."

He flipped the coin to me, and I thrust it deep into the pocket of my pants before striding out of the locker room.

"Miranda."

He would never leave me be. I hadn't even made it out of the building. "What is it now?"

"What're these?" Jason asked, holding up an item I'd failed to retrieve when my bag spilled open.

I took the bottle from his hands. "Just what the label says they are. Vitamins."

"I was referring to these," he said, holding up one of the striped capsules in his other hand. "Are you going to tell me these are vitamins, too?"

"There's no reason for me not to carry different kinds of vitamins in the same bottle. I know which are which. And I don't appreciate you going through my stuff."

"So you won't mind if I take this?" he asked.

"Of course not," I said.

The bastard called my bluff. The moment it was within centimeters of his mouth, I knocked it out of his hand, snapping, "It's birth control. I didn't tell you because I didn't want you complaining that I wasted time on men when I had homework." He wasn't buying it, but I added, "You should be thanking me. God knows what a good dose of progesterone would do to you."

"Well, I know what it's doing to you. You can't sit still for more than a few minutes at a time. Manic half the time, irritable the other half. Maybe they ought to change progesterone's primary use from birth control to weight loss."

"You're excitable when it comes to the sims, too."

"Yes, but I'm not going to fail my physical because of illegal diet drugs," he said without looking at me. "I can't believe you would do that to yourself, and I can't believe you would do it to someone who trusted you."

Without a word, I retrieved the capsule off the floor for disposal elsewhere and headed out of the building. Once I was outside, I couldn't go any farther. I sat on the steps, waiting for him, wondering what I was going to say.

I needed those pills. The brittleness of my bones revealed a great excess of phosphate, and the pills contained both a phosphate binder and massive doses of a bone strengthener for my nose and ribs. Telling him the truth was the moral path to take, but the implied fragility would probably cost me my partner.

I was so close to the end of my visa though, so close. I needed to hide everything long enough for him to help me get my papers.

My palmer signaled an incoming call. I answered it and promptly wished I hadn't.

"What is it?" Jason asked, reading my expression as he approached.

"Great news. They had a cancelation, so I'm on my way over for my flight physical," I said, getting to my feet. "Wish me luck."

I walked away before he saw how worried I was. My physical wasn't supposed to be for another three days. Marco had been called away before he had a chance to run a urinalysis, figure out what I needed to doctor, and obtain what I would need to doctor it with.

But this was a real flight physical, and Jason's presence reminded me that I wasn't the only one at risk if I lied my way into the cockpit before I was physically ready to fly. I'd vacillated for weeks about whether or not I should attempt to fool the system.

Now it was too late. I couldn't exactly cancel it since I had pestered them to give me an earlier appointment in the first place, but holy hell, I didn't expect to walk in there unprepared.

Maybe it wouldn't be an issue. With one thing or another, Marco hadn't given me a full bioscan in months, and I'd almost had passable kidney function then. Over the past year, my condition had steadily improved throughout my whole body, so my kidneys were probably already at the low end of okay.

At the flight surgeon's office, my confidence surged as they ran Big Blue over me. They weren't using the most detailed scan at all. Why had I assumed they would start with the four-hour scan?

In fact, I was under Blue's regard for a mere fifteen minutes, most of that spent on my face while they checked how my nose was healing. They took the expected blood and urine samples and sent me upstairs for an endurance evaluation while my lab work was processed.

Having no desire to wait anxiously for my lab work to save me or damn me, I eagerly approached the distraction of the physical trial. Before long, my feet hammered the treadmill into submission while I sucked air through the mask attached to the machine that checked the efficiency of my lungs.

Stay calm. Breathe deep and even, and keep your stride clean and beautiful. You've never been better at this.

The incline increased, and I gritted my teeth at the stabbing pains in my thighs. Rivulets of sweat stung my eyes, but I didn't dare try to shake my head and risk losing my balance.

I could do this. I had to. The pain in my chest scared me, but I kept going. Right when I was on the verge of bursting into tears, the treadmill's incline and speed decreased so I could cool down. Far more worried about my frenetic heartrate than the agony in my legs, I concentrated on calming down. Soon, the pain from breathing subsided, and then my heart's rhythm slowed until the pounding in my head eased.

Afterward, I was calm but exhausted to the point of stumbling as I returned to the flight surgeon's office. And when he told me I was green all the way across the board, I thanked him like I would've been surprised at any other outcome.

Out on the sidewalk, I fired off a message to Jason, partially because he was my partner and needed to know I was fit to fly, but also to gloat that they found no sign of drug abuse despite his suspicions.

I looked up into the pristine blue sky and thanked God for my health before heading home.

The flight check was going to be the easiest task on my list. Once I rocked that, the MoD had no reason to deny me a permanent position.

At home, I settled on the couch to tweak my academic resume in case there was an interview during which I could remind them what I particularly excelled in.

The next penny was inside my laptop. I raised the screen, and the penny slid into my lap. Staring down at it, I said in a shaky voice, "Marco, can I talk to you for a minute?"

"Can it wait? I want to finish this level on my game."

"Well, he's escalating."

He walked away from his game without even pausing it, and we went out onto the back deck.

"Two in one day." My hands shook to the point of violence as I gave him the pennies. "We're up to 2012."

"How nasty are your side effects?"

"What? You want to talk about that now?"

"Answer me."

"The new meds give me the jitters, so Jason is positive I'm on diet pills."

He called out to Zack. "Have you been drinking the orange juice?"

"No," he yelled back.

Marco nodded as if that was the expected response. "Mira, you do know that each serving of orange juice has twice the caffeine of a cup of coffee, don't you? I noticed it was disappearing, but I thought he was having some, too."

"Great. Betrayed by juice. That's a new one," I said. "By the way, I passed my flight physical."

His eyes widened. "When was this?"

"Between the two pennies. I expected him to ask about the bone pills, but he didn't."

"They'd need a special analysis for it. How did the endurance testing go?"

"I passed. Not by much, so I've still got a lot of work to do. But I passed."

"Congratulations," he said, breaking into a real smile.

"It seems like authorizing me to fly is a mistake. I don't feel strong enough to be a combat flyer. I still get tired easily and get dizzy sometimes when I stand up too fast."

"What did you expect when you forget to eat six meals a day, you exercise hard, and you chug caffein-ated orange juice?" he said. "Mira, you passed without the usual deceptions. This is great news. You'll keep get-ting better if you reduce your stress."

"Tell that to my pennies."

"I think they're from someone who knows more about what you're doing here than we do."

I felt that sensation of unease again, that funny tremor in my stomach. Most of the trouble I dealt with at the academy made sense. The subject of my origins was something else entirely. I hadn't looked under the bed for monsters as a child, and if I'd been given Pandora's Box, I wouldn't have opened it. I supposed that meant I believed in real evil.

Treating my beginnings among the Hernandez like a puzzle to solve and not a personal issue, I said, "So what do we know? I'm assuming I'm not worth smuggling onto Hernandez lands. Me, myself, and I. Can we agree on that?"

He hesitated. "I'm sorry, but I've been assuming that you personally are not the reason."

"Look at you trying to be sensitive. Knock it off. It's freaking me out," I said. "So my sole differentiating fea-ture is whatever it was that brought me from 2014 to 2119. We'll call it the experiment for now, and we'll agree that the experiment caused the physical deterioration you noted when we met."

"You're important for more than that."

"But we said that me, myself, and I were not valu-able."

"If it was solely about the experiment, then after you were taken out of it, you would stop being important."

"I don't follow."

"Well, let's say you were studying what goes on when a person drowns. When the drowning stops either because of death or first aid, the person is no longer producing relevant data because the person is no longer drowning."

A chill settled on my spine, seeping into my bones. "They started making repairs to me. No one invests that kind of cash on someone who doesn't have a continuing importance."

"The skill needed for these kinds of repairs is important to keep in mind, too. Your initial bioscan showed multiple organ transplants with minimal scarring."

"What?"

"We didn't tell you sooner because we didn't want you to overreact," he said with a pointed look to let me know he wouldn't appreciate my breaking down now.

I'd already drawn up my knees and hugged them to my torso like a shield for my vulnerable insides.

"They aren't bioprinted ones, either." He reacted to my puzzled look by explaining, "If there's enough warning a liver is failing, healthy liver cells are harvested, replicated, and laid in sheets on a special matrix. In effect, they're growing a new liver. Depending on the organ, the matrix may dissolve in time or stay forever. The success rate is no higher than receiving a donated organ, though. That's old tech. I'm surprised you're not familiar with it."

"How can you be certain that wasn't used on me?" I said, chewing on my hangnail. I'd snorkeled in the Florida Keys only once because it so unsettled me to see coral and other life growing ignominiously on a cinder block and other trash.

"Big Blue would've picked it up. Your body shows no sign the organs were ever in danger of being rejected, so there was no need to mention you even had transplants."

Morbidly curious, I asked, "Which ones?"

"You wouldn't believe me. It looks like they were all replaced at once. You shouldn't have survived that."

"Wow, do you suck at being reassuring. Look, why are my kidneys malfunctioning? Are you certain they aren't being rejected? That can occur gradually, can't it?"

"Your kidneys show no surgical scarring. It's possible the donor for the other organs had kidney disease so they couldn't be used."

The crease between his brows deepened, showing me his unease with the subject matter. His mouth was tight, too. Was there something else about my physical condition he didn't want to discuss? That was fine with me. At this point, I was far more concerned with the external threats than internal mysteries.

I said, "If the value I have is tangible, why haven't these people stolen me back like any other tangible valuable?"

"Probably because by the time they found you again, you had a Hernandez PDT embedded in your hipbone. All they had to do was run Little Blue over you on the train without you noticing, and they'd know you were tagged."

"Remind me to never ride the train again," I sighed, considering the number of people who bumped into me in the average rush hour trip. "So I'm safe until my papers expire and they remove my PDT?"

"Safe from being kidnapped," he amended.

"Safer from something is better than safe from nothing."

"We still have no idea why you're here in this clan or why the flight wasn't on the books. We need to grab this penny guy."

CHAPTER 28

SWAN DIVE

The trouble with stalkers was that they were undependable. Marco and I both had jobs to go to, so he couldn't watch over me every minute of every day. In fact, only a couple days passed before I was fed up with being scared, with suspecting everyone, and with trying to outsmart a shadow. I needed to blow off some steam. After all, if the pennies were a countdown, I didn't have to panic until after the next one showed up.

The sun was setting when I got off the train, and as I passed the sizeable grocery store by Jason's house, I recognized his car in the parking lot.

It took me a while, but I finally found him in the toiletries section smelling bottles of shampoo.

"You said you wanted time alone," he said absently as he replaced a bottle of shampoo on the shelf and crouched down to peruse the lower options. He took one and flipped open the lid to sniff the contents. He wrinkled his nose and replaced the bottle.

I said, "You look bored. We could go over to the academy and sneak in sim time if you want."

"No," he said, crab-stepping away from me to sniff other bottles on the bottom shelf. "All the simulators are in use tonight."

I barely heard him. A man was watching me over the low gondolas. I was used to my strange eyes getting double takes of surprise, but this was a focused stare from eyes as yellow as mine.

He was my age, maybe of Asian descent. Wiry build, slim shoulders, shoulder-length black hair.

It was him. It had to be.

He lifted his hand, flipping a small copper disc over his knuckles.

Jesus. Now what? Why didn't I write down a list of questions? For the life of me, I couldn't come up with anything to say to him.

My hand slipped into my pocket for my palmer so I could call Marco, but he'd been called out. No help there.

Knowing what Marco expected of me, I tried to memorize the man's face, but I had nothing to latch onto. His mouth wasn't too wide or too thin, his nose was just a nose, and his eyebrows weren't too thick or thin. It was an average face.

"What are you looking at?" Jason asked, making me jump.

"It's fine," I said in a strangled voice, already taking reluctant, inevitable steps toward my penny. "Stay here."

Jason popped up and took off running after the man, who went wide-eyed at the revelation I wasn't alone. The two men ran out of the store.

Breathing forcefully, I hurried to the aisle but found no penny. I rushed out of the store to see where they had gone but saw no sign of them.

"Did you see two men running through here?" I asked, grabbing a lady's arm. "One guy was in a nice suit?"

She made a vague gesture toward the crowd coming out of the train station. I trotted over there, swearing. Too many people.

That was it. I was going home and getting Marco's backup pistol. If hiding in my closet with a gun made me look crazy, well, so be it.

The feel of fingers clutching at the back of my collar made me bolt. The sound of pounding footfalls followed me.

I sprinted down the street, but I couldn't get away from him. If I darted through traffic, so did he. If I threw myself over a fence, so did he.

I accidentally cornered myself in a blocked-off alley and looked around wildly as he approached. I scrambled up the front of a truck and launched myself onto the lower rungs of a fire escape. Thighs and lungs burning, I took the open metal steps by twos, using my arms to whip around each corner. He was so close behind me. When I ran out of steps, I used the rail to get the height to grip the edge of the rooftop.

It wasn't until I was on the roof that I was truly caught. It was either swan dive off the roof and hope something slowed my descent or turn around and face Jason.

"Why did you run from me?" he demanded.

"I ran from the crazy man who was charging after me like a bull rhino," I gasped, clutching my sides and fighting for air. "I knew it was you, but you kept coming at me, so I kept running. I couldn't help it."

"I lost him and was afraid he'd come back to you. I was protecting you," he snapped.

"By grabbing my collar?"

"My hand barely touched your collar. It was crowded, and I was trying to stop you from getting on the train.

230

What did you want me to do, grab your hair? You weren't responding when I said your name."

Sucking down deep breaths to try to relieve the stitch in my side, I staggered around the roof on wobbly legs. "I would've if you called me Mira. No one else calls me Miranda. No one ever did."

"Your name is beautiful."

"No, it isn't."

"Who was that man?"

I rubbed my temples, wishing the headache would let me go. "I don't know."

He regarded me expectantly, but I didn't say another word about it.

"Miranda, I chased a man for blocks because he seemed to be a threat to you. Are these exquisite Italian shoes the proper tool for a hard run?" he asked.

"I'm sorry."

"And then you made me chase you."

"I said I was sorry."

"Someone probably bought my toothpaste, too. There was only one tube of it left."

"I said I was sorry. Return to your toothpaste-buying, Italian-shoed life. I don't need you."

He threw up his arms and stormed off.

I stumbled down the stairs to street level. In the pharmacy across the street, I bought water and a single dose of painkillers. Outside, I pounded them and leaned against the wall, pressing my fists into my eyes. My stomach was empty, so it didn't take long before the throbbing in my head eased. Stupid tension headaches.

"Miranda."

I jumped at Jason's voice.

"Our taxi has arrived," he said, raising his arm to get the driver's attention.

"I'll take the train."

"No, we'll take the taxi so I know you made it home safe."

When we arrived, my house was dark, empty. Turning on one light in the main living space cast ominous shadows, so I turned on all of them.

I made myself a cup of tea, needing the warmth and not caring that all we had was chamomile.

"When are your roommates going to be home?"

I made a high, startled sound at Jason's voice and apologized profusely when I saw how insulted he was.

"He had my eyes," I said, clutching my cup. I hadn't meant to mention the incident at all, but I wasn't going to change the subject now that it was out there. "Did you see that? He had my eyes."

"No, he didn't. His were light brown. Yours are yellow. When was the first time you saw him?"

"Tonight."

Brows knit, he stopped filling a glass with water to stare at me.

The mug rattled on the table. "Don't look at me like I'm crazy," I said.

"If I chased a man who ran simply because he got caught staring by a crazed boyfriend, I'm going to lose my temper. I'm already in a foul mood because he got away."

"No one thinks you're a crazed boyfriend."

"You said I looked crazed. That's why you attempted to evade me, remember?"

"No one made you run after him or me."

I burst into tears. It was real. Some guy was actually out there stalking me, leaving smug little reminders that he knew I wasn't from this time or place. Why couldn't I be delusional instead? Why couldn't it be Jason? He'd had access to some of the locations so I had wondered, but it wasn't him at all.

"I don't like crying," Jason said, frowning. "It's messy."

"I know."

"So you're doing it to further anger me? Or are you soliciting for a hug?"

"I don't have a plan," I wailed. "Sometimes I cry."

"Well, hurry it up and be done with it. You need to get some sleep."

"Jason, sometimes you never do come up with a good explanation. You know that, don't you?"

He relented. He wiped away my tears and cupped my cheek, saying huskily, "Sugar, what I know is that you are unbelievably anxious. You've got to calm down or your medical displays will light up like a Christmas tree when you try to flight check."

"I know. Don't you think I know?"

"Do you want me to call Dante for you? He's passed his flight check and can tell you what to expect. I could tell you, but perhaps it'll be easier to accept coming from him."

"I know what to expect." I couldn't help asking, "How did he get his so fast?"

"He didn't shatter his nose," he said, his finger so light on my nose I barely felt it.

"Thank you for helping me tonight."

"You're welcome, Miranda."

"You forgot your line. You're supposed to tell me not to thank you since you only ran after him to benefit yourself. Didn't you finally find a worthy adversary in the foot race?"

He smiled at that. "No, this time I did it for you. I do need to leave now, though. I have plans," he said delicately.

I nodded, remembering Marco's spare pistol. Not that I was going to need it. Jason had probably scared off my penny man for days.

CHAPTER 29

KAIRO'S GIFT

The next day at lunch, a shrill tone signaled an incoming video call, and I opened the connection without thought.

Kairo's angelic smile filled the small screen. "Mira. Hi. Have you made it into the simulators yet?"

"Hello," I said cautiously. He couldn't punch me through the video feed, but I nevertheless held my finger lightly on the button to terminate the call.

Realizing that was as much banter as he was going to get out of me, he said, "I've got a Comp file to share with you."

"And why would you want to do that?"

"When you see it, you'll know why."

"What makes you think I'll download anything you send me?"

"You can access it from any terminal in the academy's library," he said. "It's the one marked as Jason Chavez's greatest hits. When you're done, you can watch the original footage. You'll know which video it is. And don't kill yourself trying to understand it. He was born with inferior blood."

Of course, he meant substandard genetics.

He blew me a kiss and ended the call.

Unease became dread. Jason and I'd had sex in broad daylight by a floor to ceiling set of windows. If Kairo somehow got surveillance footage of that, it could ruin my career as well as Jason's.

I needed a second opinion about whether or not it was a good idea to open it, so I called Dante.

"Do it," Dante said without any of the usual amiability in his voice. "He's obviously got damaging info on your partner, and he's definitely messing with you, but that doesn't mean this can't be important. What if he's got proof Chavez caused an in-flight accident? It's not like Kairo wouldn't love showing you that your partner could get you killed."

"Good point."

"Have you talked to Nidra?"

"Not for ages. Why?"

"I told her, and she laughed at it. Made fun of it. Kept making fun of it. Then she said she'd loan me the money to have it removed. I broke up with her."

It took me a moment to figure out what to say. In a lot of ways I'd thought he deserved better than her from the start, but she'd been his choice so I respected that. "I'm sorry. How are you doing?"

"Better than expected. This time I wasn't ashamed of my extra toe, I was ashamed of who I was with."

My heart lifted. "I can't tell you how happy I am to hear that. I mean, I understand it hurts, but—"

"I'm over it," he said. "You're the one who called me, remember? My advice to you is to make sure no one's around when you watch that video."

I shut myself in one of the video rooms of the library and opened the file, recognizing it as the Comp Jason and Bear won in 2118. Kairo had zeroed in on the background conversations, amplified them, and filtered out the ambient noise. He was confident the revelations were so devastating without any dubbing or malicious tweaking on his part that he even included a list of programs and filters he used in case I wanted to check his work.

I watched it, but I didn't need to run my own programs. Everything there made sense with other comments Jason had made. I did watch the unaltered footage afterward, dismayed the whole sordid mess had been there all along.

I called Ethan. "Do you know why Bear and Jason broke up?"

"You need to talk to him, not me."

"Enhanced footage of their Comp shows what they're fighting about in the background is just awful. If you don't know the truth, I'll show it to you because you need to know who you're living with. Otherwise, I'm deleting the file. Bear doesn't deserve to have this broadcasted."

There was a long silence, and I was about to terminate the connection when he said, "Yeah, I know about it."

"You knew what Jason did, but you didn't consider warning me when he asked me to become his partner? Because you told me I wasn't going to have any trouble with him."

"I had no idea you were feeling him out to partner with him. He's never shopped for a pilot at the academies, even when we were pups in one. And Mira, I did tell you he was an asshole. You know I did."

"You know what I know? I know he's the only instructor who encourages me to challenge myself. He's fought for me and protected me and bailed me out. He even did

237

my community service and paid my fine so I could focus on school."

"There's no way he did your hours for you, especially since he said you were in the wrong. I will believe he hacked the computer to read them as complete. But yeah, he probably paid your fine if it was to his advantage that you were paid up. He's got the money to burn."

I rubbed the knots at the base of my skull. "This can't be happening."

"Seriously, what were you thinking signing with him instead of a Hernandez? You're not going to get any glory out of it. Nero Hernandez is never going to let a Texan win a Comp for him. Or are you hoping Jason will get you into Texas?"

"What? No, I wanted someone who could keep me alive."

"You got him."

"Until he betrays me," I snapped. "What about his other pilots?"

"He dumped them to upgrade until he found one that could get him to the Comp."

"Why do you put up with him?"

"He's as difficult to hate as he is to love," Ethan said matter-of-factly. "But he's different with me. I'm family."

"Didn't Bear consider himself family, too?"

The long silence ended when Ethan hung up.

I was still watching the original, unimproved Comp footage when a familiar voice made me jump.

"Why are you watching that?" Jason asked. "I hope you're not comparing yourself to Bear. It's unfair. He's got years of experience to draw from."

I couldn't look at him. "Shauna Wolfeson said it's difficult to find a gunner she can work with, but she won the Comp five times, each with a different gunner," I said, my voice sounding strange and empty to me. "She never had time to build trust with any of them. But you knew Running Bear well, didn't you?"

Accepting the topic of conversation as easily as I had expected, he said, "Very much so. He was like a brother to me."

I made an angry noise. "Then why would he want to stop flying with you? Falling in love is all fine and good, but if you were tight, why wouldn't he even try to do both? Work with you and then go home to his girlfriend? I'd be bent if the partner I trusted wanted to ditch me flat like that."

"It was more complicated than that, but I did feel betrayed. He changed the boundaries of our friendship without warning."

Was he really blaming Bear for this?

With pronounced discomfort, he went on to say, "I was unbelievably pissed at him. I mean, I was a real bastard to him."

"You were justified. You trusted him, and he betrayed you."

"You weren't there. I would appreciate it if you didn't mention it."

"Jason, I want you to know I never would do that to you."

"Don't be naive. Of course you would, if the conditions were right. Or wrong, I should say."

"No, there are things you don't do."

"Spare me the morality crap," he said, his expression closing off.

"It's crap to know right from wrong?"

"It's crap to follow rules meant to constrain the masses while power is obtained by those who don't follow them."

Eyes narrowed, I said, "Kairo sent me a file of enhanced footage from your Comp."

"Did he now?"

"He said it would explain why you and Bear broke up, and the satisfaction he took in sharing that with me tells me it will damage my respect for you. Would you care to offer an explanation now or would you prefer I come to my own conclusions after watching it?"

"You've already watched it," he said, sliding his hands into his pockets. "What conclusions have you drawn?"

"That you left out two key words in your explanation of why you split with Bear. He didn't just fall in love. He fell in love *with you.*"

"Don't stop there, Miranda."

"But you're not homosexual, didn't know he was, and you definitely weren't in love with him. When it became more than he could bear, he tried to turn in his wings to get away from you. You weren't about to let that happen, not when you'd received your precious invite to the Comp. To get him to stay long enough to compete, you lied to him."

"Did I?"

"You deceived your partner into thinking you loved him romantically, so he would fly the Comp with you. After you won it and he wanted to celebrate in a physical way, you came clean. You didn't let him down easy, either. You crushed him because you were pissed he made you pretend to be homosexual."

"Is that it?"

"You didn't stop him from turning in his wings, but you weren't about to turn in yours."

"But I did, didn't I? For the short term anyway. Why did I do that? Why did I come to the Hernandez? Wasn't that on the video, too?"

"No."

"I didn't want to deal with everyone trying to fly with me or hound me about the Comp, so I wanted to leave. My DM permitted it because it promoted goodwill with the Hernandez."

It was all true. I had risked everything for a man who had used his partner in a cold, humiliating way to win a trophy.

It took me a while to find my voice. "If you had to do it over again, how would you have handled Bear?"

The frankness of his expression was matched in his voice. "I wouldn't have done anything differently. Winning the Comp was worth it."

I gathered my bag and pushed past him.

He said, "We have sim time tomorrow morning, but I expect you there two hours early. I modified one of your projects, and I want to work it in the sim. We need to go over the details."

"Screw you."

He grabbed my arm, his eyes cold. "Get over it, Miranda. You're not flying with me out of respect for me and love for the craft. You don't care about helping me further my research. You don't even know what it is. Your classmates had interesting projects of their own, not that you bothered to ask them about it. All you've cared about since the day we met is your own citizenship, so take your holier-than-thou attitude to someone who doesn't know you."

I yanked my arm free.

"Two hours early," he repeated.

I shook my head. "I've finished the necessary sims to qualify for my flight check, so I have no intention of doing anything with you tomorrow. I'm calling in sick."

"Don't be a child. You will be there. And I want you to ruminate on your lies, your fights, the indications you're

241

abusing stimulants, and your mental glitches caused by your refusal to accept your husband's death."

I couldn't stop the red stain I knew was flooding my cheeks.

He asked, "Who is getting the worse partner here? How much more do you think I'll tolerate? If you don't show up on time, ready and willing, I promise you won't enjoy what comes next." He got in my face. "And you won't ever mention that Comp to me again."

"Get away from me."

He smiled fractionally at my defiance and left me standing there.

When I got home, Tony's car was in the drive. What could've brought the hermit out of his shell?

"Hey, stranger," I said, giving Tony as much of a smile as I could as I set down my bag. "I was about to make dinner. Can I tempt you with some pasta? I'll even leave out the mushrooms for you."

"Marco and Red were in a car accident," he told me, his voice raw and hoarse. "Red was pronounced at the scene. Marco died in surgery."

"Were they drunk again?" I asked.

"What does it matter?"

I snatched Marco's half empty bottle of tequila off the refrigerator and hurled it at the wall where it exploded into a hail of glass and liquor.

"This is your fault, Mira," Tony snapped. "He never used to drink like this before you got here. The stress of trying to protect all of us from the problems you caused made him drink more and more. I wish he'd left you to die."

"You don't mean that," I said hoarsely.

"That I'll take his life over yours? You better believe I mean it. I want you to understand that you're on your own now. Don't ever come to me for anything. Ever. Do you understand me?"

"I do."

CHAPTER 30

ADIOS, AMIGO

The trend watch websites indicated it was time to change my sleek chignon and stacked buns, no bangs, no highlights to a softer hairstyle. I struggled with a lot of things in my attempts to be conventional, but some were easy.

I closed my eyes against the sight of the red tint being applied to my hair, the drips looking too much like congealing blood. The resulting soft auburn color would make my eyes look yellower, but that couldn't be helped. I hadn't cut it as short as I should either, but concessions had to be made so I could still pin it up in uniform.

Still, it would be an undeniable attempt to reflect what was stylish.

The first manicure in my life was the clan's traditional mourning style of matte black with shiny black tips. To complete the funereal grooming, my cosmetics were pale and cold except for thick black eyelashes that simulated tear-wetted lashes. There was no crying at a Hernandez funeral. It showed weakness.

After the salon, I went to the recommended shop and had the professional shopper choose a proper black sheath with long crimson and white ribbons hanging over one shoulder.

I had never looked more Hernandez, and the man who would've appreciated it the most was the one man who wouldn't see it.

I was emptiness inside a titanium shell. The comments people made to me never penetrated, and I had nothing to say except for the proper words of the long, formal Hernandez death rites.

His expression stony, Tony stood alone, the final surviving member of the Rainer family. When he died, there would be emptiness there, and the ceremony would include a final recap of his line and additional formal shows of grief for the end of a valued line. It was all coldly perfect and beautiful in a way.

My healing ribs and lower back ached from wearing such high heels, and I had a walnut-sized pain high on one buttock from being poked sharply on the train. The fleshy failures felt out of place amongst the purity of the ceremony, and I did my best to suppress the sensation of them.

My palmer chimed softly, even though I had shut it off. It was the Ministry of Defense chime, one of the few no one in the clan had the option of silencing. People parted before me so I could take the call a respectful distance away.

CHAPTER 31

THREE DOORS

When I checked in at the main desk at the MoD, I was still in the black sheath from Marco's funeral instead of my uniform, but I didn't have it in me to care. I also had no reaction to the news I was to meet with Assistant Defense Minister Echo, the second in line to the Ministry of Defense throne. I couldn't afford to.

After my identity had been confirmed with a scan of my PDT and the processing of a drop of blood, I was instructed to sit in front of a massive curved desk. Like everything else in the MoD, it was black, unyielding, clean, and cold. We could've held the funeral there.

ADM Echo entered the room from a door at the rear, saying without preamble, "As you no doubt know, people in my clan can be unforgiving to outsiders. Some go so far as to sabotage their progress or take advantage of a lack of rights. For that reason, if you suspect your records don't present a fair evaluation of your worth, you have the option of selecting an additional trial. Understand that if you choose to do that and you fail miserably at it, you don't have the choice to have it struck down. It becomes part of your file."

I declined his offer of a glass of water, and he sat down with one of his own. He seemed to be in a hurry, draining his water and speaking with far less formality than the others at the MoD showed.

"You must know that Profit is our top-ranked Battle Axe pilot, so you can choose to dogfight against her in a simulation with equally outfitted aircraft and identical gunnery protocols. Obviously for fairness, neither of you will have a gunner. You don't have to win it to be offered citizenship, and winning it doesn't guarantee citizenship. It's nothing more than an opportunity to highlight your skills."

"I understand, sir."

"The DM has authorized a second option for your consideration. I don't know if you've heard of Greyson, but it's an invitation-only school for advanced aerial combat training. It's on Farragut lands, but the teams come from all over North America. This morning we received word that the Clan Hysanki pilot at Greyson broke his back. The program director there asked if we would like to send a pilot to take his place for the rest of the term. I can't be more specific than that because we don't know any more than that. I'm assuming you'd be doing the classwork, simulations, and aerial work with the Hysanki gunner."

He refilled his water, his brow furrowed as if he were looking for the appropriate words and failing to find them.

"Because Greyson prepares air crews for the Comp, the term runs until the end of April. We would have to give you a new visa," he realized, frowning. "Ms. Donovan, you'll have to excuse me. I need to consult with the DM."

In the waiting room, I considered the options. The Comp still didn't mean anything to me, but the sheer number of concepts I could be exposed to at Greyson was staggering. The Hernandez rarely sent a crew there, so I might be able to provide the clan with details about what was being taught there to improve the clan's training program. The results of my flight physical proved I could afford the delay in my final evaluation, and the extra hours in the saddle would only benefit me even if the information I was able to glean wasn't earthshaking.

Also, it would give me a reason to get out of the partnership with Jason before he dumped me for a pilot with fewer mental issues. The meltdown with the knife exercise took me by surprise, so I couldn't offer assurance it was an isolated event. My recall about Paul had returned, but some holes in my memory from that last month before I was shot remained.

Was running to Greyson the easy answer, though? I was unpopular among the Hernandez, I'd made a poor choice in partners, and with Marco's death I'd lost my most powerful ally.

Marco. I had never needed him more. I wouldn't have made this decision without calling him. Granted, I didn't necessarily choose the way he wanted—I paid bitterly for that mistake with Jason—but at least after consulting him I had always felt I could make an informed decision that balanced my past with my future. What would Marco suggest? I didn't know. My mind was clogged with messy emotion.

Seated in front of Echo again, I watched him jerk the knot in his tie up to his collar.

"The DM would extend your papers," he told me. "And I'm sorry about calling you away from a funeral, but Greyson needs an answer now. Even if you haven't decided between standing on your previous work and dogfighting Profit, I need to know if you have chosen against Greyson."

"No, sir, I choose Greyson."

His satisfied smile suggested I'd chosen the way they had hoped.

"In that case, you'll be leaving immediately," he said, getting to his feet. "Not a word of this to anyone. I don't want to have to field calls from all the other pilots who wish to go. It's very competitive."

"Understood. Where do I report?"

"Base ops at the military airfield. I'll have someone meet you there. You'll leave immediately."

I ran barefoot down the halls of the simulator building. The locker room was empty. Good. I emptied my locker of flight gear, uniforms, and toiletries.

The door to the locker room banged open, making me jump.

"Justice?"

I bit back a groan. It was Profit.

She strode around the corner, looking flushed and petulant in her wrinkled uniform. She made it work, though. "Haven't you got your gear yet? They're holding the plane for you."

Without delay, she snatched up my bag and headed for the door. I chased after her and barely got in her car before she dropped the engine into gear and floored the accelerator.

"How do you figure in this?" I asked.

"You're going on my invite. I'm not about to share my new moves in front of the people I'll see at the Comp in a few months. Anyway, Jason was brought here to fly with me, not you." She removed a packet from her bag and tossed it onto my lap before launching into a lengthy explanation of how the DM expected me to act and what I was supposed to do if there was any trouble.

"What else?" She glanced at me. "The piss-colored eyes. There are blue lenses in there to cover them up."

249

I almost told her that her eyes were the color of another bodily elimination product, but instead, I said, "Watch your back with Jason."

Most of the bitchiness left her face. "I know what he's like," she said with a tired, lopsided smile. "But he's the best."

She lingered, scrutinizing my face and then reached into her pocket. Handing me a disc, she said, "A little thank you for not naming me in that fight. The DM wouldn't have done anything about it, but my family would've. Open it later."

I didn't take it. "It's over and done with."

She stuffed it into my bag. "You'll love it. I stole it from him."

The security guy waved me forward. "We're ready for you, Ms. Donovan."

Profit handed over my bags, flicking an amused glance at me, so confident that her world was finally ending up the way it was supposed to. "Adios."

The security guy motioned me forward to sign a form. "For your weapon."

"I don't have one," I told him.

"That's what the DM's office is correcting, ma'am," he said, opening a case to show a service pistol. "Check the serial number against the form, and then sign here."

Ten minutes later, my tiny passenger jet left the runway. It dipped, and I gritted my teeth, squashing the impulse to push the pilot out of the way and take the controls. I wasn't certain how long my palmer would register the Hernandez towers, but at least I could start a game or novel to distract me from remembering that I met Marco at another crash.

Chapter 32

Puck

My hopes for a direct flight were stymied by a minor engine fault that forced us down at the Confederation capital of Denver. I was assured it would be fine if I went to the airport's restaurants, but I wasn't about to risk it. I used the bathroom on the plane to insert the blue lenses over my eyes and then let them force me off the plane. At the gate, I sat in the empty seat by the window, keeping the aircraft in sight.

As I settled my knapsack at my feet, the man next to me said, "Nice view."

"An airport full of people is a nice view?"

"It sure beats looking at the back of your eyelids for a hundred years, doesn't it?"

My gaze flew to his face.

"Give or take." He held up a pair of pennies for eyes. They were the final two in the predicted series, 2013 and 2014.

I kept my expression neutral as my hand inched toward my gun. No, it was locked up on the plane. "I wouldn't know."

"Sure you do," he said, tossing the pennies toward the maw of my open knapsack. "I remember you. You were opposite me in the icer. You look a lot different now, but I still knew it was you."

Curiosity got the better of me, and I studied his face. He was of mixed Asian descent, pleasant looking, but other than that night in the store, I'd never seen him before in my life. Well, lives.

"No, I don't know you," I said in a strangled voice.

He looked disappointed but rallied and stuck out his hand. "Robin Goodfellow."

"But your friends call you Puck?" I asked with a smile, nevertheless not shaking his hand. I didn't know him, didn't trust him, and didn't want him touching me.

"When we were in the icers, did you dream?"

I shook my head, having decided to play along with him for now. "I don't remember any of it. I remember getting shot, and I remember waking up in the woods. Nothing in between. You... dreamed?"

He nodded. "I had a lot of nightmares."

I tried to imagine having my worst dreams for over a hundred years. I would've gone insane.

"In fact, I was conscious on several occasions."

"That can't be," I said, horrified. "It must've been a dream."

"How else would I recognize you?"

"I don't know. Maybe I was already there when you were brought in. Maybe you were thawed before I was. Maybe you were..." But I didn't have any more maybes. I didn't want to consider the possibility of waking up in the icer, feeling the cold, feeling the fluid deep in my lungs, feeling all of it and unable to react.

"I watched you sleep. You did have nightmares. You screamed and you twitched like a dog."

I knew we weren't talking about the icers anymore. "Why did you watch me? Why leave pennies?"

"I had to get your attention. You never found them unless I put them under your nose."

"You scared me," I snapped.

"Good. I was trying to warn you when they were closing in, so if you got scared and spent more time analyzing your surroundings, mission accomplished."

"You could've left me a note or spoken to me like you're doing now."

"My options were limited. They watch you all the time, and they're hunting for me. "

"You could leave a note as quickly as a penny."

He shook his head. "I've got some kind of aphasia now. You did dream, didn't you? In the icer?"

"Again with that question? I don't remember anything about then, but a few of my nightmares now are about places I've never seen. It's dark and cold, and I can't breathe. I thought I was dreaming about what I imagined it was like."

"There was a little light from the monitoring equipment and computer screens," he told me. "Or at least there was until my eyes started rotting like yours. Then it was dark and cold, and we couldn't breathe."

His words weighed heavily in the air.

"How did I end up in a plane crash on Hernandez lands?" I asked him. "Do you know?"

"The crash, no. The flight, yeah, of course. You were stolen to be given as a gift to Nero Hernandez. His clan has its own biomanipulation experiments to advance, and your genetic code is phenomenal. Nero didn't want only a sample, though. He wanted the source. They needed to buy his love so much someone decided that was an acceptable term for him to set. After all, the lab already had your genetic material in other forms, and Tadman has more faith in free will and training programs than genetic destiny anyway. I doubt he possesses a quality genome," he said, sliding me a cynical smile.

Offended by the idea of my divine blueprint being used as a form of currency, I said, "I'm more than simply a vessel for DNA."

"Don't underestimate the value these people put on the code, Mira."

"But the Hernandez aren't harvesting it."

"You got in the system before they could prevent it. Instead of staging an accident or security breach to take you out of it, they probably decided to watch and see if you're as good as your DNA says you are."

"I'm good because of me, not my genetic blueprint," I snapped. "And why the hell would they send me to the Defense Minister instead of someone in the Science and Technology Ministry?"

"You're kidding, right? The first places the Confed looks for illegal biomanipulation are the places with the tech to untwist someone's DNA. The MoD can easily handle one more dirty secret."

He grimaced, pressing his hand to the side of his head.

I asked, "Do you need aspirin? Is the aphasia from some sort of organic deterioration in your brain from the icing? Is that what's happening to me? I'm definitely not as sane as I used to be. I go glitchy, and sometimes I have hallucinations or freak out."

"Things are going wrong in my brain. I don't want the surgery they scheduled me for. It's the kind where even if you do survive it you'll wish you hadn't, so I walked through the walls to see the ocean one last time before I die. God stopped me and told me it was more important to find you and warn you they were coming for you. He told me to tell you to protect your PDT."

"Who's coming after me?"

"The lab."

His mouth twisted in a rictus of pain. He pressed on the sides of his head, his hands whitening from the pressure.

I shot to my feet to call for help.

His hand clutched at my trousers. "Don't," he gasped. "If you draw attention to me, they'll know I'm here."

He relaxed, his breath evening out. The color had drained from his face, and his hand shook as he pulled himself into a proper sitting position.

"Running out of time," he said with a weak smile. "Want to get home to the Big Island while I still can. The Hernandez don't fly out there though, so it had to be a Confederation hub."

"You stowed away on my plane? How did you do that? Hey, did you cause that fault that forced us down? You could've killed us."

"Don't get your panties in a bunch. We got here in one piece, didn't we?"

"You better be serious about going to Hawaii, buddy. I'll cheerfully rat you out to keep my plane to the Gulf Coast in the air."

"Did you dream?" he asked.

"No. Stop asking me that. Does your lab know where I'm going? How soon should I expect them to apprehend me?"

"You've got a PDT, so they know exactly where you are. They've got to be on their way. Off Hernandez lands, it'll be a lot easier for them to fry that PDT and retrieve you. Avoid mass transit and crowds if you can help it."

That painful mark on my ass wasn't proof they'd already been emboldened enough to try to fry it, was it?

"Why should I be afraid of them?" I asked, tired of the subterfuge. "If my health fails, I can call them for help, couldn't I?"

"Oh, they'll help, but they won't stop operating on you when you're healthy again. They can do whatever human experiments they want because there's no over-sight. If you don't believe me, you can ask the couple who got off that elevator. See the ones with the pale faces and the bulges in their coats? They're from the lab. They can't know you know who I am and who they are."

He tried to stand, but he stumbled and went down.

"Do you need a doctor?" I asked, brushing the hair off Puck's face. "Can you hear me?"

"I'm dying, Mira," he said, a facial tic tightening his cheek. He pressed his hand against it. "And I'm not returning to that place. Do you understand?"

I fought to remain calm. "Don't do this. If I get you to Greyson, maybe—"

He shook his head, his face calm, happy. "I'm done. I'm so glad it's finally over. It hurts so much, and this world is so awful. Hey, I forgot to ask you. Did you dream?"

"Puck," I said. "God."

"I wouldn't trust God if I were you. At first I thought He was okay, but now I'm pretty sure He's insane."

"Puck—"

"David? Is that you?" the woman gushed to Puck, pulling him to his feet. "What a surprise. Sally's with us. You've got to come over and say hello. She's been asking about you."

256

"She sure has," the big man beside her said, propping him up on the other side. "Can't turn around without hearing David this or David that."

There was nothing terribly revealing about them. Their clothes were ordinary, their faces were ordinary, and their manner was ordinary. Everything about them was ordinary except for the guns under their jackets. How was I supposed to recognize them again?

The Hernandez airplane steward motioned to me. I nodded and stood, saying to Puck, "Aren't you coming?"

"What?"

Please, please, come with me. We'll figure it out.

"This seating area is for this flight, isn't it?" I said dryly. "They're calling for us to board."

He shook his head, giving me a defiant smile. "Another time."

The Hernandez airplane steward forced everyone back while I shouldered my knapsack. At the security barrier, my PDT was scanned, my paperwork confirmed, and the contents of my bag examined.

Looking over my shoulder, I saw the lab personnel urge Puck into the crowd. The sudden commotion from their direction drove me toward Puck. It wasn't ending this way. I was going to save him if it killed me.

"Did you dream?" Puck screamed at me, jumping up so he could see me over the crowd.

I broke into a run.

"Did you dream? Did you didyoudid you did—"

A single shot ended one scream and generated others.

Hands yanked me backward.

"Ms. Donovan, it's not safe," the Hernandez security man told me, pushing me toward the plane. "We have to leave."

CHAPTER 33

I LUV GREYSON

At the Clan Farragut airport, I met an administrative type who said in a soft Southern voice, "Let me help you get through Security and Immunizations, then we'll be on our way to Greyson."

When we stepped out of the airport, I was almost overwhelmed by myriad smells carried on a humid wind: a salty tang and smell of greenery as well as a thousand unrecognizable scents. I inhaled them all deeply, not minding the nip to the air. It was winter here like everywhere else in North America, after all. Seagulls took flight into the gray skies as we approached the train station, and I could almost hear the waves hitting the beaches. My husband would've loved it.

For having such a big reputation, the campus itself was quite modest, radiating around the small quad like spokes in a wheel. A big structure was instantly recognizable as containing four simulator bays, an old motel for housing, a squat old building holding both the cafeteria and library, and a block building holding the offices and classrooms. Past that, two hangars had space for ten jets. Even from where I stood, the concrete of the runway looked worn, buckling in areas and streaked with grass growing through the cracks. The whole place felt worn, comfortable.

Slick opened a motel suite for me, telling me he'd wait until I changed into my uniform. I put on my winter khakis and pinned up my hair, faltering every time I glimpsed myself in the mirror. Those blue eyes didn't look at home in my face anymore. It was like I was seeing a pale, watered-down reflection of myself.

I definitely didn't get the usual double take from a stranger when Slick saw me. "Ready? I'll take you straight to the class."

The halls of the academic building were lined with photos of the most celebrated flyers in candid ways: fighting, teasing, hugging, sleeping at their desks, all of it. It was a fascinating glimpse of people I was used to seeing solely in formal settings with identical serious, proud looks.

Slick held the door open, and I hurried across the threshold.

The instructor was middle-aged and barrel-chested and stood with his feet planted wide like he was standing on the deck of a ship. When he stopped mid-sentence to pin me with a sharp gaze, nineteen other pairs of eyes followed his sightline, and I recognized at least half of them from the videos Kairo had insisted I watch.

"The Hernandez pilot," Slick said, taking my file to the table beside the lectern.

"Does that mean we can go on break while you brief her?" one of the students asked.

The instructor gave the offender a reluctant smile before glancing at the clock and jerking his head at the door.

As they filed out, I approached the instructor and held out my hand. "Mira Donovan, call sign Justice."

"James Pookarski. Pooka," he said, squeezing my hand in a grip that told me he had no idea how strong his hands were. "What's your opinion of Profit?"

"I'm unable to answer that, sir."

He glanced at me with eyes of a stormy sea color. His sarcasm sharp enough to make his southern drawl all but disappear, he said, "Let me guess. You were told to be the best while in the cockpit, to be invisible while outside the cockpit, and to learn everything you can about the others without revealing anything about you or your clan."

A horrified giggle escaped me before I could help it. I almost showed him the list of expectations I had gotten from Profit so he could laugh, too.

"Everyone else here has been told that. Everyone who sticks to that bit of nonsense hates it here. Your DMs don't seem to understand this isn't a school so much as a learning laboratory. The more people get involved, the more fun they have and the more they learn. As long as you don't denigrate another clan, everyone gets along. Criticize a flyer or a team all you want, but don't make it about the clan."

Delighted, I nodded my understanding.

He leaned aside to reach for my records, sending evening sunlight streaming into my eyes. He stilled. "What's that in your eyes? Are those corrective?"

"Cosmetic lenses only, sir," I said. "It is my DM's request that I wear them when I'm not in the air."

"Why?"

I didn't know what to say. "He dislikes the color of my eyes."

"What color are they?" he asked, scrolling through my file for the answer. "Brown? So what? Most of the world has brown eyes. In fact, he's got brown eyes, doesn't he?"

"It is his request that I always wear the blue ones."

"And it is our flight surgeon's standing order that no one wears cosmetic or corrective lenses at all if they want to fly here. Either take them out and leave them out or go home."

Of all the things to end up fighting about, it had to be this? "Sir, my eyes are an unusual brown that some people stare at. To keep me from standing out and causing a disruption, the blue lenses were issued to me."

"Take them out and show me," he said. "If they'll cause problems, we'll work out a solution that'll satisfy both your DM and my flight surgeon."

It was the best I could hope for, so he took me over to the restroom so I could wash my hands and pull the plastic out of my eyes. When my eyes were naked again, I rubbed them to get rid of the lingering discomfort.

Out in the hall, I stood near the window in a shaft of sunlight.

"Wow," he said, wooly eyebrows shooting skyward. Leaning forward to get a good look, he added, "Those are yellow, not brown. How do you make them glow? No wonder Nero Hernandez was worried about you causing train wrecks."

"You get used to them."

"And how long does that take?" he asked, grinning.

Slick was hurrying down the hall toward us, and he stumbled when he looked at me.

Pooka laughed and told me, "Put in the lenses at your discretion."

Once I replaced the lenses and looked at my blue-eyed reflection, I felt my backbone slip away. Once again I was the woman who was afraid to be noticed, afraid to

261

raise my voice and lose the love of the people who preferred me quiet, and afraid to have an opinion because it
was certain to be a weird one. The sooner I could get rid
of the lenses, the better.

At the end of the day, Pooka asked me to stay after
class. Class started later here, so it was almost eight by
the time we were released for the day.

Wordlessly, we walked down to his spartan office,
and he motioned for me to have a seat. "You weren't paying attention to me in there."

"I'm sorry if it appeared that way, sir."

"Are you tired? Jetlagged? Hungry? Overwhelmed?
Homesick? Ill from all the crap they shot you full of at
Immigration?"

"No, sir. I'm just super excited. Well, not just super
excited. I'm exhausted and hungry and thrown off by the
time difference, and I've got this headache behind my left
eye, but mostly it's excitement."

"That was very specific."

"My gunner's particular about the details. Sir, did
you see who all is in that room?"

"Considering that I handpicked all of them, I do know
who's in that room."

"I heard you've got a great library, too. I've never been
so torn. It's like when you first look at a college catalog,
and you realize how much stuff you could learn. Endless
possibility."

"Do I need to get the flight surgeon?"

"For what?"

"A drug test. There's less chattering at a monkey
house."

"Education without politics, prejudice, or distraction? I'm going to stay here until the day I die."

"I'll spread your ashes under the azaleas by the Comp statue."

"Aw, that's sweet. Thanks, sir."

"Are you sure you're okay to fly? Usually, the immunizations tear up the gut for days, and I don't want you vomiting in my simulator."

My eyes narrowed. "Sim time already?" I asked, my mouth tightening. "Do you have real showers in the bathrooms? The kind that provide plenty of water to get clean?"

Puzzled, he nodded, saying, "There's a water purification plant ten kilometers from here. They pull the water out of the Gulf. Why?"

"You want to give me everything I really want. Right. Either I'm dead and this is Heaven or this is some kind of cult."

He burst out laughing.

"Go suit up, Hernandez. Let me see what you've got."

As the screen faded to black, I released a shaky breath and unclenched my blood-starved hands, reassuring myself that I was still alive, still whole, definitely not white-knuckling the stick as I fell out of the sky to splatter myself over a couple square kilometers of no-longer-American dirt.

I flipped up my visor and locked it into place. I was too exhausted to pop the hatch now that the adrenaline was leaving me, but I didn't mind the close, dark quarters.

I hadn't done as well as I had hoped. It had all unfolded so damn quickly that I could only react, not come up with a plan. Jason would've been disappointed.

"Get out of my head," I muttered. "I've got enough to worry about without making a list of all the ways I failed you and vice versa."

The seal broke with the familiar hiss, and the artificial light of the sim bay illuminated the cockpit. For one weird moment, I was surprised I wasn't covered in blood, but that evaporated the moment Pooka's Hemingway-like face peered at me with fever-bright eyes. "Your defensive skills are surprisingly good for a rookie. Strong finish, too."

"I shouldn't have won. I had a short that sent off that second pair."

"Dead is dead, no matter how you made it happen. Do you need a hand up?"

"Sir, I would love a hand up," I admitted, struggling to get out of the jet. He helped me reach dry land and took off my helmet and flight gear. My legs were all wobbly, so with a strong hand under my elbow, he guided me to the visitors' chairs.

Leaving an empty chair between us, he sat down and said, "I love the way you guys get all weak-legged. Shows you're still busting your ass even for a simulation."

I brought the water bottle to my parched lips and took long pulls on it, glad he'd installed a fridge in his sim bays.

He said, "I looked over your scores and the comments from your instructors at the academy. They all say you have enormous potential. Your face tells me you've heard that before. But I have to tell you that your being here really bothers me. When Twister was injured, I sent for Profit because they flew alike so it would have worked well for his partner, Ego. I also know her strengths and weaknesses and how to fix them."

"But?"

"You're different. Being fresh out of school, you've got no style, and you make more rookie mistakes than I've seen since I taught at the academy. If I put you in with the flyers here, you will get knocked to the ground. That sim continued as long as it did because your opponent is in the mood to fly. He passed on several chances to take you down. Understand?"

I nodded.

"I don't even know what you'll be able to pick up in class either because this is well beyond the basics that the academies teach. I'm not saying you're stupid or that this is a waste of time, but I want you to be realistic about what to expect here. Your self-esteem will take plenty of hits. To make matters worse, Ego absolutely does not want to fly with you. This is in no way a disparagement about your looks, but Profit's got a bold sex appeal that would've sucked Ego in despite her being Hernandez. I want you to consider all that and then tell me if you still want to stay."

"I do."

"Is this you taking time to think it over? Because you suck at it."

"Sir, I considered the magnitude of the challenges on the flight over here."

I had a nagging suspicion that I was forgetting something else he and I needed to discuss, but I couldn't recall what it was. My blood sugar was rock bottom, and if I sat still for too much longer, I was going to fall asleep.

As if reading my mind, he said, "When was the last time you slept?"

"At home."

"And ate?"

"I don't know. Two days ago?"

"You should've told me. This could've waited until after you recharged."

265

"So I'll recharge now," I said, getting my stuff together. "We good?"

He nodded. "Class starts at eight."

CHAPTER 34

WILD BLUE YONDER

Early the next morning I rushed to get my uniform on. My eyes still ached from the ill-fitting contacts, so I left the lenses in the case. With a smile, I tossed the case into my luggage. I wasn't wearing those again.

I caught up with Pooka in his office as he set his breakfast on his desk and broke out a well-worn fork from his desk drawer.

"Sir?"

"Morning. Did you come to your senses and change your mind?" he asked around a forkful of scrambled eggs and toast.

"Not at all, but after reading today's schedule I do have a teensy issue I need to talk to you about."

When I told him, he threw down his fork and said with disgust, "It did occur to your people that an advanced aerial combat school might require actual aerial combat, didn't it? What is it you people do out there for territorial defense?"

"I've put in the simulator hours and then some. I simply need the actual flight check."

He scrolled through my records. "There it is in the fine print."

He arranged for me to flight check immediately.

Just like that.

"I love this place," I told him.

"Well, it's not loving you," he said, annoyed. "You're turning into a pain in my ass."

"They make a cream for that."

He gave me a look, and I laughed, dodging the stylus he threw at me.

I left the runway in a specially modified trainer Axe with a feisty flight instructor riding shotgun. If I panicked, he could land the aircraft from the altered gunnery.

"Good, Justice," Misty said. "Climb to Angels eight and level off."

"Aye, sir," I said, relaxing. Pooka had me questioning everything with his mention of all my rookie mistakes, but the Axe handled beautifully for me, and I got airborne without trouble.

"I don't get to fly very often since they closed us down as a training academy for fledglings," Misty was telling me as we ascended. "You saved me from a tedious day of shifting files around and practicing my putting, which is already as good as it's going to get."

"You're welcome, sir."

I leveled off as instructed and started going through basic maneuvers to get a feel for the machine. The difference between sims and reality was the amplification of the vibrations, the noise, the force of gravity, and especially the speed. I was never going to that sim bay again, not when I had this at my disposal. It was astonishing and terrifying to have ultimate control of such a machine, and I couldn't imagine how Jason of all people could be content to be in the back seat.

After the debriefing, I ran to Pooka's office. Speaking calmly and professionally instead of screaming it at him in pure excitement, I said, "I passed."

He didn't look the least bit surprised.

"I'm pairing you with Ego," he said.

I had no experience, and Ego had lost the will to do his job. The seriousness of Pooka's expression told me he didn't like it, but there weren't a lot of other options.

"You're within your rights to register an official protest. Ego already has. It'll cover your ass if there's any kind of incident."

I shook my head. "Sir, my DM knew I would be flying with someone from another clan when he authorized me to come."

He got to his feet. "Well, the option's available to you at any point. Now, everyone's at lunch. Class will resume at one. I expect you to be there."

"Of course, sir."

When I returned to the classroom, I took the empty seat beside Ego, who turned his back to me as much as he could without falling out of his chair. Insulted, I made no attempt to greet him. Pooka shot us a look of disapproval before telling the class that we were going to dissect a sim.

As soon as the lights were dimmed and I heard the pilot asking for clearance to take off, I grimaced.

"Ah, Hernandez, stop scrunching down in your seat. They're curious about you, and I want them to see why I'm letting a green rookie stay here."

We watched my dogfight in its entirety, and then Pooka restarted it to pick it apart.

Pooka said with sarcastic bewilderment, "Why would you shut everything off after you lost your engine?"

Ah, yes, there it was, that tone indicating I was considered a freak in a room full of normal people.

Bring it on.

"Sir, Axe designer Miles January once said the most pronounced flaw of the Axe's design was that the Axe's secondary air-to-air missiles can't reliably lock onto a dead aerial target. Because of the blatant lack of need, the concern was never addressed when the Axe's weapon's systems were upgraded."

"Why is the lack of need to repair an identified flaw blatant?"

"There's no need to target a dead target because it cannot target you. Aside from the statistical anomaly of a kamikaze, it's no threat. Also, firing at a dead target isn't permitted by Confed rules. It would be like firing at a parachute."

"And why can't the Axes lock on to dead targets with any reliability?"

"I'm not certain, sir," I said.

His smile was beautiful. "Liar. But everyone's got trade secrets. Nicely done, Justice."

I didn't need his approval, but his contagious grin made me smile broadly in return. Something gave way in my nostril, and a surreptitious touch with my fingertip showed blood.

I was going to murder Kairo the next time I was within range of that nose-breaking bastard.

Without being obvious, I rested my chin on my hand, using my pinky to press my nostril shut while we moved on to the next sim. After a couple of minutes, a cautious check revealed my nose had stopped bleeding.

After class, Pooka snagged me. "See the flight surgeon."

"Hmm?"

He tapped his nose. "I saw that. I know you had reconstruction done on your snoot, and I know your flight surgeon cleared you, but that was before you were in the air. I want my doc to make sure you didn't aggravate it."

I made a face but nodded.

Before I left, he said, "I know you won't answer me, but I have to ask. Did the Hernandez suddenly relax?"

"I don't know what you mean, sir."

"The Hernandez flyers I've worked with tend to be dogmatic and predictable. Strong, fearless, and capable, no doubt, but rigid. Your answer surprised me."

Fearless and strong. What I wouldn't give to be described like that. "Flight surgeon. Right. I'll take care of that now."

I said it lightly, but my stomach burned. If my nasal repairs were failing, where was I going to find a specialist who would work on me? How would I even pay for it?

CHAPTER 35

ARE YOU KIDDING ME?

The flight surgeon's face changed as the first anomaly appeared in Blue's data stream, and as the seconds turned into minutes, it became apparent I was nowhere near where I needed to be.

The nurse asked me, "Ma'am, did you come here with a preexisting medical condition?"

"I don't know how to answer that," I told him. "I did have a few issues that are detailed in my file, but I passed my flight physical."

The doctor asked him to run a thorough bioscan while she reviewed my Hernandez medical records. Her expression became puzzled, and she excused herself.

I wasn't worried. Flight standards weren't universal, but I met the Hernandez ones, the only ones that mattered.

With nothing to be done but lie there in my underwear, I went to sleep. I almost woke when a thin blanket was draped over me but drifted under again.

When Big Blue signaled the end of the four-hour cycle, the flight surgeon, nurse, and another man walked into the room.

"Dr. Hargrove, nephrologist," the newcomer said, shaking my hand and smiling warmly. "I have to ask. Did you enjoy your last flight?"

"Very much so."

"Good, because it was your final one."

My mouth opened, but nothing came out. I looked to the flight surgeon and back to the nephrologist.

Hargrove nodded, his expression serious. "The lab work on your flight physical was altered. Was it you? Your answer won't go past this room. We'll explain to you how we know if you weren't the one who arranged to have it done."

I shook my head, hair flinging across my face. "It wasn't me."

He showed me which parameters had been tweaked. This couldn't be at that rate unless this value over here showed an increase, too, and so on.

"So you can see that this isn't the result of a contaminated specimen or improper lab procedure. This was a deliberate attempt to mask lab values outside accepted levels. It would be flattering that someone wanted you cleared for flight so badly they would go to all this trouble if it hadn't prevented you from getting the immediate medical care you needed. You did know your kidneys were underperforming, didn't you?"

I nodded. "I came out of a coma with damaged kidneys more than a year ago. Everything I ate and each drop of fluid I drank was monitored to spare my kidneys as they healed. Every time I was checked, they showed measurable improvement, so by the time I had my flight physical, I believed I was at the low end of acceptable. I never would've put my gunner's life at risk if I'd known."

My voice had gone harsh, and the nurse offered me a plastic cup of water. It was tepid and tasted of chlorine, but it helped.

I said, "That flight physical came within two weeks of my expiring visa. Someone believed they were doing me a favor." I grimaced. "Because of the rumors I was using uppers. Someone thought they were masking drug use."

Dr. Diab, the flight surgeon, asked, "Are you a Hernandez citizen now?"

"No. Before that visa expired, they got the call from Greyson. They extended my papers until the end of the term."

"Under the same medical care limitations?"

I nodded.

"You need to speak to your clan immediately. If they aren't willing to give you full papers yet, they can at least expand your medical coverage. We can diagnose you all day long, but your clan has to authorize any treatment. I'm authorized to brief your MoD, so I'll go with you."

The flight surgeon and I went to the administration office, and Slick patched us through to the Hernandez Ministry of Defense.

ADM Echo sat in front of the Hernandez seal and gave me a coldly polite greeting.

I got straight to the point, sending him the Big Blue scan. The flight surgeon spoke to the Hernandez medical representative there, who confirmed the diagnosis and treatment options presented.

After Echo dismissed the medical people on both ends, he said, "Ms. Donovan, I'm confused. What is it you want from us?"

"Sir?"

"You lied to your instructors, your partner, and the MoD by continually maintaining that you were fit enough to meet the requirements at each stage of your training.

You also deliberately avoided a medical system that's in place to identify and treat such illnesses as early as possible. Your original papers do state you may petition for such medical care. You chose not to. So what is it you believe we should do for you now?"

I swallowed the lump in my throat. "Sir, if I have deceived—"

"If?"

"Sir, I did not tamper with my flight physical."

"Why should I believe you?"

"Because I neither knew there was still a need to nor did I have time to," I said honestly. "Previous attempts were a temporary effort to buy me the time to improve my health to the required limits. I can now honestly pass the obstacle course and other physical coursework."

"Can you? Then why did I just listen to a lengthy description of how broken your kidneys are?"

I felt my hand lift and rub my damaged temple of its own volition. "With proper medical treatment, I can reach, if not exceed, all combat aviator requirements. I am petitioning for an expansion of my medical benefits to treat my kidney issues."

"It's obvious you don't need our help. Look at how far you got without it."

"Sir, I can't fulfill your hopes for data accumulation here if I can't function at even a minimal level. Shriek and Rocket are here this term, sir. If I miss class due to illness, I won't be able to study them and pass on my findings."

"Consider it a challenge of your resourcefulness for the remainder of your visa," he said with a cold smile. "Make no mistake; you have impressed me. I wondered why the DM kept giving you chance after chance, but not only did you beat our system, but as a green rookie, you showed Pooka enough skill that he accepted you there.

I'm so impressed that I will make inquiries to the availability of a new pair of kidneys for you in case the DM chooses to keep you."

"Sir, my condition requires more immediate attention, such as authorization for medication and dialysis."

"Do you have any comprehension of the position you've put us in? It looks like we're either too incompetent to accurately gauge the health of our flyers or that we deliberately sent in a flyer incapable of performing the assigned task."

"I cannot be held responsible for falsifying my lab results."

"No, I'm positive Jason Chavez made that little miracle occur, but it doesn't change how the situation is being perceived by others. You will get kidney-safe analgesics for your nose, seeing as it was a public nosebleed that triggered this debacle. As long as you do not attempt to get in the air, the medical staff will be bound by confidentiality laws not to report your renal problems. That should buy you time for a clever solution."

He was about to hang up on me, the bastard. "Sir, is there any way for me to be awarded citizenship early?"

"Of course."

"What is it?"

"We'll know it when we see it."

"What does that mean?"

"It's open to interpretation on purpose, Ms. Donovan. You need to impress us, really impress us. How you do so is not our problem to figure out."

"Fair enough," I said.

He had a strange smile on his face as he regarded me. "If we sign you, I'm giving you a fat bonus."

What a useless gift.

276

"No, I'll send it to you now," he said, as if suspecting the fish he was eyeing was casting around for more favorable waters. "It would be unsportsmanlike to leave you fighting a war without a weapon at your disposal. Good luck, Ms. Donovan. I look forward to hearing from you again."

CHAPTER 36

GRIEF

That night, I dreamed I studied while sitting on the floor at Zack's house, my books spread out on the coffee table around Marco's boots. He sat in his chair with a drink in his hand and sleepy eyes, the heel of his left boot aligning with the spot of worn finish on the coffee table. We spoke of everyday matters, shifts, who ate the last couple of carrots, and when there was time to run a quick bioscan on me.

I woke and pushed useless tears off my face. I dressed and left the dorm, collar turned up at the bite of the wind. Slick had told me the legendary library was always open, and once I saw what my resources were, I meant to figure out a plan of attack for dealing with the Hernandez MoD.

"What the—"

My belly clenched. The library was a mess. The thick layer of dust showed that people gave up finding anything in it years ago. Crooked stacks of books were piled on the tables and the floor, and the bookcases were crammed so tightly I couldn't remove a single book. The books weren't separated by language or aircraft or field. In fact, the book nearest me was an ancient Russian tech manual for a warplane none of the seventeen clans flew. My crazy Grammy's attic had made more sense.

With a simmering rage at the ruin of what should've been the best library in North America, I set my alarm to give me time to get ready for school, and then I broke into the janitor closet.

I emptied a table and wiped it down, and then I claimed a lamp and stole a lightbulb. That being done, I pulled the photo of Marco from my pocket and looked at it. He was unsmiling like usual, but the crinkles at his eyes showed he was happy. The corners of the photo were already broken from being handled, and I propped the image against the base of the light before it became any more damaged.

"So I know you heard about the doctor's findings," I told him. "And I know you would know who to consult for help."

"Hello?"

I spun around. "Is someone there?"

"That's my question," Pooka said as he appeared in the doorway. "I was leaving my office when I saw the lights on."

"What happened here?"

"Nothing. Who wants to dig through piles of outdated books when you can find better references online? I keep meaning to make a bonfire of these books."

"You will not," I retorted. "Not while I'm here."

"Do what you want in here, Hernandez. No one cares."

I snorted at that. "So are you up late or up early?"

"Couldn't sleep. The Hysanki are supporting Ego's complaint about you."

"What does that mean?"

"It means you being a cherry is being held against you. My ability to flight check someone was acknowledged, but they still won't risk him or their jet to you like they would've if Profit were here. You'll do sims together, but no aerial work. I just got off the phone with your clan, and they've surprisingly got no problem with that. I didn't expect such a lack of reaction from you either."

"I haven't had enough time to accept the idea of being here, let alone what I would be doing here. You letting me stay for any of it was enough because, like you said, I'm not the caliber of one of your usual students."

Pooka reached past me and picked up Marco's photo. "I hope your boyfriend was understanding about the short notice assignment."

"My roommate," I said. "I was at his funeral when the MoD called to find out if I wanted to come here. He was search and rescue, but he got called out on a lot of civilian calls. He and his partner got drunk at a party and drove through a retainer on the way down the mountain. He was a good man. An uncompromising, unforgiving man at times, but he was strong and brave. He risked a lot to stick to his ethics."

He returned the photo to the table with respect.

"Have you ever been to a Hernandez funeral?" I asked him. "You're not allowed to grieve. They spoke about his schooling and accomplishments like they were reading his resume. With the same pride a manager does if someone saved a particular number of dollars for the corporation, they counted the number of people he'd saved. I wanted one person to sniffle or stand up and share a personal story about him."

"Like what?"

"I don't know. Anything. The way he played jazz when he remembered his mom. The way he was always calm and confident when everything was falling apart around us. The way he couldn't eat pimento-stuffed olives because they looked like eyes to him."

Pooka bit back a laugh.

"See?" I said. "He was a human being. He was twenty-seven. It wasn't enough time for him to be on this earth, it wasn't."

"Why didn't you speak up?"

"I wanted to, but it was important to him that I strive to meet the Hernandez ideal."

"I'm sorry for your loss."

I waved that off before I started crying. It wasn't just the loss of Marco that got to me. His death in no way improved Tony's chances of being authorized breeding rights, so I grieved for the extinction of that entire family.

I had to stop dwelling on it. For all I knew, I was the end of my line, too. Thank God my husband's younger brother had impregnated his new wife before my twenty-first century kidnapping. I could tell myself Paul's familial blood was still out there in a brave blond man somewhere in the northeastern clans. But maybe his line had died out, too.

I blurted, "I can't work in here without a respirator."

"Tell Slick. He'll find one for you."

He left me alone, and I wiped down and sorted the books I'd removed from the table. It wasn't the kind of task that occupied my mind, so I spoke to Marco while I worked. Silently, I told him about Puck and my falsified lab results as well as what Echo had said.

But all the stacks of books brought Jason to mind, and that made me cry, too, because I wanted him to be there with me. Stupid Jason. That stupid day when I couldn't hold a knife and he found out I killed my husband, and he forgave me. He looked at me, saw me, and understood.

God, I wanted to scream at him about not telling me he falsified my results, but I wanted to thank him for doing it because otherwise I wouldn't have had what was probably my one and only flight piloting an Axe.

More than that, he was disappointed when I wasn't my real, weird self in front of him, and it did seem like I could be honest about my ugly side because he would understand. That made him the best friend I ever had. Given how much of myself I had buried to make Paul love me, in a few ways, my relationship with Jason was more profound.

Why couldn't he have told me he was going to hack my lab results and change anything outside the limits? If I'd known, I would've chosen differently. I would've gone straight to Marco and Tony, and we would've come up with a plan.

But for all his cleverness, Jason wasn't a medical doctor. He hadn't realized what those lab results meant. He thought it was drugs to hide momentarily while he devised a way to stop me from using them.

I clutched the Russian tech manual in my hands, holding it tight against my chest like a shield.

I was in so much trouble. Ego had done me an unexpected favor by refusing to get in the air with me, and I was truly grateful, but my condition remaining confidential was hardly the most pressing issue.

Knees wobbly, I sat down, pushing the books away from me to create some breathing room. It wasn't enough. I went outside.

Part of the universe, I thought as I looked up. Wondrous revolutions of planets, awe-inspiring chemical forces—

I was dying.

I was twenty-six years old, and I was dying from chronic kidney trouble among strangers in a foreign clan. I had no way of stopping it. Not on my own.

Why hadn't I agreed to the original visa evaluation? I would've done well, they would've offered for me, and I could've been in a cushy hospital room by now.

Possibly. If I'd done well enough. Echo had been impressed with me *after* he found out how much they'd been fooled, not before.

But what more could I have done? I could excel at any written exam they could create. I could even do a four-hour oral, which was over two hours longer than most. The Axe did everything I told it to, and I brought down targets. I gave them everything they wanted, and somehow I still wasn't good enough.

Sonneburg hadn't been either. He did everything right, and they jettisoned him, too. He was boring, but he was perfect. Why didn't the Hernandez want him?

Perhaps there had never been any way to earn my papers. Not for someone like me. Maybe Kairo was wrong when he said my divine blueprint must be spectacular. I was ordinary. Normal. Completely average. Perfectly forgettable. Without Jason mentoring me and without Dante's insights, all I could do was continue to hone the moves I knew, a plan that had failed to impress the Hernandez so far.

It was over.

So now what?

Well, conveniently, there were sixteen other clans in the Confederation. I would have to try again. No lies this time. Well, not about my health or my knack for solving challenging puzzles. I would forget about being conventional and hit it hard my own way, and when they rejected me, I would try it in another clan. Some clan out there must embrace the individual spirit. Like Yoshi said that first day of Axe training, there was a reason why governments choose human pilots instead of computerized ones.

I stood up so rapidly I got dizzy and sat down again.

Human. Not perfect and machine-like. Human.

Jason hadn't wanted me as his partner because I perfectly met the standards. He wanted me because of the glimpses of the parts I was used to hiding, the same glimpses that spared me from being deported like Sonneburg.

What if...?

What if I stopped censoring my ideas, stopped conforming altogether? Could I come up with a project so breathtaking, so irresistible that the Hernandez had to admit they wanted me?

What were the chances I would live long enough to try?

I scrubbed my hands through my hair. Not that long ago, it was short enough to stick out, and I was skinny enough to fit through the eye of a needle. Plenty of people would've written me off then, but I'd come so far. This kidney problem was entirely manageable.

"Stop being so pessimistic," I said aloud. "This is no different than any other problem. The traditional solution for healthcare is unavailable, so shut up, sit down, and figure out another. Glean data from medical websites to make lists for medicine and dosages, traditional medicine and homeopathic. Also, lab values to track and symptoms to watch out for. Check for any updates to the dietary restrictions Tony outlined at the start. And you got lucky with kidney disease because there's tons of data out there for it. This is going to be okay. Now go shower and go to class."

I paused, softening at the idea of standing under a long, hot shower and feeling clean and warm afterward. I did love Greyson. It was the ideal place to let go and find out what I was really capable of.

CHAPTER 37

Too Much Honesty

A month later, I had as good a sim as I ever had with Ego, finally developing a feel for how critical the damage to my aircraft was without him giving me the express details. The morning session of class after that rocked, too. At least the subject was awesome. Pooka, though, was short-tempered and quick to criticize.

"Who put hot pepper up his butt?" Ego muttered to no one in particular, and Pooka's stormy eyes locked onto Ego like a bird of prey sensing movement.

"Ego, front and center. I want you to tell the class why you're tanking Justice's career by taking your time rerouting damaged systems."

My back stiffened, and Ego stilled. "I've never sabotaged the pilot I'm assigned to, sir, and I resent you insinuating as much."

"I'm not insinuating, I'm saying it flat out. Did you assume that because you aren't in the air with her you can't damage her career?"

Ego was pale now, even paler than me.

I didn't care for the man, but he was still my partner. I told Pooka respectfully, "Sir, we should take this to your office."

"No one takes a step out of this room until I get answers," he told me. "Your poisoned relationship with your gunner is hurting the entire class, who came here to be honestly challenged. I've been patient, but I've had enough. We're having this out now."

I left my seat and approached Pooka. My voice low, I said, "He doesn't trust me to keep him alive, so he doesn't care about slowing the process of our deaths by rerouting things fast and clean. If we're going to fail—he's certain we always will, given our opponents and my novice status—then he wants to get it over with. On my end, I've lost my trust in him. He didn't give me what I needed one too many times, so I end up learning how to fly around the damage, assuming he can't be trusted to fix it. Nothing surprising about it."

"Justice, I—"

"Screw you," I snapped at Ego, my temper hitting its flashpoint now that Pooka had forced me to put into words something I'd tried not to think about. "You ruined me. My timing's off and my kill ratio has tanked since I partnered with you. You're useless to me, you're useless to the other flyers here, and you're useless to your clan. You'll be useless to your wife when you're dead on some valley floor."

"Justice," Pooka warned.

"I'm saying what everyone in this room is thinking." Turning to Ego, I said, "How can you throw your life away like this? Because if you keep this up, you *will* die. Even I can see that. You will cause your plane to go down, and you will leave your wife a widow. But at least Twister will be happy. You never flew as good for anyone else as you did for him. It's a shame your wife will have to find

287

another man to warm her bed. With a couple of surgeries, I understand it could even be Twister himself."

With a roar, Ego launched at me, but Pooka got between us before any punches landed.

"Enough!" Pooka yelled, grabbing my arm. "Get your stuff."

Out in the hallway, he released my arm with a shove, causing my stuff to spill all over the ground.

"Thanks," I complained as I retrieved my belongings. "Look, it needed to be said."

"Not like that. This school doesn't tolerate violence," he snapped. "Especially between members of different clans. If you can't..."

He reached past me to the hardcopy notebook lying open on the floor. "The Neary mod? Why are you looking at that?"

"It was listed as one of the most significant mods of the year."

"Check your sources next time. Independent analysts called it runny dog crap. You shouldn't be wasting your time looking at those mods." He handed me my notebook. "You're not coming back to class."

I gasped. "You're expelling me?"

He spoke over my protests. "You're going to sim bay four to watch sims Les earmarked when he heard I had a rookie on board, and you're going to answer the questions at the end of them."

"Sounds boring."

"Don't blame me. You're the one who said your basics were suffering."

I bared my teeth at him and headed for the sim bay.

As I walked through campus with long, ground-eating strides, I felt a tickle on my upper lip and brought my hand to it in surprise. My nose was bleeding. I'd had trouble with swelling in my wrists and ankles, too.

"No," I whispered to my body as I stumbled into a sedate pace. "It's all right. Sorry about that excitement. I'll reduce my stress, and I'll get plenty of sleep instead of studying all night. Hang on until I can secure our future. We'll get through this before you know it. Breathe. In with the lovely humid air and out with the stress. Everything will be fine. After all, I finally drove him to throw me out of class so I have time to do research, didn't I?"

Sitting in the visitors' chairs in the simulator bay, I couldn't keep my attention on the simulation playing out on the screen. My gaze was drawn to the blood in the grooves of my fingerprint. With a sample even as tiny as that, the Hernandez could use the polymerase chain reaction to create as much of my DNA as they wanted. If Puck's information was accurate, the availability of the tech to replicate my DNA wasn't the point. Getting the source of that DNA under lock and key was. Even if they had exclusive access to my genetic blueprint, what would they even use it for? Or was it simply a matter of making certain no one else could benefit from it? God, it wasn't like I had superpowers or anything. What the hell made it so special?

And if they wanted it locked up, why did they let me go to flight school like I was any other visa holder? Just to see what my DNA made me capable of? If so, that meant being an excellent pilot only guaranteed I would be harvested, not be allowed to become a citizen. No wonder they wouldn't authorize my medical care. They wanted me to die on their land without rights so my body could be used however they wanted.

God, even if Puck was full of crap and the Hernandez did let me fly, why did I even want to return to Rancho Hernandez? It was hot, dry, and resource deprived, and most people I met were more like Kairo than Dante.

289

I didn't take issue with patriotism, but ostracizing people born on the other side of some line was idiotic.

But I was fighting with everything I had to stay there permanently, so perhaps I was the idiot.

Bound by the Hernandez visa, I couldn't go to another clan for help. The sole way to be released from my papers was if the Hernandez let them expire because they didn't want me. Well, my death would release me, too, but that solution was slightly problematic.

I chuckled and said aloud, "Just slightly."

Maybe I could tell the Confederation what was going on. Granted, even if they accepted a story like mine without proof, I doubted they had the clout to do anything about it, even to the point of giving me sanctuary while the matter was investigated. It must've amused the Hernandez family to pretend its clan feared Confed sanctions. God only knew what they were really getting away with.

I could say to hell with it and run, too. I knew where my PDT was. All I would have to do was cut down to the bone to get to it. The poison core had to be triggered by cues other than a simple touch or people would be cutting them out left and right. It was feasible it was activated by exposure to air or a sudden drop in the bioelectric charge of the surrounding tissues. If I cut a big enough chunk of flesh to keep it surrounded, and if I did it quickly enough, maybe I could keep it from dispensing the poison.

I left the building and stood in the sun, loving the sensation of freedom and possibility.

Would they hunt me?

If they prized my DNA as much as Puck said, they wouldn't just let me go. In fact, I could guarantee they were going to return me to their lands. They were picking their moment.

Unless Puck was nothing more than a raving lunatic and my origins on Hernandez lands in that illegal plane crash had an ordinary explanation, like the black market organ trade. Marco did say I was full of transplanted organs.

I bit my lip, wishing that was a satisfactory explanation at any level. It was unnecessarily complicated to transplant organs into a person simply to transport them to another clan to be cut out again. Occam's razor said that all things being equal, usually the simplest explanation was the correct one. The trouble was, none of my solutions were simple. Most of my evidence was hearsay, anyway. Real life was annoyingly short on reliable data.

I sent a prayer to my husband for help, but I thought this one would've been beyond his experience.

"Okay, Marco, I'm going with your gut on this one. You had a reason to hide me from your own clan. I've got to figure out a way out of my papers, but I've also got to prepare a legendary sim for the possibility that the chance of becoming sanctioned as a Hernandez Axe pilot is legitimate. Piece of cake."

CHAPTER 38

DEAL WITH THE DEVIL

The next day, Pooka rousted me from my seat in the classroom while the others were settling in with their coffees and notes. He walked me through the quad toward the sim bays.

I said, "I just came to ask you a question."

"It can wait until after school like usual," he said with an impatient wave of his hand. "Justice, your last sim was a good one so I sent that vid to your DM to prove that you're—"

"You what?" I cried, panic making my pulse surge. "You had no right to do that without my permission. I crashed in that sim, Pooka. How could you send it?"

"It's a sim designed to appraise defensive maneuvers, not offensive ones, and I sent it to show him your skill is worth cultivating. I needed his office to understand that so my request for your gunner to be sent here would be taken seriously."

"You what?" I gasped and dropped like a stone on the nearest bench. The man was going to give me a damn heart attack. He was ruining everything. Not only would Jason's pride demand I be returned to the lectures with the rest of Greyson's students, but he would commandeer my hours outside class, too. It would be a lot more challenging to sneak in my four-hour bioscans at the flight surgeon's office, too.

"The Ministry of Defense shot me down cold, no explanation. They won't send him."

Relief and disappointment flooded me, almost making me dizzy.

"Calm down. I told them Ego was the problem, not you. Your MoD won't send your gunner or an airplane for you, but they did authorize you to fly with a gunner protocol so you can still do sims."

"What about Ego?"

"The Hysanki are sending a pilot to pick up the jet, and Ego will be going home with her later today."

I asked the expected question. "So if he's leaving, why are you chasing me out of class?"

"You're still a disruption."

"I'll put my blue lenses in."

"It's not that. Well, it's not only that. You ask too many questions that send us off on a tangent."

"You said this was a learning laboratory."

"That doesn't mean we're freewheeling it. It's my campus, and I want to teach particular concepts. Go to the library, go to your suite, go do a sim, or go do anything on this campus other than show up in the classroom."

"Greyson sucks," I called after him.

"So go home."

I pretended not to hear him.

"That's what I thought," he called out.

Pleased he had no intention of letting me return to class anytime soon, I returned to the library, finally allowing for the possibility something useful was on the disc Profit had given me as I left Clan Hernandez.

Sitting at my usual library table, I restlessly tapped the disc.

Marco continued to look at me with happy eyes. He must've believed I was capable of big, meaningful contributions if he'd always been so disappointed when I screwed up.

"Thanks for the vote of confidence," I told him, and I slid the disc into my palmer.

The file was Jason's working copy of an extensive critique of both my midterm project and Yoshi's comments to my project. I didn't know why she assumed it would help my position with her clan. It proved he'd been digging around in records he wasn't supposed to have access to, but a punishment for that would be negligible.

Since it was intended for his eyes only, Jason's narrative was a meticulously annotated mix of professional and personal reactions. It was a surprisingly boring read. The origination of my hypothesis was checked, and yes, it was consistent for me to have come up with this project given which texts I was issued. All my math was checked, the source of my equations confirmed. A few were marked in yellow or red depending on how far he thought I pushed the math.

When I got to one section in particular, an audio file activated in the corner of the screen because he had yet to transcribe and condense his notes. I had to restart it three times before I stopped listening to the velvet of his drawl and actually heard what he was saying.

"What an ass," Jason said as Yoshi's comment to the side became highlighted. "'What are you flying, Donovan? The rest of the class is flying a Battle Axe.' What a nice, useless, sarcastic comment to give a student, Yoshi. So his complaint about this section is that she wrote like she was driving a military aircraft other than an Axe. Yoshi's mistake is that he didn't notice she wrote it like she was facing something other than an Axe."

I stopped the file there, writing hasty notes before I forgot what was tickling my brain. Everyone knew the Axes were superior, but there had to be a spec or a maneuver unique to another warplane that could make it a threat to the Axe. God, I'd love to blow one of the Greyson aircrews out of the sky in a sim.

I looked at the photo of Marco again, pleased he was still happy with my efforts. "Should I name the move after you since you're the one who initially saved my ass? Marco Lional Rainer. Rainer. Rain. Black Rain," I decided, seeing his dark, dark eyes smile at me. "I'll call it the Black Rain."

"Miranda?" Jason asked, scowling at me from the screen. "Why do you have my file?"

I stared at him. Whatever deterioration had been destroying Puck's mind was destroying mine, and I was losing grip on reality.

"That wasn't rhetorical," he snapped.

"J-Jason?"

"You're seriously playing the crazy card? Or is this supposed to be amnesia? Do you think either is going to work with me? For the last time, why do you have my file?"

"Profit gave it to me."

His eyebrows shot toward his hairline. "Why?"

"She said it was a thank you."

The anger faded into annoyance. "Oh. I suppose she does have moments of generosity. You know. With other people's possessions."

A giggle escaped, and I clamped my hands over my mouth.

"You missed a sim," he snapped. "Forrester gave you a no show. Your phone was disconnected, and when I went to your residence to find out if you were too sick to function, all your personal effects were gone. Your locker was empty, too. You disappeared. Your roommate was killed in a car accident, and you were missing. I was terrified for you. I envisioned your deportation or murder plus the government termination of someone who was saving you from them."

"I'm sorry."

"Can you begin to imagine how inadequate that is?"

Silent, I looked down at the table because I couldn't face him.

"I would've gone to the funeral with you," he said, his voice gentle. "I know there's a strain between us, but I want to believe you know I would stand with you. This happened so close to you recovering your memories about your husband's death, and I didn't have a chance even to tell you how sorry I was."

Between the way he handled Bear and the tampered lab results, I should've hated him, but being in contact with him comforted me. Maybe it was because he reminded me anything was possible.

"Miranda," he said. "Miranda, you don't look well. Are they working you too hard there?"

"There?"

"My file tracer indicates you're at Greyson." He hesitated and then said, "I guess we now know how the Hernandez removes visa holders from their lands."

"I was given three choices," I whispered, raising teary eyes to his. "Wouldn't you have chosen Greyson, too? God, there's still so much I want to learn." I laughed sadly, wiping the wetness off my cheeks. "You know how people gush over the legendary Greyson library? It's legendarily dirty and abandoned. They don't know what they have, and they don't care, so I'm taking what I want."

"Is there a flight surgeon there? You're pale and puffy and the marks under your eyes are like bruises. Do you want me to liaise with the consulate about getting a doctor for you?"

With a fractional smile, I changed the subject. "Pooka keeps blocking me from lectures for getting everyone wound up about ideas that aren't on the curriculum."

"What do you do with your time?"

"Independent research and then sims to test my theories."

He regarded me solemnly. "They abandoned you."

"They did me a favor," I corrected. "I do what I want, and I study whatever I want. If I have a choice between learning and belonging, you know I'll choose learning every time. I passed my flight check, by the way."

"Of course you did. But they won't let you fly, will they?"

"I want to be in the sims for a while longer. It's a consequence-free environment to explore my ideas."

"That's quite a lie you've told yourself."

"I can prove the mod two is a piece of crap, and I can prove the radar signature of the E series can be faked to pass for a B. Do you think I learned that in class?"

The tension brackets around his mouth eased as the corner of his lips lifted in a smile. "I have missed you, Miranda."

"I need you to check my work, the sooner, the better."

"You're not still working on a showcase sim for the Hernandez, are you? How can you believe you still have a chance of being accepted by them?"

297

"Echo gave me a massive cash bonus. It was to be part of my citizenship bonus, but I told him I wanted it now so he gave it to me."

Jason didn't know what to make of that.

"Will you help me?" I asked. "I can pay you."

"I don't want your money."

My hands tightened on the edge of the table. "Jason, please. This is life or death to me. Anything I have that you want is yours. Help me. I don't need the idea. I have the ideas. I need you to check my work. If you need me to admit that I can't do it all on my own, that I understand what a team is and why one is important, I'll write you a paper on the subject."

"Now isn't the best time," he said with narrowed eyes. "I've got better things to do than help someone who couldn't spare ten seconds from her day to message me she was going to Greyson."

"It won't take long," I promised him. "I'll have my hypothesis ready to send to you in two days. You just have to read it and glance over my supporting material before giving me a yea or nay that I'm on the best track."

"Why should I?"

I crossed my arms and glared at him. "Because you're curious," I snapped. "And because nothing you have got going on is as exciting as what I can do with a Battle Axe."

"That's not the point."

"That is totally the point. Contact me in two days," I demanded.

He smiled that big, beautiful smile of his, always pleased by my defiance. "I'd love to."

After he terminated the connection, I sat back, smiling. I had time before my appointment with the flight surgeon for my weekly lab work and bioscan, so I scanned the local obituaries for people who were beyond needing the kidney medicine they'd been prescribed.

CHAPTER 39

YOU AGAIN

Pooka motioned me toward him while the other students settled in their seats the next morning.

"No," I told him, maintaining the charade I didn't have somewhere better to be. "Ego's gone. I don't deserve to be banished from class again. You know what? I'm not leaving willingly. You're going to have to drag me out of this room."

"Ease down, you raving loon. I've got a surprise for you."

"Great," I said. Given his previous surprise was his pre-emptive transmission of one of my simulations, I was wary about what he'd say next.

"Justice, I'm pleased to introduce the 2118 North American Aerial Combat Competition Champion Weapons Control Officer, Jason Chavez, call sign Voodoo, Republic of Texas. Voodoo, I'm pleased to present one of the best rookie defensive pilots I've ever met, Miranda Donovan, call sign Justice, Clan Hernandez."

Pooka stepped back with an enormous grin on his face.

Jason's expression showed a polite if chilly interest. It was like we were strangers again. He was beautiful though. Tired-looking, but his Texan uniform was crisp, and he was impeccably groomed like always.

"Ms. Donovan," he sniffed.

"It's my honor, sir," I said. But I couldn't be polite and distant. I burst out laughing and lit up with delight. "You're the best gunner on the planet."

He gave me an odd look. "I know."

That made me laugh again, and I threw my arms around him. I refused to have him as my partner, but I would take him as a mentor.

"Boundaries," he chided, stepping aside.

He nodded his goodbye at Pooka and put his hand under my elbow, steering me out of the room.

"She's excused from class," Pooka called after us. "For as long as you want."

I shot him an amused look. He couldn't find enough reasons to keep me out of his lectures.

"You'll have to share a suite," Pooka added.

Jason and I swung around in surprise.

"I take teams here," Pooka reminded us. "The only accommodations I have are suites of two bedrooms separated by a common area. I've got a full house this term, so I can't put you in different suites. If you don't like it, get a room downtown and ride the bus back to campus."

Jason glanced at me. "I can tolerate sharing a suite."

I nodded, failing to come up with a way to express my privacy concerns in a way that wouldn't tip off Jason that I was hiding something or insult him to the point where he wouldn't work with me.

Outside, I asked Jason, "What are you doing here?"

"You asked me to look over your project. I'm not going to have sensitive information crossing the border between Clan Farragut and Texas on unsecure lines."

"Texas? Weren't you in Rancho Hernandez?"

"You sound disappointed."

"I am. I was hoping you'd know how Dante was doing. I learned a lot from him."

He raised an eyebrow at that. "Such as?"

"He kept me grounded. He also reminded me that when other people don't like something about me, it's usually a deficiency in their makeup, not mine."

His brows knit together. "Who doesn't like you?"

"Why are you saying it like you're going to go confront them about it? I meant in general."

"I arranged for him to get a great gunner before I left."

"Thank you. So what went wrong? I thought you were in Rancho until the Comp."

"The Hernandez robbed me of the pilot I wanted to work with, so I robbed them of my company."

I snorted. "You have the world wrapped around your finger, don't you?"

"Big chunks of it, yes," he said, frowning as he got a good look at me. "You look even worse in person."

"Flatterer. How long are you here for?"

"As long as I want, but don't assume my time is yours to waste."

"Well, vice versa, cowboy. Come to the library so I can show you what I've got."

"No, we'll start with a sim to see where you're at."

It was nothing short of frustrating to work with Jason again. I had expected real-world scenarios with a computer program that built the challenges as it registered my competency, but Jason had me alone in a cloudless sky while I drilled the same maneuvers over and over again.

"Do it again," he said for what sounded like the millionth time.

Biting back a nasty comment, I spurred the plane into the hard, twisting loop of a bimini.

It was the morning of the third day, and I was getting tired of his nitpicking. No, that wasn't quite accurate. Thanks to an ungodly number of hours in the saddle, he'd brought me online, but now he wouldn't accept anything less than perfection. It hadn't bothered me the first two days, but waking up with a terrible pins-and-needles sensation in my leg scared me. I needed a day off to recover, and if that wasn't feasible, I wanted to move past all this preliminary stuff and get to dogfighting.

"Look at your hands," Jason told me. "You're flying like your left hand is dropping. I know you're tired, but you've got to lift and tighten your left hand's grip. Now do another."

Pissed, I fixed my hands and did ten biminis in a row, trying to make him hurl.

"Better," he said. "Much better. Moving on."

"I must take issue with this," I said. "If I continue to perform these maneuvers to a particular standard every single time thanks to endless hours developing the muscle memory, then I become predictable. If my adversary knows I always finish delta plus twenty if I do a bimini, then he can meet me there with guns poised."

"A valid argument," he surprised me by saying. "We'll discuss it over lunch. Moving on."

I rolled my eyes, gritted my teeth, and went to work.

Three hours later, Jason frowned at my meal. "There's not enough protein there."

I ignored him and started eating my grilled shrimp on salad. The man would run my entire life if I let him. "Why are you training me to be predictable?"

He pushed a pair of his shrimp onto my plate, examined my face, and then added one more.

"You don't expect me to believe you read my protein levels by looking at my face."

"You're a lot easier to read than Bear. Your skin is so fair I can almost see the blood move through your veins."

"And count my heme groups?"

His eyes crinkled.

I considered eating the shrimp he gave me and adjusting my mental count of my daily protein, but I was careful to the point of obsessive about what I ate and drank for a reason.

"Why am I practicing to be predictable?" I asked again.

He passed me his parsley garnish since I had eaten mine, but again I ignored it.

"You're practicing to be efficient in your maneuvers. Cumulatively, it saves you time and energy and saves the jet wear. While I do acknowledge it is a risk, it is less than you suspect. Those aren't standard parameters, but ones I calculated for you individually driving that series of Axe. Someone would have to study you for months to recognize and capitalize on it."

"Have I told you lately that you're a god?"

"It's always nice to hear. You look better, but you need a day off. No planes."

"No sims," I agreed.

"I meant a break from studying and everything else."

"You're a bastard."

"You said I was a god."

"That was before I knew you meant to punish me so. I'm not doing a sim for at least twenty-four hours, but I will continue with what I'm working on."

He gave a weak grin at my defiance. Was it my imagination or did he look pale?

"Jason? You okay?"

"I'm deciding whether or not vomiting would make me feel better. You should've warned me the immunization shots lived up to their hype. I haven't been able to eat well for days."

"They didn't bother me at all."

"What a blessing to be such a statistical anomaly." His attempt to take a deep breath was aborted by his abrupt departure.

I had the server pack up the remains of our meal, and I met Jason out front.

He barely glanced at me, coloring.

"So what if I know you barfed?" I asked. "You've seen me do it and were callous enough to critique it."

"You have these cute coughs that produce vomit. I make the most awful sounds. And we're done with the subject," he said, wiping the sweat from his forehead. "I need to go sit down."

"Are you going to pass out, or can I still brief you about my project?" I asked. With those monotonous sims, I'd already done my penance for walking out on him to come to Greyson, and he knew it.

He flashed me an exasperated look. "Briefly. Cocktail party briefly."

Before he knew what hit him, I had him seated in a chair in my simulator bay watching the Japanese version of the Comp.

"The Rising Sun," he said, nodding at the maneuver playing out on the big screen. "I know it. It's showy and beautiful, but its tactical use is extremely limited."

"I was envisioning an opening spiral instead of a tight, upward screw. I need the centrifugal force and rotation to spin away up to six active, untargeted missiles in rapid succession."

"By untargeted, you mean releasing active warheads without having locked them onto a specific target."

"I love the way you said that like I was a moron."

"You are making me wonder if I came out here for nothing. What missile?"

"Standard air-to-air Cories."

"Even better. When Cories are fired without a fixed target, they automatically go for the nearest heat signature within a specific temperature range. Your jet will be in the middle of a field of missiles looking for an Axe heat signature. Firing six missiles in a row will also mean that the first missile may have time to target you before the sixth is released."

"Dead engine after the sixth. I can drop the exhaust temp with a coolant dump. I also did a sim where a short made two missiles launch with one trigger pull, so I'm playing with that idea, too."

"Deliberately creating two faults in a fully functioning Axe?" he asked in a strangled voice.

"Taking out six bogeys at once."

"And screwing up your aircraft in the process," he said, his disapproval sharpening his voice. "Not yet knowing the specifics of your coolant dump, I still have to wonder if you can get the engines to relight before you auger in. I'm assuming there is a relighting."

"Of course there is."

"Yes, how foolish of me to suspect you were crazy. A dead engine means you'll have dead instruments. How can you possibly know if all bogeys are snuffed, if all live missiles found targets, and if you have enough altitude left to relight your candles?"

"My gunner and I will still be able to look out the canopy."

"Very comforting. And if you run out of altitude before all the bogeys or missiles are disposed of?"

"Emergency light, fast burn. That has to be assumed. Altitude is less of an issue than you presume. If I check my gauges before we go dead, I can calculate how much time we have. It's not like the force of gravity isn't consistent. Here, I'll show you," I said, calling up the sims I had prepped to send him, including my original one for Pooka that showed the missile misfire.

"I'll watch these. You go lie down. I'll meet you in the suite."

Instead, I sat beside him and rested my head on his shoulder, so grateful he had come.

He put his arm around my shoulders without thought, his eyes already on the screen.

"Oh," he blurted, snatching back his arm. "I don't know where that came from."

"It's fine. Your body puts out a lot of heat. It feels good. Don't worry. I'm not in love with you or anything."

He didn't replace his arm.

I didn't lift my head.

He swore softly, brushed the hair behind my ear, and went to work.

I was woken by a nudge and a complaint.

"You're snoring."

"I know. I couldn't wake up enough to do anything about it."

He laughed.

"Laughter's good," I said. "Not so crazy now, am I?"

"You've been out for a while, so I went through a lot of your other sims. Ego's frighteningly inept, by the way."

"He didn't want to fly with me. And yes, I figured out he was bleeding power from me. I even figured out how. I repaid him by crashing upside-down a lot because it made him throw up."

He snorted. "That bastard. He should be glad he left before I reviewed these."

"We were laughing," I reminded him.

"Well, your confidence in your recovery may be warranted if nothing else," he allowed. "Walk me through your thought process for the rest of it. When the Hernandez hear I helped you here, they're going to wonder whose work they're seeing. You have to be able to prove it was your idea and your work that got you there."

"My palmer can prove that."

He transferred his frown to the screen. "Miranda, this is incredibly dangerous. Are you sure this is the best you've got to show the Hernandez?"

"Is it feasible?" I persisted.

"I need to run some numbers."

"Look, Axes have been popular for decades. The chance of coming up with a new move is nearly zero, especially because I don't have experience or extensive education. What I can do at this point is exploit the weaknesses I've come across. Am I correct about that?"

"Yes. Now show me what else you've been working on."

By the end of the day, his face was set in a perpetual scowl.

"Black Rain it is," I said cheerfully.

CHAPTER 40

BLACK RAIN

"Shh, Miranda, shh," a deep voice coaxed. "You're safe."

I batted at the hand stroking my hair. "What are you doing in my room?"

"You were having a nightmare," Jason told me.

"That's not an implied invitation."

"Your moans and cries kept me from getting any work done."

"Oh," I said, relaxing. "Sorry."

He left my bedroom, and I went to the kitchenette for an ice cube to suck on. His computers and tablets used all the available space on the coffee table, so some of his books and whatnot were placed around him on the couch like fortress walls. For his being so fastidious about everything else, the apparent chaos of his surroundings while he worked made me want to tease him. I wished he would leave the glorious disarray on display, but when he was done working for the day, he would stack his books tidily and put away his notes. Then he would wipe down the tabletop and fluff the throw pillows to return it to a living room again.

"What are you working on?" I asked him.

"Do you need to be distracted from your nightmare?"

"No, I'm merely curious."

"Then go to bed," he told me without looking up from his screen.

"I'm doing my showcase sim today. How am I possibly supposed to be able to get any sleep?" I asked.

"Then go clink your ice cube against your teeth in your bedroom with the door shut."

"Black Rain," I said, savoring it. "That's a kick-ass name, isn't it?"

"Very gothic. What if it fails?"

"Then I'm naming it after you."

He snorted. "Do you know how many hopeful parents have given their babies my name?"

Amused at his sheer arrogance, I said, "Your name is from the Bible, isn't it?"

"No, I mean the whole Jason Alexander Chavez plus the mother's surname."

"The gall. Don't they know you're saving that name for all of your own children?"

"There's no government cap on how many babies I can have. You wish your genetic code got as high a rating as mine."

"Rating? You told me those tests were crap."

"For measuring potential? Absolutely. For providing a statistical probability someone's child will have a particular physiological disease, well, I do give that some credence. What makes me curious, though, is why your genetic analysis results are missing, not sealed. I can hack anything sealed, but the only part that made it into the system was your g-force tolerance. I know you were evaluated. You had to be."

"Don't be sloppy. *Had to be* is not a valid conclusion."

"There's no way the Hernandez would let a visa holder into a military flight school without knowing exactly what her genome contains. Plus you weren't put on the waiting list for school. Plus they said you have amnesia when you don't. Plus every cadet who makes it past the Decision has at least a DNA sample on file for remains identification in case the PDT is destroyed during a training accident. Well, every cadet except for you."

"You didn't know my hereditary strengths and weaknesses when you decided you wanted to fly with me," I countered. "And honestly, aren't you the reason I got into flight school in the first place?" I asked, masking a yawn. "Why were you searching for my genome?"

He was silent, mouth slightly parted. How could he be surprised by the question?

My belly sank. "Why are you so curious about it?"

"Why are you so angry?"

"I'm not angry, I'm disappointed in you. All this emphasis on people's divine blueprint is another way to try to force people into categories, a new way to discriminate. And then there are the people who want to splice bits of DNA to bioengineer the perfect-looking woman or the fearless, obedient soldier or the talking dog every kid wants for his birthday."

He burst out laughing.

"Don't laugh. It's not the least bit funny."

"Miranda, stop. I'm curious about you. The test's absence naturally makes me more so. I have no idea where you're from, who your people are, or what your educational background is. I'm entitled some curiosity."

"I grew up in the traditional family of married parents and a pair of sisters, but they're all long dead. My dad had a job where we moved every few years, so when people ask where I'm from I never have an answer for them. Investing in friendships and community is new to me. Getting the most out of the books I read isn't." Remembering the disturbing story Puck told me, I added, "I don't know anything about how or why I ended up on Hernandez lands. Do you?"

He shook his head. "If the information doesn't exist in the digital world, I'm limited to the read I get on the people involved if I ever cross paths with them."

I made a face at him. "So much for you having the world wrapped around your little finger."

Stung, he pointed at my room. "Get some sleep."

"No, I'm up now."

The rest of the morning vanished while I cleaned and sorted books in the library. I was careful though, keeping a buffer of dusty stacks at the forefront so the casual visitor would be repulsed and leave. Even bibliophile Jason wouldn't set foot in there, although he'd had the decency to be on the verge of tears when he saw the mess.

Stepping around the tall cases brought to sight my immaculate, sorted part of the library, where Marco's photo now sat on the scarred mahogany desk I used as my base. "Today is the day," I told him. "If you've got nothing better going on up there at harp school, look down on me about three o'clock. I'll resemble a whirling dervish in that jet, and Jason will probably be swearing up a storm, but it'll get me in, Marco. Thanks for keeping the faith."

Finally, it was time, and I climbed into the simulator. Jason and I had agreed it couldn't seem like he carried me so he wasn't in the cockpit.

"Pooka and I will both be on the comm line. I do want you to reconsider doing a short sim to get used to the gunner protocol I installed."

I shook my head. My energy reserves weren't infinite.

311

"Miranda, look at me."

When I complied, his shining face and strong gaze showed his complete faith in me.

"If it feels off, don't force it. You've got a great understanding of the Axe, so don't be afraid to follow your instincts down a different path. But if do you, make damn sure you sound like it was where you meant to go all along."

I laughed.

Pooka loaded a no-holds-barred dogfighting sim, and I charged into it without hesitation. Moments later, the strain made me shake, and lights flashed the aircraft's distress from every angle. As the computer initiated the repairs that Jason would've, I countermanded a lot of them, knowing from those sims with Ego what I could live without. I needed to divert power away from every nonessential system to find a path through the hurricane of ordinance and debris.

The hammering of my heart burst a blood vessel in my nose, and the pins-and-needles sensation spread through my hands and arms. The jet shuddered, threatening to come apart. It wasn't part of the sim, but the simulator itself. It wasn't meant to handle a sim like this, but I wouldn't back down. Not this time. If I could hold, the machine could hold.

A whispery voice came out of nowhere. "We're going to make history tonight, Miranda."

Blue sky finally opened up above me, and the sunlight was so piercing I had to turn away while my visor adjusted. My bogey klaxons were eerily silent, but lower tones signaled my jet's distress.

"Ease off." Pooka's voice came from far away. "You've got to ease off."

Jason's voice teased my senses. "Ease off the throttle, sugar. Nice and easy. You're clear."

I released the throttle, letting the warbird do as it would while I tore off my mask, spraying blood. "What a ride. Voodoo, would you mind taking the reins?"

"Computer, override primary cockpit control, authorization Chavez, Jason Alexander, Republic of Texas serial number TA549-767-3709, code 99. Set autopilot for best course and descent rate to angels ten."

"Thanks," I groaned, happy for the chance to recover while the simulator decelerated. I pinched my nose to encourage clotting. I was going to have to account for the mess in a way that wouldn't require a medic. "Pooka, do me a favor, will you? I bit my lip, and I'm drowning in blood. Will you have stuff ready so I can clean up the drips on your equipment when I dismount?"

"Don't worry about it. You want a medic?"

"No, it's not that critical. Now if you all don't mind, I need a moment to myself. I'm clicking off for thirty seconds."

"Go ahead," Jason said. "I've got control."

I disconnected from my communications line and closed my eyes for a moment, trying not to tense for what I had to do. I savaged my lower lip between my teeth until the taste of copper filled my mouth fast and hot.

Thirty seconds on the mark, I plugged in. "Miss me?"

"Can't live without you," Jason said. "You ready to land this plane?"

"Oh, aye."

"Computer, release primary cockpit control, authorization Chavez, Jason Alexander, Republic of Texas serial number TA549-767-3709, code 10."

"Thank you," I said, relaxing into my seat as I took the stick in hand.

At the end of the sim, Pooka helped me from the cockpit, his gnarled hands as strong and hard as oak. "Ugh, you weren't kidding about the blood."

"Sorry."

Jason removed my helmet. "Oh, sugar, your poor lip. What's the damage?"

I took off my gloves and peeled back my lip, showing the ragged gash. "See? It's nothing. I just may hurl from the taste though, so if you'll excuse me."

Alone in the locker room, I let go of the facade that I was okay and dragged myself to the bench in front of my locker so I could lie down. I concentrated on my breathing, and the sharp tingling in my arms and hands faded. Moving carefully, I sat up, waited for the dizziness to fade, and then I shrugged off the layers of flight gear. With regret, I touched the drying stains that dirtied my pretty gear.

"Aren't you clean and ready for your adoring public yet?" Jason said as he stepped around the bank of lockers.

"Burned through my adrenaline. I'm worn out."

"It shows. You're very pale," he said, adding my helmet to the stack of my gear and walking to the sink. A wad of wet toweling in hand, he straddled the bench and cleaned my face, his hands gentler and more thorough than mine would've been. "You need to stop going so deep, Miranda. It's not healthy."

Eyes closed, I said, "Was I good? Good enough, I mean? You'd sign me?"

His warm hands framed my face, and he kissed my forehead with infinite gentleness. "You are magnificent."

"I meant from a professional standpoint."

"That was my professional opinion. But you should've seen Pooka's reaction when you started your move. He never saw it coming, which in itself is a hell of a feat. Then, even though your plan was working as expected, you not only saw a better solution, you hit it hard."

"Is it reproducible? It can't be written off as an anomaly."

"A very skilled team could reproduce it with some success, yes. I know perhaps three teams who can at least come close. It'll come down to their ability to time it."

"Perfect. Pooka's already sent it to the DM's office?"

"Yes. We still used the Black Rain label."

"Thank you. I'll be taking their call soon, I expect."

CHAPTER 41

FINALLY

Jason's expression shifted between thoughtful and troubled as we walked through the quad a few minutes later. A cold wind pushed black-bottomed storm clouds toward us, but a few shafts of sunlight still made it through.

"Think out loud," I told him, sitting on the nearest bench to rest.

"The way you get your hopes up is torture to watch," he said, accepting my invitation to sit by me. "I want you to petition Texas. There'll be no problem getting papers if not outright citizenship. My DM knows I don't go high-tailing it after a pilot for no reason. That sim is a bonus orgasm."

I smiled. "I've fought hard for my place among the Hernandez."

"You're not one of them. You're so much better than they are." He wiped a trickle of blood off my lip where my smile cracked the clot. "Think of what we could do together, even if you don't want me as a partner, and even if you don't want to fly at all. The schooling. The research. God, Miranda, there's so much we could do."

My eyelids felt like stone as I raised them to regard him. "I'm going home."

"Even if you don't want to work with me at all, I want you to come to Texas," he said, caressing my cheek. "I worry about you working too hard and forgetting to eat and sleep. Marco's gone, and I'll be in another clan. Who will watch out for you?"

I laughed. "I've suffered a lot from well-intentioned people taking care of me."

"What did you think about Kairo's arrest?"

I gave him a long, measuring look. "What arrest would that be, Jason?"

"Homeland Defense found enough incriminating evidence on his computer to arrest him for domestic terrorism."

I jerked my eyes away, not liking what I saw in his. Jason always had a sense of latent power around him, but seeing this flash of it was unnerving. He preached violence as a last resort, and now I understood retribution, ambush, and other unsavory digital responses were his preferred alternatives.

"The way he hurt you was unforgivable," he said softly.

"Some would argue that was an overreaction," I said carefully, deliberately blanketing the statement over Jason's action as much as Kairo's.

"Perhaps there was some strong emotion involved."

"And if I were to provoke emotion of that magnitude?"

"Miranda, he knew you had inadequate medical coverage, and if the clan had heard about it before Marco took care of it, you probably would've been deported for being unable to complete your contract. Who would've repaired your nose then? What would you have done if it became infected? He meant to leave you with no home, no friends, no money, and no chance. You don't think that could be a death sentence? You wouldn't do that to someone."

He leaned forward, and I resisted the urge to move out of range.

"It was a close call," he said. "I suspect you don't fully understand how close."

After a moment, I met his gaze and nodded. I didn't agree with the terrible vengeance Jason had sought on my behalf, but I understood it. But I also knew that if he'd understood the depth of Kairo's malevolence, Jason would've prevented Kairo from getting close enough to land that blow to my face in the first place.

Needing to lighten the mood, I said, "Jason, I need to tell you something, too."

"You can tell me anything."

"The sole reason I signed with you is because of who your family is."

He snorted, the edge of his mouth lifting.

"I'm serious," I insisted. "It's all about your Comp win and your family for me."

"Enough. I chose to be a gunner instead of a pilot specifically so people couldn't compare me with the other flying members of my family."

"Elegant solution. Do you ever regret it?"

"If I was in any way dissatisfied, don't you think I would change my path?"

Of course he would.

I asked him, "Do you want to know why I wanted to sign with you? Because honestly, if it was all about my safety, then I either would've chosen the engineering job or the Plough."

"I'll bite. Why?"

"Well, let me preface my answer by telling you a story. Once upon a time, my parents were playing with a math problem. Both had worked on it for weeks, and their competition was becoming less playful as time dragged. I wanted to try to solve it, and they indulged me. I found a solution."

"They must've been proud."

"I was eleven."

"They must've been very proud," he corrected.

My lips flexed in what only a charitable person would call a smile. "They said they were, but I knew the situation had gone terribly wrong. From the looks on their faces, I knew not to tell anyone what I had done. They certainly didn't. My relationship with them was never the same again. So I got my A's like they told me to, but I did just enough to get the A's. They told me they were proud and told my sisters they should emulate me, but it felt like they were merely going through the motions. Like they didn't dare show me any real encouragement to flex my mind and see what I could do."

"Because you would've looked smarter than them," he said. "I can't be the first person to encourage you. What about your husband?"

"By the time I met him, I knew how to act normal. Smart with math and physics, but not freakishly so."

"That's a crime."

"That's how to get loved," I said. "But these have been the best weeks of my life. I have never been more myself, and it turns out that being alone is—"

"You're not alone."

"Did you interrupt me, Mr. I-Don't-Tolerate-Interruptions?"

"You're not alone," he repeated. "Miranda, when Bear told me how he felt about me—"

"This discussion is over," I told him, getting to my feet.

"I betrayed him because of the Hernandez."

I sank onto the wooden bench.

"The Comp is the pinnacle of our field, so it was a huge deal to me personally," he allowed, "but I would've been satisfied if I won it a different year."

"Jason, don't do this. Can't you let me hang on to a good mood this one time?"

"Bear did his big emotional reveal to explain why he was turning in his wings before I could tell him we received our invitation to the Comp."

"I know how this story turns out," I reminded him.

"But you don't understand why. The Hernandez had been flexing their strength up and down our border, and it was in part because my clan tried a new mod and ended up in the seventy-fifth percentile at the Comp for three years running. Bear knew Texas needed a very strong showing, and we were the ones who could produce it, but he didn't care. So I told him everything he wanted to hear to get him back in the cockpit."

His voice was hoarse, and he swallowed with difficulty to clear his throat.

My jaw was clenched from the need to stop him from ruining what regard I had for him.

He said, "The morning we were to fly north for the Comp, I reconsidered because my lie wasn't sustainable. I knew if I told Bear the truth then, he would be super pissed at me, but we could recover from it in a year or two. Pressing forward would have me telling him the truth about my lack of romantic and sexual feelings for him after he was emotionally and physically wrung out by the Comp. It would be catastrophic. My brother Cris was there to see me off, and I asked him how far he would go for the clan. I was hoping his response would give me any kind of reason why I could back down, but obviously, it didn't."

"Why are you telling me all this? Why now?"

"If the Hernandez decide to fast track you, you will have to make decisions like mine. You and I have barely had a chance to touch on the human cost of victory, but I need you to understand that sometimes there are personally devastating decisions you will make for a clan that doesn't really care. They'll care about how it makes them look stronger, but they won't care how it weakened you."

"Jason."

"Let me finish. Make decisions that are best for your sustained ability to serve the clan in the manner you are best at."

"Is that regret in your voice?"

"I did what I needed to, Miranda. But there isn't a day that goes by that I don't grieve for what I lost with Bear and my family. They haven't spoken to me since the day they found out what I did to him. Now, I want you to promise me you won't tell anybody. About Bear, I mean. He's very private. I've always been very comfortable in my villain's role."

"I know how to keep a secret."

"Obviously, or I wouldn't have brought it up. I need you to keep one more secret."

"Please don't make me hate you with your next words."

"No, this is a conclusion you will eventually come to yourself if you live among the Hernandez for too much longer. I don't want you doing something in the post-coital glow of being offered citizenship you'll come to regret. It's about your other ideas beyond Black Rain. I want you to keep them to yourself, except for the one you labeled Cloud Fall. That one I want you to delete and abandon entirely."

My eyes narrowed. "You want me to be a one-hit wonder. Why?"

"I want you to have a better understanding for how the Hernandez will use the weapons you can provide. Between politics and resource scarcity, the balance of the seventeen clans is precarious. Giving an aggressive, imperialist-minded nation a distinct advantage on the battlefield has only one possible result."

"With knowledge comes responsibility," I said. "Politics takes all the fun out of learning."

He squeezed my hand in appreciation for accepting the reality of the situation. "Think about Texas. At least consider it."

"I will."

It was ten that night when Slick told me my call had come through. Sitting down in the comm office, I saw that Nero Hernandez looked even more imposing on the vid link than in the news feeds.

Without preamble, he said, "Wonderful job, Ms. Donovan. Go to the Hernandez consulate at your soonest convenience to sign for your citizenship papers."

"No, thank you, sir."

It took a moment or two for him to realize what I said.

"You want the notary to deliver them to you on a silver platter?" he asked with a tight smile. "Very well. What time is convenient for you?"

"I'm rescinding my request."

His dark eyes attempted to level me from afar. "Ms. Donovan, it doesn't matter how lucrative offers from other clans are. You're bound by the terms of your visa, and I have no intention of releasing you early so you can sign with someone else. Are you expecting to survive your disease long enough to simply wait out the expiry of your papers? I wasn't aware you had the luxury of time."

"I won't live long enough to see them expire."

"All the more reason for you to sign for your citizenship immediately. We have a medevac standing by to bring you home."

"No, thank you."

He gave me a withering look. "I suppose you have terms you want to set."

"Not at all. I used that sim to get an audience with you, nothing more."

He tapped a button on his desk. "Echo, I need you. I had hoped to present to Ms. Donovan myself, but there's an issue, and I have to prep for the Confed liaison."

"Aye, sir. Of course."

Echo replaced Nero Hernandez behind the desk.

"Ms. Donovan, you wildly exceeded expectations," he said with a real smile. "What an exciting simulation to watch. Citizenship is assured."

"I've decided to rescind my request for it, sir."

"Why?"

"Well, it was my sincere intention to be useful to your clan and repay the generosity of the people in it. I'm sorry my deception toward that goal was unforgivably dishonorable in your eyes. I didn't care for it either, but I knew I had so much to offer you once my health improved. You can't imagine what I felt when I learned the only reason you let me go through this charade was your curiosity about the manifestation of my exemplary DNA."

Echo's confusion showed before his face went blank, but Nero's head snapped up, and the look in his eyes said Puck had told the truth.

I said, "You bastard. There's no way to work toward a better genetic code because you either have a good one or you don't. And I doubt there was any way to earn a second chance if I hadn't lived up to the supposed promise of my DNA. There must be something broken in your own genome if you don't recognize how immoral this is."

Echo stiffened at the insult, and Nero's glittering gaze continued to level me from afar.

"Seeing as it's my body and I'm still of sound mind, I'm the one who chooses how my body is used," I told them. "Therefore, I donated my future remains to a Confed organization created to handle the corpses of intestate people. They've already been auctioned off and my death rites assured."

Both of them spoke at once, but Nero Hernandez's commanding voice took control of the conversation. "You cannot enter any contract without permission of the Hernandez while you are a visa holder."

"According to both the Confed and Hernandez consulate lawyers who looked at the paperwork you wrote, I can in this case. Clans don't want intestate corpses cooling on a slab while any salvageable organs are losing viability. From the moment I die, I become intestate. Privacy laws protect the identity of the clan that won the bid, but the look on your faces tells me it wasn't you."

"You're still under Hernandez law as a visa holder, and we have the right to retrieve you immediately. Once you're dead on our lands, there's no way any clan will fight us to get to you."

I used a pair of metal forceps to set a bloody transmitter on the table, fat globules sticking in its cracks. I lowered my trousers and peeled back the soaked bandage so they could see the hole it had come from before blood filled it in again. I needed stitches, but I enjoyed the effect of the gory cavern.

"Good luck finding me without my PDT," I said, smiling. "And that, gentlemen, is that."

"Stop!"

"For what?" I asked Nero, my hand hovering over the disconnect button.

"Echo, leave." After his second had fled the room, Nero snapped, "I was promised the DNA was coming from a woman who was so damaged she was already days away from death. They said her legacy was on the verge of being lost forever."

My eyebrows shot up. The lab gave up repairing me so they gave my corpse away? "What makes my genetic blueprint more valuable than anyone else's in your clan? Why would you go to all this trouble?"

"I'm not about to respond to that. However, I will tell you this. When my mother dies, I will be Chieftain," he said. "You can't imagine the responsibility I face. Look around you. Babies with degraded DNA are dying in the womb at an ever-increasing rate. Don't you believe I'd prefer to be able to give my clansmen fertile, uncontaminated soil to grow food in? Clean water and air? Don't you think I want women to react to their pregnancies with hope instead of fear that their bodies are too full of environmental poisons for their eggs to reproduce accurately? Whether you approve or not, I will use the technology available to give my people a chance for a better life. You're already dying, Ms. Donovan. Don't let your DNA go to waste. It would be such a beautiful legacy, wouldn't it?"

Fed up with listening to the propaganda, I terminated the connection with the man who never believed I had any value unless I was dead and cut into pieces.

My DNA hadn't been wasted. I was put on Earth to experience the gamut of emotions alongside the rest of humanity. I lived, loved, and learned as I went along. The last year or two, I'd lived for myself, but that was by necessity, not choice. I liked easing other people's burdens. I liked living with hope as much as intelligence and with love as much as a desire to solve problems. How was that wasting my divine blueprint?

CHAPTER 42

FAITH AND PEACE

From the administration office, I went to the library. I opened the water-stained copy of the Russian tech manual and removed my inventory from its hollowed-out core.

I sorted the medication bottles and blister packs, all prescribed to other people. The nephrologist had written out recommended drug regimens as my lab values decreased, so in my current condition, I estimated I had ten percent more medicine than I needed. I debated whether it was worth offering to buy the remaining meds from more families of the freshly dead just to be certain.

Being wrong about the Hernandez wanting a final bioscan before offering citizenship cost me some time, but I'd had to risk it.

I jumped as the flight surgeon came around the stacks. "There was blood on your chair in the admin office," she explained. "I followed you here."

I indicated the transparent baggie with my PDT. "I've gone rogue, Dr. Diab."

"Finally." She saw the pile of medication and froze. "You've been taking all this?"

"Building up my supply. I expected the Hernandez to want one final round of lab values so I couldn't show signs of improving health, or they'd never stop looking for me. I'm about to take a bolus dose of this one," I said, lobbing a bottle toward her.

"Let me call Hargrove."

"He's the one who made certain I knew what to get, how much to get, and when to take it." I raised my water bottle to her. "Cheers." I swallowed the four blue pills and grimaced at the taste of chemicals. "And since you're here, would you also be willing to help with these?" I asked, pulling two syringes from the drawer refrigerator I'd installed under the table and handing her one.

"You're a remarkable young woman," she commented as she wiped my arm with an alcohol pad.

"Merely a bitter one. If you're available, I also need stitches in my hip, and this other syringe needs to be diluted in an IV."

"Let's get started."

It would be a grueling effort to drag myself back from the edge, to be sure. My immediate goal was to get healthy enough to survive the transplant surgeries. As Dr. Diab prepared my IV, she told me she'd heard rumors of an illegal medical station with dialysis out in the Gulf of Mexico near Tampa, but I'd still likely need a new set of kidneys at some point.

It was time to leave Greyson regardless. By lunch, I would have said my goodbyes to Jason and moved my personal effects to a hotel. There I would contact the Confed so the retrieval team for my corpse knew where to find me in the unlikely case I died before the hard-core pharmaceutical assault on my kidneys worked its magic. My vague plan for my recuperation was to read stories to kids in the library, watch beach sunrises, and go to church to pray for Jason, who needed all the help he could get.

After leaving Dr. Diab's office, I returned to the darkened suite. Jason's door was shut, but I wouldn't be able to relax until I was behind the locked door of my bedroom. I locked the door with shaking hands, my head pounding so hard I felt it in my eyes. I slid to the floor as the shakes returned, along with nausea and dizziness. Puck's two pennies were clutched in my hand, my payment for Charon.

My spell lasted significantly longer than past episodes. Was this a reaction to the drugs or was I dying? Just in case, I prayed with all my heart. I begged for His forgiveness and for His mercy in letting me rejoin Paul. I prayed for His protection of the people I cared about over and over again until it stopped being words, stopped being thought, to become waves of emotion.

The awful sensation eventually faded, and I pulled myself to my feet. In the bathroom, I used handfuls of water to rinse my mouth and clean my bloodied nose. I couldn't help glancing at my reflection. I wasn't going to let Jason see me with my hair this matted down or my skin dull from drying sweat.

I sucked down glucose gel packs, and I showered, meticulously cleaning my body between rest periods when I had to sit with my head between my knees to let the dizziness fade.

Looking closer to human and feeling better as my blood sugar came up, I left my room and went to his. It wasn't locked.

"Jason?"

"Come here already," he yawned, lifting the sheet. He was bare-chested and wore pajama pants. "I've been waiting up."

I got into bed beside him, and he spooned around me without making any attempt to turn it sexual. I pressed my face to the sheets, inhaling that familiar Jason scent. "Go to sleep. I promise I'll be here in the morning."

He said something in Spanish that sounded soft and sweet, and then he sank into his pillow and drifted off.

I let the comforting warmth of his body seep into mine and felt the cadence of his heart gentle mine into a peaceful rhythm. As grateful as I was for Jason's presence, I still ached for my husband to the point of tears.

I screwed up and delayed too long to take the meds, so I might be coming home to you, Paul. Probably by the end of the week, if not sooner. I've changed, no doubt, and I've had moments of weakness, but you have always been and always will be my love. God willing, I will feel your arms around me again.

CHAPTER 43

THE REAPING

Jason was still asleep at daybreak, his hand curved around my belly with an intimacy that alarmed me. I tried to ease out of bed without waking him, and he chuckled at my attempt.

I said, "I just... I..."

He raised an eyebrow at me. "Get a hold of yourself, Miranda. You know I can't stand it when you get all romantic."

I burst out laughing. I felt weak and tired but far better than I had through the night. Death seemed very far away again.

"So how did your conversation with the Hernandez turn out?" he asked as if it didn't matter.

"They offered," I said with a shrug.

"Congratulations," he said, turning away. "I'll be headed home to Texas then since there's no reason for me to stay here."

Even though it was clear he was looking for me to give him any reason to stay, I nodded.

"Miranda, Pooka would let you stay for the rest of the term if you wanted to."

"No, I'm going home," I said, fingers curling around the pennies in my pocket. "It's time. But before we part ways, I was hoping we could do a sim."

"Hell, no."

"Not that kind of sim. We could chase a sunrise over a mountain to a vast tropical sea."

"I would love that," he said, rolling out of bed.

In the hallway at the end of the simulator building, Jason delayed until the cleaning woman was all the way inside the women's locker room before wrapping his hand around my nape to draw me close. "Are you sure you want to do this? Because I'm going to give you the kind of sim that makes a woman turn her back on her clan and come to mine. After all, there's no shame in admitting there's no one you want more than me in your bed, your cockpit, and your library."

"The trouble with you is that you lack self-esteem. I'm only attracted to arrogant men."

He chuckled and released me. He must've seen how puffy I was, how pale. How had I got away with it so long? Perhaps like when Bear fell in love with him, there were moments when Jason saw only what he wanted to see.

"Don't stand there smiling at me," he chided. "Hurry up and get changed."

"Whatever you say, Jason."

"If only you meant that," he grinned as he backed into the men's locker room.

I donned my flight suit, smoothing the wires in place and guiding them through their grommets with deft

331

fingers. My flight gear came next, and I settled its familiar weight around me.

I reached for my pistol, checked the barrel and clip and snugged it into its holster, tight against my left side.

"I didn't think you flew with guns when there wasn't a war going on," the cleaning woman said, clutching her mop handle with a white-knuckled grip.

"It's not loaded," I told her absently as I checked the fittings on the regulator Jason had loaned me. "I'm doing a simulation today, but if I don't wear it, it feels funny. Don't you remember the way your tongue always went to the hole where your tooth used to be when you were a kid?"

"Oh," she said, her expression clearing.

There was a knock on the door and then a male voice. "Maintenance. Anyone in here? Ruthie?"

"Hold up, Fred. There's still someone in here."

I waved that off as I attached the regulator to the hoses. "It's fine."

Fred and Ruthie exchanged pleasantries before he set up his ladder under a burned-out lightbulb.

"I'm sorry about this," the cleaning woman said.

I shut my locker and gathered up my helmet. "Nothing to be sorry about."

"Ma'am, you're going to have to come with us," Fred was saying.

I looked at him in surprise. "Excuse me?"

The distinctive click of a gun being cocked behind me required no translation.

"We don't want to injure you, Ms. Donovan. Just the opposite, in fact, so come with us quietly so no one gets hurt, especially you."

"Under whose authority are you acting?"

"You know the answer to that, Mira."

I shook my head, pressing against the lockers so they couldn't get behind me. The PDT hadn't been out of my body for twenty-four hours before they showed up.

"Ma'am, the Republic of Texas doesn't recognize your affiliation to the Hernandez Clan as you were already a citizen of the former when you entered into a work visa with the latter. You were grandfathered into the Republic following the dissolution of the United States."

"Time," Fred said to Ruthie, his urgency plain.

Ruthie brought her pistol up. No, it was a simple tranq gun like Marco carried in his med kit.

"Stop!" I yelled, holding my hands out to ward her off. Adrenaline charged through my veins, making me weak-kneed, and I said, "Standard type five cartridges will kill me. I've got end-stage kidney disease. Even one dart will kill me."

"Nice try. We know the Hernandez offered you citizenship. They wouldn't do that if you were that sick," she said before firing the first tranq into my neck.

I yanked the dart out before the pain even registered. My gun was in my hand a moment later, the shot deafening in the tiled confines of the locker room. Of course, I'd lied about being unarmed. I was a lone Hernandez island in a sea of foreigners. One of the DM's rules had been to always keep a round chambered and a full clip.

Fred fired two darts into my thigh as I whirled around and capped him, too. I didn't have time to regret any of it. I was already convulsing before he hit the ground. The pain was unbelievable. Every part of me was racked with the explosions of dying cells and disintegrating nerve endings. I had no time to think or pray or anything. When Jason responded to the sound of shots by bursting into the locker room with his own pistol in hand, I was already fading to black.

CHAPTER 44

HEAVEN OR HELL

The deep, hollow sound of my breathing filled my head like I was submerged in water except for my mouth, but there was no sign of liquid warmth surrounding me. Filling my lungs deeply and slowly, I felt the rawness of my throat and a bone-deep ache in my chest.

God, I was tired.

Strange smells penetrated my haze, and my brain strained to separate and identify them. I couldn't mistake the harsh scent of disinfectant and the medicinal scent of antiseptics, but underneath that was the comforting, musky smell of human sweat.

I tried to open my eyes, but they didn't respond. A claustrophobic kind of panic hit me while I repeated the attempt.

I tried to bring a hand up to my face, but I couldn't do that either. I was restrained from end to end, and I felt the frantic fear increase because nothing responded. Nothing about my body felt familiar, felt right. It was a jumbled mass of electrical burns and dead spaces.

"Come on, Mira," a deep male voice coaxed as a warm callused hand squeezed mine. He sounded tired. How long had he held my hand? His words were well-worn from repetition. "Come on back to us. Fight."

I couldn't swallow. I was drowning, and I couldn't turn my head or swallow or spit out the fluid. A Big Blue bioscanner pinged an alarm.

"Get Chase in here stat."

The air moved around me, and I caught the scent of another man.

"I got her," he said breathlessly. The man tipped open my mouth and eased out the tube. "Shane, get me a number nine."

My esophagus contracted, working the saliva down my throat until my mouth was empty. I could breathe.

"Stop. Look."

There was a pause. "Jesus Christ, it worked."

The first man had never released my hand, and he squeezed it again. "Mira, can you hear me?"

A tear slid out of my eye and down into my ear.

"Oh, Jesus. She's back."

I swallowed and swallowed again to ease the soreness of my throat. I felt the need to say something, but I had trouble thinking through the painful fuzziness in my head.

"You are such a fighter," the man squeezing my hand said. "We thought we'd lost you for good so many times, but you always come back."

"W-where?"

"Texas. You're in a medical lab deep underneath Texas soil. Your original body was unsalvageable, but we got you a new one, and it was a perfect match if a little young. The mature one was used for your initial repairs."

New one? Mature one? I was confused. For a moment, it sounded like he was referring to bodies. All that crap about the Hernandez's need for my DNA gave me the strangest nightmares.

"You should've seen it," he babbled. "It took the surgical computers six days to splice the nerves to switch bodily function controls from her brain to yours, but it worked. Look at you. You swallowed on your own. Your eyes are moving behind the lids and your tear ducts are producing tears. You're even speaking. You're in control of her body. Your body now."

Wake up. Grab this nightmare by the balls and wake up.

"You are something else," he was saying in wonder. "Oh, Mira, wait until you see the life we've got for you. We have government support to place you anywhere doing nearly anything. Of course, you can't reconnect with your friends. Miranda Donovan is dead. She died of multiple organ failure in the Farragut clan weeks ago. But you, you can be anyone you want. We're giving you a new face, a new name, anything and everything. The Ministries will handle the creation of your background and give you the money you need."

This couldn't be happening. Not again. I *died*. I was going to be reunited with Paul, my dog, and the rest of my family. I was *free*.

"Are you listening? Your future is limitless. There won't be any more plane hijackings dumping you on the Hernandez. This time around you're going to have the best medical care all the way to the finish line and all the rewards of citizenship. It's the least the clan can do for its oldest member."

A different voice spoke up. "Don't worry about being stolen from us again. We more than proved that your genetic code alone was worth the expense of topping every bid on your remains to make sure you ended back here with us. But don't assume it's exclusively about your genetics. We are beyond excited to have you with us conscious and interactive. But we can talk about that later. For now, know we've got extra security measures in place and that you're safe. You're worth any and all expense to keep you safe."

I understood now that it was never going to end. Every time I died, they would find another way to revive me, always telling me I had to abandon every trace of my previous life. I was a novelty to them. I was the never-ending Miranda. I was a hundred-and-thirty-one-year-old woman in a much, much younger body, and every time I died, they would put me in someone else's body, to see if it could be done, to see if they could sustain one individual soul for a hundred fifty years, three hundred years, or even a thousand years. An eternal soul living a hundred lives watching scores of empires rise and fall, seeing endless atrocity and human suffering as people fought to carve better lives out of a dying planet.

I couldn't bear it.

The scream left my head and poured out of a mouth that wasn't my own. Reassuring voices promised that everything was fine, that all my dreams were coming true, but all I could do was scream my rage and fear.

Epilogue

The woman in the hospital bed wept, but Jason didn't care what the surrogate felt or did now that the child was born.

His eyes locked on the screen of the computer processing the blood sample. His name appeared, but there was a maddening pause as they waited for the maternity to be confirmed.

"Why is it taking so long?" he demanded. "I gave you samples for both."

"Yours was fresher."

Her name manifested as a burst of black font on the pale blue screen, the arrival of all nine delicious syllables as abrupt as her appearance in his life had been.

"Thank You," Jason breathed, directing his gaze heavenward as his heart swelled. Not that he hadn't controlled every single thing he could, but life occasionally delivered nasty surprises.

He caressed her name on the screen and collected their son before they finished cleaning him. He held the newborn to his chest to let the boy hear his heartbeat.

"Nicolas Jamison Chavez," he told Juliana Fischer, the Texan Defense Minister.

"Jamison? You hate him."

"Not the pilot, ma'am. The 'Ja' is for Jason, the 'mi' for Miranda, and the 'son' is because he's our boy child." Jason kissed the baby on the head. "You'll arrange it?"

"The birth record will be sealed as promised if you still wish it."

"Thank you, I do. I wanted him born on Texan soil, but I'm not ready to share him with my family or anyone else yet. The expectations will be massive."

Jason sensed her eyes on him and looked up.

The DM asked bluntly, "How did you get a hold of her egg?"

"I bought the services of someone with the knowledge and the immediate access to her to get me what I wanted."

"You stole it from her corpse. You're frighteningly amoral."

"Ma'am, you keep saying that, but you keep presenting me with the finest women in Texas with the hope I settle down and impregnate one of them. You do know that any baby I have will have the amoral streak as well as the genius and the flying ones, don't you?" he teased.

"I prefer to believe God's design includes the mother's genes prevailing."

"I hope so, too. I very much want this child to be her legacy. My God, he is beautiful. If you'll excuse us, our plane is waiting. Labor continued longer than expected," he said, sparing the surrogate an accusing look.

He soothed the crying baby with a skill honed from caring for his sister, born when he was a teenager.

Wrapping the toweling around Nicolas, he said, "Your mama was always cold, too, but don't you worry. We're going far away to warm, sunny beaches. You're going to love Italy. They make the most wonderful suits. See, that's the part where your mama would've laughed. I'll tell you all about her until you love her as much as I do, I promise. Once you're old enough to handle the crap and the pressure that comes from being a member of the most notorious family in Texas, we will return so I can teach you to fly like her. You, my darling son, are going to make history."

Visit author Jordana Wells at:

JordanaWells.com

Be on the lookout for

Metaphase: DNA Strand 2

Brought back from the dead, combat pilot Miranda Donovan finds the price for her resurrection is a steep one. The biomedical laboratory has creatively interpreted the law so the experiments on her can continue. Her determination to escape only intensifies after a horrific, blood-soaked night reveals how much their work has made her a target. The uneasy truce with the biotech lab hinges on her ability to track down the murderous security agent, but her only path to freedom may lie in trusting a man whose secrets are even darker than her own.

Coming soon!

www.ingramcontent.com/pod-product-compliance
Lightning Source LLC
Chambersburg PA
CBHW020826180626
46814CB00001B/128